D1634775

About the Author

A snapshot of a gene over three centuries from a Highland clothes line to Glasgow business and a Kenyan mission to the starting of a world-wide volunteer support body and the establishment of two different and successful schools. The author was born in Kenya and educated in Scotland.

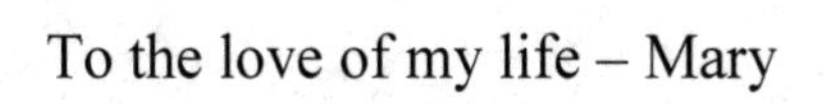

To the love of my life – Mary

David S. C. Arthur

An Avenue In Time

A CIP catalogue record for this title is available from the British Library.

ISBN 978 184963 401 4

www.austinmacauley.com

First Published (2014)
Austin Macauley Publishers Ltd.
25 Canada Square
Canary Wharf
London
E14 5LB

Printed and bound in Great Britain

Contents

Prologue

Extract from Presbytery of Caithness Records, July 25 1699

"Primo – Rev Neil Beaton, – on being interrogated on his session book, replied that what, he was asked, he had not in readiness, and on being asked about other unparalleled and worse – gross, an ignorance of God, of breaking the Sabbath and of sorceries, of incest, and adulteries.......

Oh dear! And the next forty years saw little change....."

There was another meeting of the same Presbytery – this time on the 24th of November 1741- the Rev James Brodie, who had succeeded as minister to Latheron Church, was asked "if the report that was so common that he had slit the ears of a thief, was this true?"

Could I have started on my research into my ancestors and find a better introduction?

"Not to know your history is to remain forever a child". However that may be, some of us do want to write our story. Perhaps it is to ensure that our name, our story, ourselves live on, or perhaps it's just to correct the wrongs of that story, or perhaps, simply to tell others a little about that life which may well be hidden or unknown to them. I am sure that there are elements of all of that in my story.

I could perhaps put it another way. I have had a good life, an interesting one, and one which has seen the growth of a number of the projects in which I was involved, themselves evolving and taking on a more definite shape. Life for me has not just been interesting, but challenging. At times like for so many, it has been sad, yet it has left me with a sense of achievement and even of optimism. As Father Frost grew older, he became a pessimist and a rather depressed one. For my part I see that the world for which I was so optimistic, as we all did in the 1950's and the 1960's, has not quite turned out as we had hoped. I also do see so much good to balance the bad and to recognise that, as the French put it – "plus ca change". The more it changes the less it does. Classically Afghanistan is a good example. In the 19th century much of our military commitment was to subdue the Afghans and to protect India. That failed. Then the Russians went in and invaded it in the 20th century. They failed. And now finally, in 2012, here we are back again trying to bring order and peace to an innately difficult, if not impossible country.

I think what really switched me on to writing my story was reading my grandfather's diary which he wrote at the age of seventy to tell his family a bit of his life story. There he was walking to Glasgow University, down near the Cathedral, as it was then in 1860; going to school and being rolled in the snow as a small boy for throwing a snowball at a girl, setting up a business, going through a spiritual change through Moodey and Sankey in the 1880's, and playing rugby for a rudimentary Scotland.....My father had seventy-one first cousins, and Grandfather could visit more than forty houses in the West End of Glasgow where he would find a close relative.

It is a truism that the world changes, but for my generation it has done more than that – it has seen a cosmic change in life style, in manners, in technology ever more dramatic, indeed in almost everything. We have been so successful in harnessing the forces of nature that we now perhaps face the reality of world climate change. Despite being more than four score years, I feel no different to that little boy going away to boarding school. But that world is very different, and I am different too.

No longer climbing hills, marking that international centre at rugby, standing on that barrack square with my short back and sides and in grubby BD. Age does not seem to affect one's memories in that way. Memories may fade but there are still bright pictures of events and characters. One of my pleasures is to watch "Grumpy Old Men" on TV. I am not grumpy but their words and comments light up the memories that they evoke! In my lifetime, I have lived in a house with no electricity, no TV to watch nor had a computer; I have dipped my pen in an inkwell, had my teeth extracted without an injection, and driven a car that had running boards and flip-flop indicators. I have had to make arrangements with the bank manager to draw money on holiday, and yet can now take it from the machine in the wall. Will my grandchildren see a world that is so different for them as the one we have to-day? That is what looking back in time is about, not the queens, the squires, the bankers and the politicians, but the little simple things of our own life that have changed.

Looking back is fun, it brings back memories – Learie Lamplighter in a Glasgow street, the hurdy-gurdy man and the little old lady with the Shetland pony who came round Woodburn Terrace and played the organ for the girls, the man with the accordion, pipes and drum in Roseburn after a rugby international. Where are the Onion Johnnies on their cycles, the Fisherrow Fishwives with their creels and blue striped coats, the knife sharpeners with the grindstone on a hand-cart? It is no longer jumping into bed across the cold linoleum to avoid cold feet, it is not lighting the paraffin lamps and the delicate business of not putting up the flame and so damaging that delicate cotton globe. It is not groaning when the accumulator on the radio ran out in the middle of ITMA, and the wind-up gramophone with the scratchy needle. It is sitting by the fire, hands outstretched, with the hank of wool that Gran turned into balls of wool for knitting. Mind, that was when people still knitted and socks were darned.

Life was good, though like most youngsters you would never admit it. We could play football in the streets and cycle for miles on empty roads. Life was much quieter, and there were fewer choices of what to do in life. There were few leisure opportunities, and we had to make our own interests – reading, playing an instrument, games in the home – like – ludo, dominoes, whist, jigsaws, the beetle drive and the shaking dice – snakes and ladders!

We live to-day in a dangerous world, of weapons of mass destruction, of nuclear threats, of suicide bombers. My childhood world was one third of it red, and it enjoyed Pax

Britannica, but that has all changed and I have seen that red empire shrink to just a few islands. I have watched democracy, or what goes for democracy, come to that empire, yet an almost endless stream of wars and conflicts – Communists in Malaya, Mau- Mau in Kenya, Eoka in Cyprus, Korea, UDI in Rhodesia, civil war in Nigeria, Iraq and Afghanistan. And so it goes on and will do so for the foreseeable future. Does human nature ever really change?

I am happy to record the passing of the world where I grew up, one in which we had to wear black shoes with a suit and brown with flannel trousers, a detachable collar – often starched – and no button down shirts. Then the wearing of hats, which I hated, from trilbies and flat caps to modern visors, ties that were refined, old school, regimental or club, or none.

That was a world where women wore hats and gloves, and skirts. Forget all that. Welcome to my world and its metamorphosis.

I had been reading John McCarthy's account of his being taken hostage, and how he spent his first few weeks looking back on his life, and it set me thinking. Any good therapist is able to find all kinds of horrors in your early life, and upbringing to explain your problems, and to find the reasons for your twists and turns. In fact, if we are honest no childhood and no kind of parenting can ever be entirely successful in bringing up the perfectly rounded personality. Whether it is nature or nurture, we all have these little imperfections and it is foolish to blame anyone else for them. It is fun, however, to look back with the benefit of hindsight, and so to trace some of the features that have played a part in one's life. If I were to apportion blame I suppose I could do so, by saying that I never really had much of a home life, being sent away to boarding at the age of four, then to prep school and finally to another boarding school, Loretto. Even when I was home, Dad was always busy and Mum overwhelmed with all the tasks about the house, so I was very much left on my own. I do have to say that I never really got to know Dad and my relations with Mum were sometimes tense. My big brother was seven years older and none too keen on a cheeky sibling. School, both Lathallan and Loretto, were tough schools. The really happy time for me was being at home for those four years of university. I think, however, that it was not until we married that I really understood the full meaning of happiness and the fulfilment through that perfect relationship in which both Mary and I found happiness. It was a relationship which was based on understanding and commitment and mutual respect. How much I owe to her for her support, her love and her wonderful companionship, something that I can now see when I no longer have it. We argued, we discussed, and we had that well known combative interplay. It was wonderful. We loved.

So what kind of person did it make me? I have always had this commitment to doing something for others. I am a bit of a loner. I can face failure, and have had to, both at Lomond and now with the deaths of both Mary and Catriona. I am obstinate and determined. I have been so fortunate in achieving a great deal – the foundation and expansion of the Samaritans, and the establishment of Cystic Fibrosis in Scotland as a recognised charity. Two schools from scratch, one a very difficult amalgamation. Then that wonderful and supportive family. It's not been a bad life…

The Arthur Parents

Rev. Dr. J.W. Arthur OBE DD MD Mrs E M Arthur

The Frost Family

Mr R.G. Frost Mrs Rose Frost

Golden Wedding – 1977

The Cutting Edge – Rev. James Brodie – A Look into a Surprising Family Story

"The Reverend Brodie was asked, as the report was common, if it was true that he had slit the ears of a thief........" -From the Presbytery records in Thurso, 24th November 1741

Scotland in the eighteenth h Century was in the middle of dramatic change. The Monarchy had been completely altered with the arrival of the Hanoverian Kings, and the possibility of a return for the Stuarts was to dominate it for the first half of that age. At its core was the Reformation only a century into its shattering alteration of both religious and political life but still seeking the move to both philosophical and constitutional structures.

Latheron Church lies on the cliffs of Caithness high above the North Sea, some ten miles south of Wick. As a parish it was "supplied" or established in 1567. Like many other churches in rural Scotland it was very isolated, yet it was set to meet the needs of a far-scattered congregation. The records tell of a surprising membership of " 2,000 catechisable", but with only two hundred able to read, while with a delightful gibe that those eighteen hundred who were" mostly Irish" or Gaelic speaking or even "popish". This big number of those who could not read recalls the voice of John Knox that, with the Reformation, there would be a school in every parish. That part of Scotland is wind-swept and treeless, so the next part of the story is perhaps not too surprising, taking account of the few alternative outlets of activity available. The church was built in about 1734, and the records from the presbytery tell an interesting story. These records are wonderful, being phrased using a unique language – a strange mixture of Scots, English and Latin.

As if that story at the top was not enough the tale grows with his predecessor, Rev. Mr. Beaton, who had not even conformed to Presbyterianism and was now challenged by the presbytery on the 25th July 1699 with tales of a series of scandals, "Primo", the first and least of which was a failure to keep his records up to date, but far worse – then with supine negligence, for failure to catechise. (That is to teach the fundamentals of religion) But also with "Secundo", "that he never preached but once a day, and sometime to marry on the Sabbath Day, with loads and frequent fishing." That part of Sutherland was very dependent on fishing from the North Sea. But it could only get worse, and it did –"dancing at the solicitation of the company at a wedding"....and Sexton, there were "the number of adulteries, incests and rapes in his paroch." With that quote it is no surprise to read that Mr Beaton was suspended but, there is astonishment that, in consequence of him behaving himself, he was soon reinstated.

My great, great, grandfather's crime seems relatively minor when compared with Mr Beaton, but he was nonetheless suspended for seven months. The tale is a delightful one. It concerned one, James Sutherland, a known thief but who had been employed in the manse garden. The Rev James was in the garden with the family washing hanging out when the said James Sutherland arrived, to be accused of stealing shirts off the line. An argument ensued, and it was unfortunate that the Rev James was shaving at the time – presumably with an open razor – and on becoming angry, he threatened James " to give him a mark that would let it be known for what he was in the whole parish." A tussle followed and the razor "occasioned to wound the top of the ear." Here is a lesson to us all never to argue with an open blade. Strange is it not, that that perhaps justified a suspension while a tale of orgies sank without loss?

The Rev. James died in Aberdeen in 1775 but married one Anne Murray, by whom he had seven children. Of these six were boys, with one daughter. It reflects on the times that three boys died young, and one emigrated to the West Indies, while only one, Patrick, had a family. She, Ann Murray, claimed direct "descendance", as described in his diary, from Eyanard, Duke of Orkney, the brother of one William, Duke of Normandy, who became William 1, of England in 1066. So the genes are there! From the North of Scotland to Normandy. Before one gets too excited, we should look at the size of families and the spread of descendants over the years to understand the enormous spread of the DNA from one mediaeval sire. It bring us back to earth to realise that, if you assume three generations to a century, and families of at least five to ten, the numbers of blood relations assumes impossible proportions.

Families

We are lucky that there has been a great deal of research into the family background on both sides. I can date the Arthur side back to a John Arthur who lived in Paisley in 1610, while another arm goes to the Borders with a James Walker in 1625. He was a Covenanter and his son was also of the same group and fought at the Battle of Bothwell Brig. There are other threads that link up – the Tennants, they were farmers, from Ayrshire in 1635, and lived in Ayrshire at Glenconner and the family had close connections with one Robert Burns. From that family was Sarah Tennant who died in 1864 and is my great grandmother. Her sister, Nancy was the poet's "auld acquaintance" and she married George Barrie, of whom the poet wrote he was "a guid chiel wi a pickle o' siller!" Then the Sloans emerge in 1700 into the family tree, and there were more than enough of them.

On mother's side – the Coullies – there was a view that the family were French Huguenots and came, via Belgium to Scotland after the eviction as a result of the Edict of Nantes, though there was mention of an Arch-Bishop Coullie in the Netherlands. On mother's mother's side were the Brodies, now that family were wealthy, as Kenneth Brodie was an indigo trader and owned a large country mansion near the Lake of Monteith, he – well his wife – had eight children including three sets of twins. Once more the DNA spreads through family connections in Caithness – the Smiths, from whose family came Sir William Smith, who started the Boys Brigade. His sons were great friends of my fathers, with Douglas working for the BBC and becoming famous at Loretto for his support of boys through the half- crown high tea at the Co-op in the High Street. A man who attracted a lot of support from hungry school boys.

On the Frost Side the connections were English with a strong link with the South-West – Mary always enjoyed the photo of herself sitting on her own tomb near Dartmoor. The family moved to London and then to East Anglia and finally, looking for work, came to Scotland.

It is fascinating to look at the two families and their backgrounds, furnishers, calico printers, indigo traders – now there's a interesting source of cash – the ministers, doctors and weavers, to mention but a few and to compare with the next generation – teacher, doctor, academics, sales persons, land owners...... Welcome to the 20th Century.

AN ANCESTRAL DIARIST – J. W. ARTHUR

John William Arthur

It was watching " The Diary of Ann Frank" on TV which reminded me again of how important are the diaries and personal records and how I would fear if they were to be superseded by the modern alternative – the blog, an entry on Facebook, Twitter, or a message text on the IPad. Will these, like e-mails with their short life survive to be a record? Our ancestors, on the other hand, were very good at recording their lives, and sometimes their thoughts. My grandfather, J W Arthur, was one of those who kept meticulous records, either separately or in neatly kept note books, and in a beautiful hand. During a life from 1848 to 1921 he completed one part of his diary at each year's end, and a further separate one in which he summarised his life and what he had achieved. In one of these, written on reaching the age of seventy, he listed all that he had done over those years and he felt this important as being a record that would be for the benefit of his family.

A number of points immediately strike one. There is the beautiful hand-writing, in which there are amazingly few mistakes, written or otherwise. In the one which he made each year end the record is equally correct in his grammar and punctuation. He was no academic, but a proud, elderly Glasgow businessman who had made his own way in life. His family were from the west of Scotland, with their original roots as weavers in the Paisley area, while his own business led to him becoming a calico printer, calico being a superior kind of linen.

His diary is very honest, he writes, a little sadly, at one point, of "a life with but little adventure." Such modesty is not to any eye true, for it also tells of another world, a world as different to us to-day as is that of our parents is to us. Born near Barrowfield, Glasgow near the Clyde, he moved at an early age to India Street, close to Sauchiehall Street. There he had a dose of scarlet fever and writes of eating, while visiting with his grandmother "dabbities" – these were some kind of shortbread petticoat tails. He mentions the arrival of an early telegram from his father telling his mother that he had been delayed in Edinburgh while on business, and his aunt remarking that there must be something "wrong with Allan as it was not in his own hand!". In our world of instant communication the introduction of wireless telegraphy – as he described it – is almost beyond our understanding. On one visit he was the recipient of souvenirs from his local doctor after a call and of being given "mementoes from the Crimean war" which had just ended along with bottles of Jordan water – something that was popular for a long time for use at christenings. Father Frost had brought such a bottle back after his visit to Palestine. That water was gratefully used for Bobby and Gillian.

Then for him came calamity when he was to be sent to school, at Mr Longs in Thistle Street. What tears there were on being forced to wear "breeks", the custom in those days, being skirts for both boys and girls.

In about 1855 the family moved to a house in Laurel Bank, at that time a house in the country, in the middle of wide green fields, for the north side of Byres Road had not yet been built upon, while Gilmorehill House stood alone not as not yet being part of the University. This area was all in the independent community of Partick, which had its own schools, its own gas works, magistrates and even a Volunteer Company. He records of a neighbouring family facing a very modern day crisis with the crash of their business following the bankruptcy of the Western Bank, and their forced consequent emigration to Canada. Shades of our own credit crunch.

Having moved to Partick this meant not only the move to a local Partick school but to the ownership of his own patch of garden to cultivate, complete with a pool filled with minnows.

At the age of eleven he made the big step forward to go to the Glasgow Academy – but not the fine building of the Academy that stands now on the banks of the Kelvin. Here was a school started only thirteen years before in1846, but standing at that time in Elmbank Street to which the old High School was to move, and is now part of the City Offices, but was then surrounded by open fields and orchards. He records that the school building had only recently opened, and that previously the earlier classes were held in Renfield Street. Shock, horror! If the present Health and Safety had done an inspection of the new Academy, for there was but one small trickling hose tap for "ablutions" and drinking purposes at the back of this school for six hundred boys. There was no uniform, no caps and much roughness to boot. He never saw a piece of soap or a towel in all his days. Differences were sorted out at the back at 4 o'clock in the Orchard – the most serious being between two cousins, Jack and Lawrie Buchanan. There were fearsome games against the wall known as "Crash A", probably like the Eton Wall Game with the ball carrier crushed on the bricks. There were games of football and "bools" on the asphalt playground.

For to-days educationists his year of Latin 1 had one hundred and five boys divided into four classes, but all were taught in the same one large hall. This caused major problems of discipline for the unfortunate Frenchman, "Mooshie Suilay", who was responsible for the French while Mr John Gow, who taught writing, should have had as his armorial bearings "a Cane Rampant". Delightfully he records with some sorrow, that that arithmetic master dealt my grandfather a belting with the tawse by mistake. However, Mr Gow agreed that if it were to happen again he would be let off. What he actually meant, when the worst did take place, was that he only got six instead of twelve! Such were the human rights of the nineteenth century. There was little public transport in those days, even if the family could have afforded it, so he walked the five miles there and back, and these led to at least one encounter with a "mill girl" (how did he know?) who rolled him in the snow after he had snowballed her.

The curriculum was basically classical. Each Year was Latin 1, Latin 2 and so on. and the desk from which arithmetic was taught was known as the "Areopagus" – or Marr's Hill after the master, Mr Marr. For lunch he had sometimes a glass of milk with scones and cookies, and the occasional "succulent" sweet.

What impresses is the warmth with which he remembered his days at the Academy after leaving in Latin Fifth, with all its hardships and, to the modern eye, the grimness of the situation. He recalls with pleasure the friends, many of whom were to remain with him all his life. From that group came a Lord Provost, a bishop, lawyers, financiers, and business men. No wonder that in later days he played a big part in the governance of the School, becoming the Chairman of Governors.

So from the Academy to the University in October 1864, situated then at the East end of the city down near the present Royal Infirmary, an even longer walk – nine miles this time.

He prided himself that he had never taken a hansom cab, unlike some young gentlemen, but walked every day. Again, his course was heavily classical, and he enrolled as Johannes Gulielmus Arthur into Logic and Rhetoric with a gentlemanly old man but a fine scholar, Professor Lushington – he was Wordsworth's brother-in-law as his instructor. He only remained at the University for a year. He was anxious to make his own way in life and to earn some money and there were still seven members of the family who needed the money to be educated. He writes of a number of events, a Rectorial election which was he thought was rather good fun but hardly justified the noise that surrounded it, of a Professors Dinner with the students held in the Professors Court at night, of a football match against the university and an assortment of West End fellows, and of one Stewnose Sandy Taylor, whose job it was to bang the lecture door shut on any late comers immediately the five minute bell had rung.

So at the age of seventeen he left the academic world for that of business.

J.W. ARTHUR 2

It may only be one hundred and fifty years since grandfather wrote his diary, but the world has changed in an almost unimaginable way – indeed, in a way that each generation could not possibly have imagined. I grew up in a world where there was no electricity and the telephone was rarely used – indeed, Alex Drysdale would allow his kids only to make two calls a week. Mary and I did suggest the same, only to be met with a united scream of disapproval. Today the iPad, the Internet, the digital camera and texting have taken over. Even the humble telegram has gone into total world of the blank.

Now, if you compare my grandfather's world with his father, grandfather and so on, the differences are marginal. Life was very limited in twentieth century terms. The world has started to shoot, and I suspect that my grandchildren will see even greater strides or changes.

The diary, therefore, brings back very sharply to another world, one with the need to make one's own world of activity, to fill the time with books, with games, with activities, with action. One can see in this life the drive to fill the unforgiving minutes. He was particularly into sport, and rugby was high on the agenda. One forgets in those days that there was a great lack of sporting facilities – no games hall, no indoor cover; indeed, there were very few sporting clubs of any kind. There were very few ground for games of any kind. The late 1800s was a time that saw the emergence of clubs – rugby, football, tennis. All that there was was a rowing club on the Clyde, and a skating and curling pond. In that is a reminder that climate change in the last thirty years has seen the end of the local skating pond and outdoor curling club.

In 1866, The Glasgow Academical Club was formed in the Writing Rooms of the school, with a division of activities into various clubs, in particular for rugby, and even one for literary skills. Sadly, that did not last. The grounds set aside for rugby was a rough area opposite Burnbank Drill Hall, though this was soon transferred to the present Old Anniesland.

Between 1867 and 1873, the Rugby Club played 51 matches, won 33, lost 4, and drew 14. They reached the heights with wins to become Scottish Champions for the years 1871, 1872, and 1873 without losing a match. On the 6th of December 1870, they crossed the Border – the first club of any kind, rugby or soccer to do so – and played a win against Manchester and a draw to Liverpool.

The success was such that it was decided to issue a challenge to the English Rugby Union for a match to be played between the two countries. There were six signatories to the letter, my grandfather being one. They represented the other Scottish Clubs. The match would be played at Raeburn Place in Edinburgh, the home of the Edinburgh Academicals.

That Club was going through difficult times as they wanted to develop, and all the Nimbies on the South Side were up in arms.

The match was fought on a beautiful afternoon and Scotland won by one goal and a try to one try. J.W.A. placed the ball for Willie Cross to convert to a goal. I mentioned fought. H.H. Almond, headmaster of Loretto, was the referee, and he threatened to stop the game if there was more rough stuff.

Grandfather walked to school and University far off in the East End, so was a very fit man, and took part in all kinds of sport – golf at Prestwick, West Gales and Cardross, angling on the Tweed and on the streams near Garelochhead, curling on Loch Lomond and at Carsebreck, and even on the pond near Old Anniesland. There was too cricket, croquet, and on one occasion lacrosse, because he had met up with a group of North American Indians. Just in case of boredom he yachted on the Clyde. Life was not bad, and a contrast with much of the rest of Scots.

The Scotland XX on 27th March 1871

Grandfather is the bearded one in the centre. *The Herald*, in a recent article on the match considered that, as there were no numbers at the time, he should be awarded the No. 1 shirt!

He kept a record of his walks – he was a walker as well in Scotland – in 1964 from Ardlui to Oban, via Glencoe, Connel, and Loch Awe at the rate of eighteen miles a day for seven days. Two years later, he covered much the same ground, but this time at twenty four miles a day. He extended his walks to the continent – in 1867 in Switzerland, from Meiringen to Interlaken, this time at the rate of twenty four and a half miles in ten days. He found one of the benefits of being a member of Partick Church was that the doors of manses on these routes were always open to them. His was a lesson in economy as the total cost of these journeys worked out at £1 a day!

He was exceedingly proud of one journey that he and his friends did one Glasgow Fair Friday. This involved twenty one of the boys who holidayed down the Clyde at Blairmore. They took three boats, "all varnished and 23 foot long" up Loch Long to Arrochar, carried the boats across the neck of land to Tarbet – incidentally also done by the Vikings in the tenth century – slept for a few hours at Rowardennan, climbed Ben Lomond to breakfast the top with the sunrise, then back down to Loch Lomond and off to Balloch. Once again they were forced to portage the boats to the River Leven and so to the Clyde and back to Blairmore. He sounded very indignant to learn later that another group had completed the same trip in one day.

As a hill walker myself, I cannot but be impressed at the extent of his journeys and the scale of his activities, all carried out without the aid of a car, or indeed any vehicle. He was lucky too to be part of a class that could afford the time to engage in it all.

There is very little about money or his income and the censuses do not shed any light on the servants. Oddly in 1881, there is only mention of two sons and his wife, though it adds that he was Turkey Red and Calico printer employing twenty five people. But in 1901, he has Mary Macleod, Companion, Catherine Macleod, Cook, Rachel Nicholson, servant, and Janet Munro, housemaid.

He was certainly not distracted by TV or the cinema, and not by plays or music. There is no mention at all of any such interest, this being mainly related to the church. I can find no mention even of books or lectures. He and his family were hugely part of the life of the church. His great-great-grandfather, James Monteith, had founded his own church – Anderston UF Church – all because he had failed to attend his own church and instead had gone to the service in a neighbouring but closer church on a very wet day. That failure led to the said James "being sessioned" by the officials of St. Enoch Church. This meant a public appearance before the whole congregation to explain his failure. He was so furious that the result was his own church to which the family lived in and loved so loyally. The mid-1840s were a time of endless ecclesiastical argument and discussion, always directed to the narrow or fresh interpretation of the scriptures. The national church faced the famous "Disruption" over the right of lairds, or landowners, to appoint the local minister. As a result, the Church split into the Free Church. On the other side, my own grandfather, the Rev James Coullie, became the minister of Pencaitland in East Lothian as the result of being presented by the laird. In his case, the last time in Scotland.

J.W.A. was deeply affected by the arrival in Scotland of two famous American evangelists, Moody and Sankey, who brought with them a new and infectious approach, all similar to the 1950s and Billy Graham and the twentieth century Evangelicals. For J.W.A., this meant a deep interest in the work of religion in young people and the resultant establishment of Sabbath Schools and Bible Study groups – these being mostly for boys – but also the Mills Girls Society for girls. This interest was a central part of his spare time and takes up a large share of the diary. A very moving area was the end of year account, when he summed up the successes and failures of that year in relation to his own work. It is also interesting that he had become a very central part in the life of Glasgow, both on a business and sporting side

In his earlier account, there is another surprising side, an interest in the nineteenth century Volunteer Force. This today would be the Territorial Army, and was established in 1856 to meet the need to provide backup for the regular Army. Britain was the centre of that huge expansion of the Empire, and the Volunteers provided the excitement and opportunities for young men. He gives no reason for his joining – perhaps his seniors felt that it would be an outlet for his energies. He was only nineteen in 1867 and he was immediately commissioned as an Ensign – today a Second Lieutenant – with promotion in 1868 to Lieutenant, and one year later to Captain – all the standard procedure for the recognition of the differing classes. I could find no mention of what the life was like, or indeed of any description of the activities. His regiment was the 4th Volunteer Battalion of the Scottish Rifles, which eventually became the Glasgow Highlanders. He did attend the famous "Wet Review" in Holyrood Park before her Majesty, a day of torrential rain, when the scarlet of the uniform merged with the white of the pipe clay and wiped out all the excitement of the day for the forty thousand men on duty. A sad result was a large number of deaths, and a poem by the Dundee McGonigle.

An unusual side to his character emerges in 1888 when, in annoyance at the failure of promotion to Major, resulted in his resignation. In contrast in 1914, aged sixty five, he came out of retirement and found, to his great joy, that the "44 year old blue patrol jacket" proved that that old dug-out, like its owner was still fit! The contrast to the new khaki set one difficulty, as wearing it in the street proved a problem of recognition – was he a Senior Naval Officer or a Commissioner of Police, or a bandmaster, as one drunk in the street decided? Or even worse, the cruellest cut when the bus conductor offered him a free bus pass, as he was obviously a policeman.

J.W. ARTHUR

The more I went into that diary of my grandfather the greater has been my admiration for the energy and vitality of his life and this in contrast with the life that we lead in the 21st century. To consider but one side and look at the size of the connections within the family and the numbers that were common to many families of that day and time – contraception was for another generation. He married a Margaret Sloan in August 1877 and, with that marriage he immediately became part of huge family. Within the two generations of that family there were 73 relatives and he claimed that he could visit 44 houses in Glasgow in which there would be a relative. My own father always boasted of 71 first cousins. To equate our current family can only once again feel inadequate – a mere 24 at a similar stage. In those days theirs were not all that large families, ten, fifteen and more, that inevitably meant that there were the ravages of death, sometimes at an early age. One can feel in his pages his deep sadness in the recording of such events. This was an age where medical remedies were neither universal nor even successful, and life was lived with a knowledge of the closeness to death. This can be seen in the heartfelt way in which he writes of the death of his much loved wife and that of a sister and daughter.

He obviously had a sense of humour and a number of Punch cartoons are copied into his diary over the years of 1878 starting with an entry for 3rd October of that year. – "yesterday the City of Glasgow Bank suspended payments, causing great surprise and excitement."

Mr Punch. "What are you looking for Father?

On October 3rd 1878 there appears an entry – "Yesterday the City Of Glasgow bank suspended payments, causing great surprise and excitement." It could be to-days Lehman Brothers.

Their company business account was kept with that Bank. They, their company, had an overdraft limit of £3, 400, and his clerk, Andrew had drawn out £1, 000 the day before to pay some bills – for once in cash and not, as usual by cheque. The number of bills owed was small and a small cheque to him was returned with Andrew as being not properly signed. That closure wiped out 10% of the Scotland's banking capital, had liabilities of £6.2 million, and the £100 shares which had been previously worth £240 immediately were worthless. Happy grandfather. But altogether it was a bad year, his beloved father died in December which cast a pall over everything, the business ran into difficulties.

JWA's life was a full one but there is no mention anywhere of his financial situation. From his holidays, his houses and his activities he must have been reasonably comfortably well off. He began his business life as an office boy in a related family firm, Robert Hannan at 75 St Vincent St in Glasgow, in 1865 it was a small one but it gave many opportunities for learning his trade, which for the whole of his life was with calico or fine linen and in particular, handkerchiefs. He describes it as a good business which later fell on evil times. He himself transferred to his father's firm, Henry Monteith & Son, and while it was reorganised into various shapes, it became Allan Arthur & Co but it always kept the linen connection. At one point many firms who were involved in what was called the Line Spinners Association, linked up with the successful Coats of Paisley to form the Calico Printers Association. At this point he mentions that they did receive £ 1, 500 for the take-over, and that this sum was then divided among the employees right down to the office boy. His part of the business was very much within the family with his brother, Andrew, joining as a partner. It's clear from his diary that he was held in high regard with a number of Directorship and Chairs, including The Board of Glasgow Academy and the Glasgow Chamber of Commerce.

There is much in the books about the importance of family and friends, whether in his numerous activities and holidays. The friendships in many cases go back to his schooldays and those holidays. Work for him and his friends was there to give a high quality of life yet also to be within high standards of behaviour. While many of the sentiments that he expresses about his part in the life of the church also relate to business, these were strong feelings that this was in no way mere sentiment. He expected high standards for himself and his employees and the same were expected of his family. There were four sons and two daughters, one son, Allan set up his own electrical business and became an obsessive mountaineer and, by picking up 2 planks and garden poles from the garden, was responsible for the establishment of the Scottish Ski Club. The second son died as a result of war wounds. While the third, my father, became a highly successful medical missionary in Kenya, and the fourth became a prominent business man in India. In the style of the times the two daughters were not expected to follow a career, though one worked as a VAD and eventually became the matron of a hospital in 1939. I always remember my father laughingly recounting that when the family went on holiday, usually to a rented house with all the servants, the two daughters insisted on travelling first class while the boys went 3rd class!

Clearly the study of the diaries is interesting of itself but there is an equal interest not just in the genealogy but in the transfer of the genes over the years. Here was a very physical man who combined energy, hard work and achieved considerable success, who delighted in keeping a record of that life for future generations. In rugby terms, three of his sons played first class rugby and two reached Scottish trial level, both his grandsons played for first class clubs, while his great-grandson plays at a reasonable level. The military side has been continued in both the army and air-force (the latter unknown in his day), business, medicine, and teaching –at one point three of the independent schools in the West of Scotland had cousins from this Arthur/Sloan family as heads –the High School, Laurel Bank and Lomond.

Times have changed in the life and the world of the generation who have peopled the 20th and 21st centuries but I do not think that my grandfather would feel any concern that his legacy had not been maintained and indeed honoured.

Rev John William Arthur OBE DD MD (1881 – 1954)

My father was a modest person, but he was very proud of the names which he had inherited from his father and which he later gave to his eldest son, and of the various degrees and medals that he had. He was the third son of the other J. W. Arthur and went to Glasgow Academy, and then on to study medicine at the University. He was a keen and a very good athlete who got a blue for athletics and played for Glasgow Academicals at rugby. He might have won a cap for Scotland if he had stayed in this country. But he was very imbued with his father's evangelical fervour and was determined to become a medical missionary. At first this was to be in China, but the appointment that came through was instead to Kenya. The Mission in Kenya had come about through the financial support of Sir William MacKinnon, a Scot from Campbelltown in Argyll, who had founded the Imperial British East Africa Company. The initial establishment of the mission was to be at Kibwezi, south of Nairobi, in 1898, with some of the cost coming additionally from the Free Church with £40, 000. Sadly the site chosen was a bad one, being both very hot and open to disease with the result that five out of the six pioneer missionaries died. The Mission then moved North to Dagoretti or Kikuyu, as this was higher and more open with sweeping views – to the mountain of Kenya. Some 3, 000 acres of farm land were purchased or leased on a ninety nine year basis. The ground which they were actually given was slightly physically lower than had been agreed – the suggestion being that the Chief could then look down and see what was going on.

By the time my father arrived on the first day of 1907, by that time the site was established, the manse had arrived and been erected. Incredibly the ship which had been carrying it had earlier sunk in the Red Sea, and the structure been salvaged and built on a site at the top. There was a little wooden church, and a small house built for Dad, designed both for living and acting as the surgery. He had come up on the recently built steam Kenya Uganda railway, the famous Lunatic Line, for which no one knew the purpose. It had been a twenty four hour journey from Mombasa, and he was met at Kikuyu station by a party of ten "boys" dressed in dirty long lengths of cloth slung over the shoulder. He had already noted that the white men, presumably settlers, at Nairobi station had shown their antagonism to missionaries. Perhaps some explanation for this being the presence of ten priests and four nuns on the train. He described in his letter home that the country at this level was beautiful, with fine ridges, streams and rich vegetation. He also saw the women staggering up from the streams with those big pots of water and loads of firewood held on their heads with leather bands. One of the signs for women being the indent in the forehead from carrying that weight. His introduction, that day, to the Mission was a sports afternoon, with three legged races, flat races and a high jump of 3'10". It was one of the positive aspects and activities of life in Kenya that he quickly picked upon was the extraordinary athleticism of the Kenyans. Something well recognised in the Olympic world of the centuries of the nineteenth and twentieth, and his generous request for boots for his football team was, however, soon abandoned when he found that the boots caused more injuries than the original bare feet!

His time in Kenya saw major changes, many of them due to his energy and drive. From a start as the GP who had to train his first orderly to clean and bandage, he had to bury his first death, as it was considered unlucky for Africans to touch a dead body. The Kikuyu took the dying out into a simple hut in the forest and left them there to die. One of his first visits was to the local Chief, who was then being treated for cancer of the liver, that being proven by having his back jumped upon by the medicine man. This was all at a cost of two goats and a calf. He quickly learnt to ride a bicycle, and this meant that at night, when he had to go out to an emergency, he had to carry a bag and a paraffin lamp on his handlebars. On these journeys he sang childhood choruses at the top of his voice to frighten away the lions, or at least to keep his own spirits up. His next methods of transport was a motor bicycle which he rode on the railway line, there being no danger from the few trains. He was also one of the first to own a car. I remember, as a boy, going on wonderful rides across the prairie after picnics to race the zebra and giraffes. He argued that this was purely to find what speed the animals could reach. He had a wild side and he showed that when, when I was aged twelve, when he got out of the car and said to me " get into the driving seat it is high time you learnt to drive!" By this time he had returned to Scotland. I should add that, being wartime there were no other cars on the road, and he was driving, lucky enough to be a county councillor, and so he had petrol coupons. He once wrote of one adventure when the Mission was being pestered by a wild rhino, and he and two others from the station set off to frighten it away. Fortunately they never found the animal, as he only had a revolver and no one had shown him how to operate the safety catch. On another occasion, and his first holiday, he went up to Uganda, a city like Rome on seven hills. Happily riding his bicycle, he found himself being pushed up hills by a small boy. Apparently this was the custom for helping important people.

My father could be a formidable figure. He was a thoughtful man, who tried to understand people of different backgrounds and cultures, and was happy to discipline himself so as to avoid difficulties. He and my mother never drank alcohol in case it gave the wrong impression that white people drank too much. His comment on being accused of failing to understand or appreciate different customs was blunt; "They (the Africans) are pretty hard headed individuals and they think of you as the "mzungu", or strangers, who have come and stolen their land." He was very much in support of the appointment of Africans to the ministry. Johnson Kamau who later became Jomo Kenyatta, had started his life as a boy at a Kikuyu school. He, Kenyatta, kept in touch with my Dad and was happy to meet him in 1948 when Dad went out to celebrate his 50 years of the mission. Jomo was rather proud of the photo that my father took of him as a boy at school and was to use it on a postage stamp when he became President.

By 1912 he found himself given the task of heading the Mission, and taking the responsibility for its leadership. There then followed major changes He began the Mission Hospital at Kikuyu, the operation was rather different to European styles as there was a veranda upon which relatives and friends could camp, and cook food for the patient. He and George Grieve, who was out as a teacher, established a school for secondary pupils – in this case for boys. The school for girls came later. That school became known as the Eton of Kenya as the Alliance High School, and from which so many leaders of the nation were to come. Perhaps of all that he did this was to have the most lasting benefits. As a small side light my father always wore a buttonhole in his jacket, and it was customary for later politicians to follow suit. His Kikuyu name "regitari" and was still recognised when we went back to Kenya in the 1970's.Perhaps the most beautiful reminder of his time is the magnificent Church of the Torch, set in the middle of the green grass below the manse. Built thanks to my father's efforts to raise the funds and that took him back to Scotland to raise the money from churches and industrialists, like Carr's biscuits. It stands to-day as a lovely memorial to him and to the lone Scots master mason, John Gordon, who trained and over- saw the actual building. The stone was carried by locals from the quarry at the back of the manse for three shillings a stone, the total cost for the whole exercise being in the region of 700, 000 shillings. He was very involved in the establishment of a United Church including all religions, though this was a long term project which would not materialise for years. Of all his work perhaps the most difficult and dangerous was the strong line that he took on female circumcision. This was very much part of African culture, often as part of the process of male domination and to match that of boys at a similar age. Unfortunately for girls the process could be painful and have long term damage, both to the reproductive system and, more importantly to the whole birth procedure. My father had no doubt that this was wrong purely from a medical point of view and took a strong line. Unfortunately, African opinion in Kenya saw it as part of further interference by the white man on their culture and it became embedded in a strongly nationalist view. The Church, under my father's influence took a strong line which split the church. It engendered anger among the settler and government ranks and my father suffered. Probably it was the major reason for his departure from Kenya, and was to be a part of his regret at leaving the country in 1937.

A true valuation of the part that he played lies in the veneration in which his name was held for years after he had left. When Gillian, our daughter, did part of her medical training in Kenya she found how much this respect remained. He did a great job for the Church and for Kenya.

How do I remember him. He was tough and he could be driven by his job and by his temperament. He did not marry until he was forty and he was fifty when I was born. He wasn't really a family man. He was of an age when children had to take second place and it was no problem for him to see them either be sent away to school, or left with friends or relatives if he had to be somewhere else. He was very clear on his religious philosophy and was not very understanding of the difficulties of a young son. I think that I would sum him up that I respected him and had great affection for him, perhaps the word love does not seem to be a very appropriate term for what he was – a Victorian father. I used the word tough, and I remember hearing someone who had been studying African history describing him as hard and tough. I am not sure about the hard. He would not be dissuaded if he believed his was the right course. The argument over female circumcision was one of those, and it would be difficult to argue with him that it was a culture that could be defended. In other ways he was tough. He had always been a keen walker, and was even as he grew older and he found relief in the Scottish Highlands. He had no difficulty in climbing the Cairngorms until he was in his sixties. In Kenya, he attempted to climb Mount Kenya on a number of occasions, but like me, he was walker not a rock climber and Kenya is a formidable climb. He had numerous photos of the mountain and there was no doubt that he loved it. He also climbed Mount Kilimanjaro, with the help of the usual train of porters. He also showed his determination when he established the Carrier Corps of Africans who served the forces in the invasion of Tanganyika in 1915. He not only commanded it but was the Medical Officer. This force played an important part when the motor vehicles of the time could not play any real part because of ground conditions or the lack of power in cars and lorries. They, the Carriers, were the main source of supply of food, equipment and ammunition to troops at the front. There is a statue on the main avenue in Nairobi to the Corps.

By Royal Invitation

In the twenty first century the word telegram just does not ring bells. The computer with its e-mails, the mobile and the text, have all taken over. But in 1937 on the 28th of March a cable reached Kenya Radio asking,

"Will Arthur and wife accept colonial office invitation to attend coronation, Westminster Abbey. Cable reply". A bit blunt, but still a royal invitation.

I suppose we all, particularly the Scots, are a bit republican and see ourselves as being above that sort of affair, but if we were offered the chance....

From J.W. Arthur's diary of that Royal Coronation on the 12th day of May 1937

They had travelled south to stay with friends behind St. Columba's on Pont Street. In London. First, was the major question of clothes which hung over their minds – and, of course ladies first "she was to wear, by Royal Command evening dress, but no low frocks!" So there she was, in a long blue dress, with long white gloves and three ostrich feathers in her hair, together with a tiara of diamonds – lent by a friend. He wore dark knee britches with silver buckles, and a long cassock, "so the slim elegant legs and ankles never got displayed!" His sash had a St. Andrew's cross and a Torch (for the Kenya Church of the Torch). The picture was taken at Harrods – of course – by a dapper little gentleman with a pointed beard.

Many slept the night on the pavement, but the Arthurs went to their elegant beds early, while many peeresses were said to have spent the night at the hairdresser!

The call came at 5.30am for a taxi which also carried a companion lady, and was one who knew her way around, for she had once taught the Queen French.

They followed the prescribed route, but had taken the precaution of a good breakfast and had carefully stuffed sandwiches either into his three cornered hat or her handbag. As they neared the Abbey the crowds on the streets saw – peers carrying their coronets, admirals, generals, and even two old coaches with wigged coachmen. They took their seats by 7.am in the gallery of the north aisle. Here they were surrounded by old friends from the colonies. They all had a beautifully prepared book of the ceremony with timings and details.

At 8.55 the Royals, foreign and domestic, began to arrive and to be seated – the Queen Mother and the two princesses, and at 9.55 the regalia – the Crown, the Orb, the Sceptre, were carried in with pomp and ceremony. At 11am, the King and Queen and their attendants processed to their thrones, all at a very slow pace so that they could be easily identified.

The service itself then began, and must have lasted for an hour and a half with all the due ceremonies of oaths to the King, and all the array of cloaks, and crowns and the King and Queen going through the ceremonies separately. At 1.30pm – four hours from their arrival the coronation was over but the processions on the streets were still to come all appropriately solemn and pompous.

They remained seated until they were instructed to leave at 3.30pm – some effort at eight hours! How did they last out? It began to rain at 2.45 while the procession round the streets went on. The Arthurs filled the time by wandering up to the altar and having a good look at the regalia. There was chaos outside with peeresses sitting weeping on the stairs while they waited for their taxis which had not turned up.

So it was home by 5.15 and supper, and then a trip to see the King and Queen appear on the balcony about 10pm and a quick tour round Hyde Park and Piccadilly.

Some day!

I personally have vivid memories of that day. My parents were very good at "dumping" us if they had need to go away, and Carol, my sister, and I were put into a boarding house at 26 Blacket Place in Edinburgh. It was run by a rather tough minister, and the main room of the house was the meeting place for a large number of elderly ladies all dressed – in my memory – in black, and smelling of moth balls. On Coronation Day itself, of course there was no TV to record it for us and the radio was boring, so brother Jo had been given the day off from Loretto to celebrate with us. He had decided to take us to the cinema to see a film, called "They Died at Dawn", All I can remember is that there was an endless sequence of sailors being lined up on a submarine and being shot. Unsurprisingly, that seven- year- old boy and the eleven- year-old girl burst into tears and, to his sophisticated elderly horror, our brother was forced to take us out in disgrace. He always claimed afterwards never to have forgiven us. I suspect he felt that he had wasted his valuable money. In his favour, he did at least stand us tea at a nearby tea- shop!

IMPERIAL BRITISH AIRWAYS

DR. I.W. ARTHUR'S flight in February 1935
Journeys from England to Kenya
1906 – By boat – 28 days
1935 – By air – 7days
2001 – By air – 12 hours

The Church of the Torch from the Manse
February 1935

Monday 4th February 1935

I have been weighed in so that a proper weight distribution can be achieved on the aircraft. I admit, though grudgingly, that I am a little disconcerted at this, being one who thought he had kept an eye on his weight, and now to find that I was 1 kilo over – about 4lbs. That cost me 12 Kenya shillings and 50 pence. Including your luggage, you must not weigh more than 221 lbs when travelling by air.

Travel broadens the mind. I have now learnt that Nairobi is one of the great airports in the Cape schedule of Imperial British Airways. There are two flights each week to the north and to the south. They go to the north on Monday and Friday mornings, and the other way on Monday and Friday evenings. On last Boxing Day, there was an air show with twenty to thirty planes.

I have suddenly realised that I am an old stick-in-the-mud. I arrived by steamer twenty years ago in 1906 after a sea voyage that took between twenty four and twenty eight days from Tilbury in England. Then I was coming to a country that few knew anything about except that it was in Darkest Africa, and one where wild animals roamed and few Europeans returned without some dire disease. Today, Kenya is becoming a target for tourism – shooting elephant, fishing, polo – the good life. What took twenty eight days then, I can complete by air in seven.

What a chance I am being given. Events have conspired that the Church of Scotland wished me to be in Scotland to discuss important developments in the mission field, and have asked me to return as speedily as possible, while other native matters which I have championed in Kenya could be combined with the Colonial office while I am at home, hence the unheard of chance of a flight home.

A whole group of people from the various missions have gathered to wish me god speed, and I suspect that not a few harbour secret wishes that it could have been one of them that was the lucky one to make such a great adventure. Like Peter Pan I shall fly, but without wires. The Africans were greatly excited and walked round the plane cheerfully, making laughing comments on the chances that it would never get off the ground. I felt greatly heartened by their confidence. Evelyn, my wife, and David, my five-year-old-son, had said goodbye earlier and driven off up the hill to get a better view. David could hardly contain himself with excitement that Daddy was actually going to fly in the air.

We took off exactly at 9pm. Because of altitude, Nairobi is at 6, 000ft, and aircraft take off and land mostly during early morning or evening when the air is cooler and heavier. The aircraft was a four-engine monoplane of the Atlanta class and was called *Artemis*. I drew on that classical education of which Glasgow Academy was so proud to recall that Artemis was better known as Diana – the goddess of the hunt and the moon. I hope that my old Classics master, probably away up there above in the sky, enjoys the tribute to his good teaching and the depth of my memory. The plane can carry twelve passengers, with four rows of three seats – two on one side and one on the other – but there were only six of us this time – a charming Scots lady, a Mrs Harcourt from Stirling and myself going the whole way to England, two gentlemen going to Paris, and two others just as far as Kisumu on Lake Victoria.

The air was crystal clear and Nairobi, with its thirty thousand inhabitants, stood out green and bright as we flew just north of the Prince of Wales School, and then almost before we knew it we were over the Mission and there was Jenny Smith from the Alliance High School, good soul that she is, waving her towel as promised. For a moment I felt nostalgic, and then the excitement hit me – here was I, flying back to England, travelling 1, 000 feet up and all of seventy miles an hour. Even in my wildest dreams neither on my old

BSA motor bike or in the Ford could I even reach 60mph, and flat out at that! What a thrill it all was, and I felt myself to be so lucky.

From this eagle eye view, I could see all the old familiar territory of Kikuyu land. There were the paths that I have cycled, sometimes at night with a hurricane lamp precariously perched on the handlebars, my medical bag on the other end when called out to an emergency. Putting a brave face on it all, I sang choruses to frighten off the lions and leopards – perhaps that achieved its purpose by frightening them.

Over there was the flat bit beyond the mission where I and two others had vainly chased a rogue rhino which had bothered the hospital, me with an old Webley revolver that I had never in my life fired and did not even know how to release the safety catch. Needless to say that while we saw the beast – at a distance – we did not achieve anything.

The first part of the flight was across the coffee and tea plantations which were green and fresh. I could make out the maize and areas of sweet potatoes, but then we were over the dry area of the Great Rift Valley all burnt up and brown, the whole area striated like an old man's face. I wondered once again how the great cattle tribes of the Masai survived the dry months. And of course they don't, and the cattle dry in droves. To them a cow is cash, each one like any old pound note – torn or twisted, it is still worth a pound! As you may imagine, my camera was in great demand and I had photos of the extinct volcanic cones of Suswa and Longinot, while below lay Lake Naivasha, silvery in the light and ringed with its pink eye of the flocks of flamingos. We were only about 1, 000 feet up, and everything stood out sharp and clear. The flight had begun to be a little bumpy but my stomach was in good heart – if I can put it that way!

Mount Kenya

Away to the northeast were the twin peaks of Mount Kenya, rising to 17, 040 feet. Sadly, I have managed five expeditions to it, all failing at about 16, 000 feet, though I suppose that my one claim to fame is that I did skate, at 15, 000 feet on the "curling pond" or the Equator. We had seen the sugar lump of Kilimanjaro as we took off and even though it is over 19, 000 feet, I have climbed that. It is a much simpler task.

One of the pilots came to the rear to tell us that we were over the police station at Narok, with its school and neat barrack blocks and the country had changed to a rich green with little pillars of fire from the scattered huts. The huts were like circular mushrooms, but as we progressed along the Great Rift, the villages were different, this time with a large central hut surrounded by the smaller ones of the wives, bright green hedges all very clean and symmetrical. Interesting for the anthropologist to see his studies on polygamy laid out before him in such a fashion.

By this time, we had started to drop towards the ocean-like Lake Victoria and landed smoothly at Kisumu at 10.35am.

Standing on the aerodrome, its wings glinting in the morning sun, was our next aircraft – one of the Hannibal class, the Hengist. I remembered dimly that Hengist and Horsa were twins – some kind of invading knights in the Middle Ages perhaps? Our new aeroplane was bigger with accommodation for up to twenty passengers. Our brief stop was for half an hour, but it gave us a chance to drink a cup of coffee and stretch our legs.

We took off for Entebbe at 11.15am. We were in luck – the Hengist was a beautiful new plane, this time a biplane with the new experimental seats, two cabins – the fore one with six seats and the rear for ten. The seats were lovely, with buttons in the arms which could tilt them to any angle that you wished, and a writing table in the back of the seat in front. How easy it now is to write my diary. There is even a head piece which you can raise to allow me my post lunch nap – how very thoughtful!

We flew at about 6, 000 feet or 2, 000 metres above the Lake, first over the Kavirondo Gulf, and then straight across the great Lake Victoria itself. Our view was restricted, with heavy smoky clouds though we passed over a number of islands, their gardens all ready for planting and looking very neat and tidy. The flight was lovely, and there were only five of us on board, so we were aft for the sake of weight. There was almost complete silence, unlike the Artemis, and no vibration, so that this diary was completed apace. We landed at Entebbe at 12.55pm. The aerodrome is at the back of the hill on which Entebbe was built. In fact, Entebbe is not the capital of Uganda, which is Kampala, like Rome built on seven hills, with the King's Palace on the highest. I remember on my first visit, way back in 1908, being given a cycle to ride from one part of the town to another. It was great fun freewheeling down one hill, but not so great pedalling like mad up the other. Strangely, on one hill, I found myself being pushed upwards by a small boy.

I later discovered that it was the tradition for small boys to be posted the foot of the hills and to be tasked to give "distinguished" guests a push up the steep side. In Glasgow that would be a "hurley", but a hurley with a difference. It had been a wonderful feeling to be so distinguished. The lunch at Entebbe was excellent, with a delicate fish dish. I sent off a wire to let the family know that I had survived 157 miles in three hours!

From Entebbe we flew north across the green well-cultivated fields of Uganda. Here was the source of the thousands of bales of cotton that feed the mills of Lancashire and Paisley. My own family came originally from Paisley, and we can trace their descent as cotton spinners back to the 1700s, my father having been a calico printer in Glasgow. Soon we could see the mighty Nile, narrowing and then expanding into Lake Kioga, and then narrowing to pour over the narrow gorge of the Murchison Falls.

We left Entebbe at 1.45pm, having lost one passenger and gained five. Among the new passengers were two Swedes – a Baron and Baroness no less – who were returning home after a shoot. After the Lake we dropped to just 200 feet, perhaps to let us see the game. The two Swedes said that they had seen some fifty elephants, though I saw neither. Perhaps as my family will unkindly guess, it was the time of my after-lunch sleep. For the first time there was a shower of rain, though the plane dodged one belt of rain and it got a bit bumpy. Thankfully my tummy has remained unaffected.

Tea was served as the plane continued to try to avoid the worst of the storms. Below us, the Nile had become un-navigable, and I looked carefully to see where I had walked fifteen years before. What has taken the aircraft one hour took me nine days of hard walking, hot and bedevilled by the swarms of flies. I sit in comfort now like a god – at times a bit awe inspiring.

We landed at Juba at 5.30pm, having covered 340 miles in three hours and forty five minutes. Juba is a new township ten miles beyond Rigof. In 1920, we stopped at Rigof, but Juba seems to have taken over, perhaps because of its importance to navigation on the Nile. We were taken to the new modern Sudan Railways Hotel, run by a Greek, as are most of the hotels in the Sudan. The room was big and airy with a little veranda and a large bed, complete with the necessary mosquito net.

Because we had had tea on the plane I was free to walk down to the wharf on the riverbank and see the small boats tied up for the night. The big river steamer had gone earlier, but we will see it tomorrow on our way north.

The dinner this evening was lovely – soup, fish, a meat course and Melba ice cream. Here we were in darkest Sudan with electricity and a Frigidaire. The southbound plane has not yet arrived, so I can complete this part of the diary, post it on the southbound plane, and you will get it within two days. I slept well.

Tuesday 5th February

Wow! Knocked awake with a cup of tea at 4.30am. Imperial British Airways certainly believe in getting their passengers on their way early. Breakfast at 5am and off in motorcars to the airfield. The engines are being warmed up, and we are in the air at 6am. It is too dull to take any photos but we kept low, about 200 feet, and sure enough, within half an hour, the little bell tinkled and we all rushed across to the left hand side to see the first herd of elephants – only about ten, one being a toto. The plane circled slowly round which, not surprisingly, seemed to worry them. Over the next hour, we saw another small –herd, and then as we crossed the Nile at Boi, there were two big herds, one of over two hundred and the other even bigger. All the herds were clear to us with the flocks of white birds that flew above them. These elephants did not seem much worried by us – perhaps they thought that we were just another large bird? As we passed Boi, we saw the river steamer that had left Juba two days before.

The weather was still the dry season and we could see the huts of the Shilluk tribe. Many of the huts were being re-thatched, probably because of the Dry and in preparation for the Wet, and the cattle were corralled in a separate boma. All the huts were walled up to three to four feet with white clay, and near each village there was a small depression of the water hole. I had always heard that you could walk from one end of Africa along the network of paths and these little winding walkways stood out clearly in the dust, intersecting at various places like railway junctions. Not much has changed since Livingstone had criss-crossed the Dark Continent, and I felt quite historical that I might be seeing the very paths along which Baker and his wife had travelled in their epic journey to trace the Nile.

The flight followed the course of the Nile, meandering – the river, not the flight – here and there, dividing round islands and meeting again, the banks were all fringed with papyrus and occasionally there was the blunt grey shape of a hippo, but I found it difficult to pick out either the hippo or any crocs. After a bit we climbed to 3, 000 feet until we dropped down to land at Malakal at 10.45am, having covered 326 miles in just under four hours. This was a petrol stop, but it allowed us time to stretch rather weary legs and be given a tea of coffee and biscuits from a nearby tent while the plane was refreshed with fuel. We all congregated and shared our excitement at the herds of elephant. Even the B&B (Swedish) said that they had never seen anything like that in their journeys.

We were off within half an hour and flew at 5-6,000 feet away from the river, and so it became boring. Boring? While enjoying such an experience? Afraid so! Never mind – there was lunch about 12.30 on the plane, and some lunch at that!

Soup, salmon – caught on the Nile that morning – well, they would say that, wouldn't they? That was followed by a salad of meat, ham and tongue, and then fruit and cheese. I cannot deny, though the family would merely say that I was following my usual routine, that I slept soundly. Well, I had been up at 4.30am. The new seats simply encouraged me. But I did read a bit, and write my diary – honest.

The second stage on this long part of the journey was a ten minute stop at Kosti to allow – would you believe it? – the smokers a break for their filthy habit. So speaks a life long non-smoker, probably I'm a bit priggish as well. The only bit of excitement for me was a photo of some camels and donkeys etched behind the plane. Incidentally, we had lost one of our passengers, or rather we had offloaded him at Juba, so we were down to eight at this stage. You become a little blasé as one of the "originals" from Nairobi and we were intrigued with three of the passengers who had got on at Entebbe. One was a rather pretty fair-haired lady, her chauffeur/courier and her maid. She disembarked at Kosti, as her car had been left there. Now had it got there? Who had driven it? How had it survived the heat of the Sudan? What had she been up to after leaving it a few days before at Kosti? Step forward, Sherlock Holmes – how would you have worked out the story? Was there a body entombed in the vast wastelands of the Sudanese desert? Ah, well, a vivid imagination does while away the hours. We had passed the South bound plane about 11am – very late.

The sky was clear and the sun shone brightly at 6, 000 feet, and just before Khartoum we could see the reason for the site of the town with the appearance of the Blue Nile, clear hence its colourful name, joining to the white or brown Nile from the desert. We slid gently down to the aerodrome and landed at precisely 4.20pm. What it is to be so accurate – 756 miles in eight hours and five minutes. The ease of the journey reminded me of some of the early missionaries who had walked up from the Coast to Kikuyu and learnt to count their steps to keep an accurate log of their progress. Granny Watson, one of the originals at the Mission, was so accustomed to doing this that she even counted her steps when she walked round Mount Kenya.

Khartoum looked beautiful in the last evening light and we were taken by bus the two miles to the Grand Hotel which was on the river front, near to the Palace. It seems odd to think that only fifty years before, General Gordon had been speared to death at this very spot. For many families in Britain, it still held memories. My own younger brother had been given Gordon as his second name. Today, the Sudan enjoys the fruits of Pax Britannica, with the government by the British held in high regard. Long may it remain so.

I am looking forward to this evening, perhaps a highlight on the journey. Friends from Scotland – Mr & Mrs Angus Gillan – had promised me a dinner when I arrived in Khartoum. So, on arrival at the Grand Hotel, a superb building, I was conducted to a huge double-bedded room complete with bathroom attached. How often in 1935 is luxury such as that granted to one? Anyway, I phoned Angus as soon as we had been refreshed with tea and cakes to be told that he was playing tennis but would ring back as soon as he had finished. True to his word, he rang to tell me that a car would collect me about 8pm. Just time for a bath and to finish my day's diary,

The car arrived on time and took me to the Gillans' house and I was ushered into a large roomful of people. The Gillans were charmingly welcoming and I was introduced to the Governor, H.E. Sir Stuart Symes and his ADC, who arrived moments afterwards. Fourteen of us sat down to dinner and I sat between Miss King, who is the Scotch Matron of the Hospital, and Mrs Gibson, whose husband is busy building dams in the country. The price for a pleasant company is that I will be responsible for their two boys, who join the flight at Alexandria to return to school. After dinner, when the ladies had withdrawn to allow cigars and port for the men, once again I "suffered" for my principles of non-smoking and abstinence from alcohol. I have to say that I did not really suffer, as the opportunity for good conversation more than made up for any loss. H.E, the Governor, was interesting about both the current state of Kenya and in giving some rather blunt views on some of the settlers. I also spoke to a Colonel Bacon who has served with the KAR – The King's African Rifles – in Kenya in 1905-7. Lastly, I renewed an old rugby feud with Sir Robert Archibald, who had graduated from Edinburgh University and had played against me in various varsity rugby matches. He is now the Director for Medical Services in the Sudan. They say that Scotland has no need for independence as it already runs the British Empire. How true!

All in all, it was a great evening, and I went to bed tired but pleasantly invigorated by the company. Never had a bed felt more attractive or more comfortable. One of the great benefits of being teetotaller is that mornings after hold no fears, and knowing Imperial British Airways, it will be an early start tomorrow. I really must stop sounding so smug. On that deep philosophical note I shall go to sleep. Well-dined, well entertained, good company – what more could a man ask?

This was the family taken on holiday, probably on the way to the Treetops Outlook near Nyeri, as you have to cross the Equator to reach it. You will see our youngest, David, in the middle, holding the signpost. My trip in 1935 gave me the chance to see our eldest, Jo. He had been sent home in 1931 as there was no suitable education in Kenya at that time, and the experiment of a governess was not a success. By that time our middle youngster, Carol, was at school at St Andrews at Turi. David joined her that year.

Wednesday 7th February

On awakening this morning, I felt quite disorientated and my first thought was, "where on earth am I?" And then, true to my forebodings of the night before, we were awakened with a cup of tea at 4.15am – 4.15 of a dark Sudanese morning, but still warm. Once I had woken sufficiently to realise that we were in Khartoum, I gave a thought to the last time that I had travelled this way. That was in 1920, with my good friend Sir Fowell Buxton, who was later to be my companion on my next attempt on Mount Kenya, and best man at my wedding later the next year. That time we took a month to travel by boat and on foot down the Nile to Lake Victoria. After that journey I was tired, foot-sore, filthy dirty and nigh exhausted. We followed very much in the track of the Bakers, the first full explorers of the River. Little had changed. We were always near the river, but frequently we had to make long detours round the swampy bits. The natives were friendly and we were always welcomed wherever we stopped, the days of Livingstone and the long lines of the slave caravans were long gone. It was not a trip that I would have wished to repeat – there was too much heat, dust and sheer physical exhaustion, not to mention the insects. Yet here I was twenty five years later, a little over two decades on, but only one day needed to cover the whole way by air, still fresh and in good heart. A lovely thought – the cup of tea – but just a little early. It's this need for the new system of transportation, the airway, to prove that it is just that bit more efficient than its predecessors. Breakfast was served at 4.45am, and by that time, the boys had collected the luggage from our doors. What a breakfast! Fresh fish followed by ham and eggs, toast and excellent coffee. This super efficiency was a little spoilt as the bus did not appear until 5.30am. Oh, if we had just had that extra time in that wonderfully comfortable bed.

Dawn was just breaking as we got to the airfield – the special dynamos had got the engines ticking over and we were away, the doors shut, at 5.45am. It was a gorgeous sight to the east as the sun rose, pale and the pink followed by rich golden bronze, suffusing the darkness of the desert with colour radiating all the colours of the sun. There is not a lot of heating that early on these modern aircraft, and the steward tucked us all in with warm blankets. There was complete silence – not I think that we were all enthralled by the beauty of the dawn, but more likely that most of us had gone to sleep.

The two pilots, Captain Powell with his co-pilot Captain Matheson, a real Glaswegian from his accent, were men after my own heart and believed in saving time and fuel by short cuts, and with a small passenger load they could afford to do so. Our normal target for refuelling was 260 miles away at Shereik, but they made a beeline for Wadi Halfa, straight across the desert. They saved 60 miles and we did our longest flight of 420 miles in six hours. We were flying rock steady at 7000 feet, the desert spread out in stark colours below us. I took some photos but fear that all they will show is rather boring mile after mile of sand. Why is it that photographers can never refrain from taking photos even when they know that they will prove anything but earth shaking? The only signs of life were the little clusters of villages, clay houses roofed with reeds, and these stood out clearly below us.

About 9am, we were provided with a cup of hot Bovril and a water biscuit, very welcome and warming, though we were soon able to dispose of the comfort of the blanket.

Because there was little to see, we soon found ourselves sharing details of our lives, or perhaps a little gossip is part of all our existence – the more so at 9, 000 feet. The B&B (the Swedes) whom I had romantically suspected of being a honeymoon couple, had in fact children, one of two and half and a younger one, so that piece of imaginative fiction went out of the window. We learned that her Ladyship, whom we had left behind for a leisurely break at Khartoum, was a Lady Nott or Knot, and was the widow of a shipping magnate who had left her comfortably off. In my book as an impoverished missionary, that probably meant a few hundred thousand pounds, or perhaps even millions. She came from Jersey, as did her maid and chauffeur whom she could afford to fly with her. It had cost her just £20 to have that extra break of her journey at Khartoum for a week, while the two servants went on to collect her 25 HP Rolls car, which had been left at Cairo. She obviously was a good mistress, as she had paid up front for the two to have a trip to the Valley of the Kings that evening.

There were two more passengers, an Englishman travelling to Cairo, and a Frenchman whose name I never learnt.

We landed at Wadi Halfa at 11.45. This is an important terminus, for roads and steamer as it is the end for the Khartoum line and the start/end of the Nile Cataracts. The Steamer goes from here to Aswan and the dam and all the temples. The native taxi drivers were clearly infected by the I.B.A bug and we positively flew over and through the ruts of an awful murram road. Lunch as usual was excellent – iced soup, hot and wonderfully tender chicken, cold meat followed by a fritter with a secret sauce. As a good teetotaller, I dared not ask its ingredients. I certainly slept well after lunch. It was not long before our friendly Captain Powell, or should that have been Bligh, had us on our way. My heart went out to the smokers who were unable even to finish their cigarettes.

In minutes we were off again at 12.43 and soon up at 8, 000 feet. The afternoon was glorious; we avoided Aswan flying direct to Luxor where we arrived at 3.43, just a three hour flight which included a welcome cup of tea at 2pm. The 6 mile journey into Luxor was rough and we passed the fellaheen, some of them hard at the double wheel worked by a buffalo, others with the shaduf, hauling water up at the end of a weighted pole. The Winter Palace lived up to our expectations, standing on the river bank looking out to the Valley of the Kings, while the Temple and Karnak were on the same side.

Tombs of the Queens

I.B.A. had laid on a trip across the river to the Valley of the Kings, but being a Scot with an eye to the pennies and having seen the tombs in 1920, I decided to opt out. I don't suppose that they have really changed that much since my last visit. I felt the need for some exercise after all those hours of sitting – and eating – so I walked into town. It was very disappointing, dirty, and smelly with an endless run of small boys tugging at hands asking for baksheesh, or making suggestions that I felt it better to pretend not to understand. So another day, scenery pretty boring after the glory of the sunrise as it was all sand, sand and yet more sand. The day covered 700 miles and took about nine hours. Tomorrow is a short day with an 8 o'clock start so we might hopefully be allowed to sleep until 6.30.

Thursday 8th February

A long lie in at the Winter Palace with tea at 6.20, but the luggage boy at 6.30 so slug-a-beds had to be up sharpish. I have taken to shaving at night so I have just that little extra time in the mornings. I also have all my things packed up ready. I had, fortunately, pulled down my mosquito net last night as a fellow passenger was quite badly bitten.

A good breakfast and off at am; it was distinctly chilly and I was glad of my woolly gloves, muffler and warm coat. I was in the same car as Captain Powell so I was able to pick his brains about the journey. Each plane does 400 hours running before it needs a change of engines – clean ones, not necessarily new. That means the plane will cover about 400, 000 miles, or eight trips to the Cape and back. The changeover of engines takes about a day, the carburettors are fixed and never need to be fiddled with – perhaps my Ford could be given a set! The fuel tank holds six hundred gallons and uses about one hundred gallons an hour at the rate of one mile a gallon. Going north into the wind, the speed drops to 80-90mph, while a tail wind, often going south, sees an improvement in speed up to 135mph.

We took off at 7.45 and flew over the Temple of Karnak and then the Tombs, and then a sharp right, or should it be to starboard, to make a beeline for Cairo, The bitter cold of the dawn had gone and flying at 8-9, 000 feet, we were warm and cosy. Another beautifully clear day, but still just sand and more sand. We were served hot cocoa and biscuits at 9 o'clock, and then back over the Nile as we approached Cairo. Below were the Pyramids and the Sphinx. Oh traveller, what has two legs and walks on four and then three? "The ancient famous challenge of the fearsome Sphinx to the wayfarer, whose failure to answer the riddle meant instant death." "Why, dear Sphinx, it is man of course. As a baby he crawls on four legs, as a man on two, while in old age he has the help of a stick." What a fund of interesting/useless knowledge one does accumulate in one's life. We landed at 11.15am, having covered about 380 miles. The aerodrome is jointly owned by Imperial, The Army and KLM. Once again we were whisked off, oddly after going through customs for the first time on the journey, to the fine Airport Hotel for lunch. I had been told that the family of an old Kenya friend was a Flight Lieutenant in the RAF and based at Heliopolis, and on enquiry, I found that their house was only five minutes away. A kindly member of the I.B.A. staff ran me down and I had half an hour with the family, and then hurried back to the Hotel where I was entreated by the waiter to have my lunch. I just made it.

There was a new Captain, or Master as they will call him, as Captain Powell was on the other flight to India. The new pilot was a Captain Alcock, and we soon discovered that this was part of the famous Alcock and Brown partnership who were the first to cross the Atlantic. If my memory serves me right, they finished up nose down in an Irish bog. I hope that he has learnt to land more delicately with passengers on board.

We took off at 1.40pm and flew direct to Alexandria, landing there at 3.15, and were driven to the Hotel Cecil through a very rough part of the town. The Hotel itself was pleasant and situated on the sea front, with a wonderful view of the calm blue Mediterranean. We were able to watch our next aircraft land on the sea at 5.30.

I had dinner with some friends but was off to bed pretty quickly. They, the friends, had been upset the previous week with the crash of a KLM plane in the Mediterranean. The wreckage had been found by the RAF. The thinking was that it was due to pilot fatigue or lightning, the plane took off from Amsterdam and had one brief stop before the crossing the sea. The crew decided to go ahead even though the Imperial flight was postponed because of the storms ahead. Sad and a bit scary for us with our prospective flight next day.

Friday 9th February

No sleep for the wicked – we were woken at 5am with a cup of rotten tea and a stale cake. Breakfast was late as they were waiting for the Palestine connection. The two Gibson lads whose parents I had met in Khartoum appeared from another hotel and I introduced myself. They seemed pleased to have company, or perhaps they had been well brought up and were simply being polite. How things have changed from my day when I walked to school, and now you can fly!

The bus collected us and took us to the launch that carried us out the 50 yards to the plane. It is one of the Scipio class and called Satyrus, with the capacity to have fifteen people, though there were only eight on board.

One of the arrivals was from Lloyds Register of shipping. He had come from Aden the previous day, and was thankful to be flying British. His last flight was gippy and was overcrowded, while the pilots had not the slightest interest either in the plane or the passengers, and were only interested in making sure that it landed.

We took off on a flat calm and there was a pleasant swish through the water, and in a moment we were in the air with a gorgeous sunrise to the East, a blaze of reds and golds. Only 6.25 in the morning!

That flight was marvellous – the sea was, of course, Mediterranean blue and like a mill pond. We had a 10mph tailwind, so our speed was about 110mph and we were able to fly at about 500 feet. I saw no ships this side of Crete, but Crete itself was lovely, with the hills green lower down but with snow on the tops. I slept a bit, as my family would have expected, but was woken by breakfast at 7.30. Very nice too, with hot coffee from the thermos, then grapefruit followed by ham and liver, the liver being particularly tasty. Funny how journeys revolve round food.

The Captain, a stout Scot, was able to leave the controls to his co-pilot and came and sat down beside me for a bit. He gets 2½p per flying hour over and above his salary. So he will make about £10 for today's work. If my calculations are correct that puts him on about £ 2, 000 a year, quite something compared with a humble missionary at £230 pa. I must curb that jealousy side of me. He flies bodies and I save souls. We really should get together as he reaches heights that I cannot.

The flight was very swift and we were able to make Athens direct without a stop at Mirabelle in Crete. We were over Athens and could see, despite some haze, the Parthenon and that small hill called Mars, from which a famous predecessor of mine called Paul had preached a sermon about the Unknown God. I wonder what Paul would have made of missionaries flying about their business. I guess that Athens has changed a little in 1900 years, but has man?

The landing, despite a slight swell, was smooth, and we taxied to our thirteen anchorage and were taken ashore by boat while the refuelling went on. It's fascinating how the moment everyone is on dry land out come the pipes or the cigarettes, it makes one very smug. So that was a flight of five hours and forty minutes – 600 miles.

There were barely thirty minutes before we were off at 12.35pm and flying over the Gulf of Corinth, and once more my thoughts were with Paul. What job would he have had today – perhaps a fabric maker for aeroplanes?

Does anyone write letters like he did? – and two of them to the Corinthians.

We lunched at 1 o'clock, and a very nice one too, and by this time we were up to 6, 000 feet, crossing the hills of Greece. Because of the good weather and the tailwind, the pilots were able to shortcut the journey and fly across the Adriatic and onto Brindisi. Despite a bit of buffeting, I never felt sick at all and we landed at 3pm, though that was really 4pm as we had gained/lost an hour. It was incredible to think that we had flown just on 1, 000 miles in a day, about nine hours flying time. That is almost the end of flying as we go by train to Paris with a last leg to London by air. The last time that I had been to Brindisi was by fast Anglo-Indian packet which connected up with P&O at Port Said and rushed across at breakneck speed and much racketing in forty eight hours.

Brindisi is a small town, so a walk through the streets added nothing to one's knowledge. We had a cup of tea before the walk and are dining at 7pm before boarding the Blue Danube Express at 8 o'clock, and that will take us two nights and a day to reach Paris.

Saturday / Sunday 9th & 10th February

I have surprisingly little memory of this trip and my diary seems to have a blank. Perhaps having enjoyed the sophistication of air travel I am satiated with a train. Perhaps one day there will be trains that travel at 200mph or even 100 that will match the aircraft, but that is not yet.

My memory of the journey is one of boredom. I.B.A. have a reserved coach on the Blue Danube and we each have a compartment to ourselves, but the days passed slowly, eating, reading, talking to our fellow travellers, but nothing of note. Perhaps Agatha Christie's detective novels on the Orient Express are more interesting, but this was not.

The train pulled into Paris on Sunday morning at 6.30am, and a cold and frosty one it was. We were transferred to the Hotel des Ambassadeurs near the I.B.A. Headquarters and given a good solid breakfast, none of your weak French croissant and coffee, but bacon and eggs and toast. Very welcome after the stiffness of the journey wore off. We said farewell to the Swedish B&B, who were now bosom pals. We then discovered that the other young man, another Scot, was MP for Broughton, but he intended to sample the pleasures of Paris for another day. I hope that a Parisian Sunday is a little more exciting, or should I say damning, than a "good" Scots Calvinist one, otherwise it will be a wasted day for the poor man. So there remained the faithful three – Mrs Harcourt, Mr Hughes, the hydroelectric engineer, and of course the two boys.

We left by bus for Le Bourget at 8.45, along with eight other newcomers. Why does one feel superior when others join a group who have travelled far?

We reached Le Bourget at 9.20 to find the Hercules waiting for us, its engines warming up. I felt that we had come full circle as it exactly matched dear old Hengist with which we had almost started our journey. In this case, it could carry the huge load of 38. It was clear and frosty, but we travelled higher than before so saw little. It was pleasant, with a cup of Bovril and biscuits to warm us up. The last bit was very cloudy and we could see nothing of the ground, always a bit daunting for the passengers, but then suddenly there were cottages, fields and streets, and we were bumping down on British soil at 12.30pm.

There remained only customs and the last bus into the centre of London. For the statistical like me, I had left Kenya on the Monday, having preached in the Church of the Torch on Sunday and here I was in London, 4, 945 miles away and seven days later, able to attend the Scots Kirk in Pont Street in London that evening.

It has been an extraordinary journey, untroubled, easy, luxurious. What an experience. I can only end by congratulating Imperial Airways on their staff on the way in which they had looked after me. I had had visions of the future and been blessed with the chance to see them.

J. W.A in London

Kikuyu Then and Now

Rev John W Arthur OBE MD February 1935

Dunbog, A Rural Idyll?

September 1938 to July 1948

'The warld's aboot the queerest place
Ye couldna just say foo tae tak it
And queer the fowk o'human ract mak'it'

Dunbog

Green fields, a gentle countryside, the hills of home, the bleating of sheep in the fields and the lowing of cows. What more could you ask of retirement? In the nature of the world, reality is more than slightly different. The bleating of sheep just brought in from the hills and pastured in the manse fields kept us awake the first night of our arrival. The Fifer is notoriously slow to welcome strangers – "it takes 30 years, if you are not born in the kingdom to become a native!" So the new world of Scotland was not quite what any of us expected.

Dad gave up his post as head of the Church of Scotland Mission at Kikuyu, Kenya, in 1937. He had recently become very involved in the fierce arguments over female circumcision which had begun to divide the traditionalists among the Africans, which proved almost as good a recruiting ground for anti-colonialism as the major question of land and those who recognised that the initiation was neither Christian nor medically right. I was never quite sure whether my father decided that it was the right time to make a move, or whether he was given a gentle push by the Church. He was certainly not much liked, either by the administration or by the settlers, both for his efforts on land reform and for the female circumcision problem. For thirty years of work in Africa, he received no recognition at all from the government. The OBE which he had been awarded was for his work in raising the Carrier Corps in 1915. What did emerge in later years was the deep affection in which he was held by African leaders. Two major institutions that stand as his memorial are the Alliance High School, the premier school in Kenya, and the beautiful Church of the Torch.

Dad returned to an uncertain future. The home Church, while paying a weak lip service to missions, had no intention of rewarding returning missionaries in any practical way. The parishes – and this was an age when every small parish in

Scotland had a minister – looked askance at those who had not served their time at the coalface in Scotland. It was regarded as an easy option for a minister to work abroad. The prospects of finding a parish were poor. Initially he worked as the Assistant Minister to Dr Fleming at Pont Street in London. Jo was a boarder at Loretto and Carol and I were entered as day pupils at St. Trinneans in Dalkeith Rd in Edinburgh. For a few weeks, we were put into a dreadful boarding house at 26 Blacket Place, filled with elderly ladies in black bombazine and smelling of BO and mothballs. It was an awful place, and both Carol and I hated it. I think at one point we both climbed the tree in the back garden to escape. The next move was briefly to 59 Findhorn Place.

Finally, in May 1938, my father was invited to preach at the small parish church of Dunbog in North Fife, and was formally inducted later that year. His position at first was as assistant to Rev Tocher. Rev Tocher received half of the £300 stipend as his pension. The Church at that time had no pension policy nor fund.

Dunbog is a narrow strath running almost east to west between Cupar, six miles to the west and Newburgh four miles to the east. It is hemmed in by low hills on either side, while to the north lies the valley of the mighty Tay. Its name comes from a boggy section at the west end of the parish. The area was a long valley with no central or focal village, but a scatter of farms with a number of attached tied cottages. The nearest to a rallying point was at the foot of our road from the home farm to the main road – 4913. Farms at that time were heavily labour intensive, but with a strict pecking order – first the farmer, mostly on a lease basis, in the farmhouse, then the grieve or foreman with his own superior cottage; the dairyman, who was a skilled man, the cattleman, and then the lads in the bothy who were starting out. Finally, each farm had a string of tied cottages where the families lived.

They had little security but could move – at one time they were entitled to remove the roof beams of their cottages. The move was at Michaelman or Martinmas – the 11th of November. Life was hard, dependent on the weather, though they were out in all weathers. Life was governed by the seasons – spring and ploughing, summer and harvest, and autumn with tattie picking, though this was also for the kids or incomers.

The time that a boy remembers best of the seasons was harvest time. First, the field had to be opened with the scythe to make a road for the harvester and binder. Once that was done, in came the machinery, pulled either by the huge Clydesdales, or if they were lucky and wealthy, a Fordson tractor. The horses were great, huge, powerful yet gentle, and so obedient to commands. Mind, the hooves were enormous, and yet so delicately placed. The field was cut in a gradually diminishing circle, with the women and boys coming behind with rough string in their pockets for a final bind but collecting the sheaves in eights and stacking them into stooks. At the very end, when the cutting was almost finished, the fun began for the rabbits and hares caught in the middle trying to escape all the boys with sticks and the dogs. Fun for everyone but the poor animals. At a later date, the threshing machine puffed and blew its way from the previous farm and the thrashing began. That is after the stooks had been led in, piled high on the carts. If you were lucky and if you had helped, you were allowed to bounce on the top of the pile. Master of all you surveyed above the puffing horses.

The celebration of 'harvest home' brought home just how important the land and its produce was. In those days, you were very much part of the soil. Even more so when you went "tattie howking". Schools in October had three weeks off to allow the children to earn some cash. It was backbreaking and bitterly cold work. It was always wet, and you were given a wire basket and section of tatties to haul. If the machine was horse drawn, life was reasonable but if it was tractor driven, you never really caught up. Backs and fingers were covered in soil and blue with cold. You earned every penny. What was worse, we were volunteered by the school to give the money to the war effort.

The parish was hierarchical – first the laird, then minister and then the dominie. In our case the laird lived at the "big hoose", Aytonhill, which lay in the centre of the parish. Mr Carnegie was a real gentleman, complete with monocle, moustache and very upper-class speech and manners. He was always treated with the utmost respect, and the rare occasions when he was invited to tea were special occasions, except when Carol made ginger biscuits with pepper. Even then he behaved impeccably, ate one and laughed it all off. He had his own pew in church, at the front of the gallery on the left looking at the pulpit. Each

Sunday he sat there solemnly. I think that he slept a lot. He was a genuinely nice man, unusually married to a German, who was equally delightful, but who sadly died early in 1940. Aytonhill house was a large one, built on the small manor house style, east to west with a conservatory on the west side. A long drive, lined with beautiful daffodils in spring, led up to the house, while there was a small artificial lake below the house. He very kindly allowed me to fish when I wanted, though I never caught much, either there were very few fish or I was not… Dad did not have much luck either.

Mr Carnegie ran the estate with the help of a factor but it was done in a very genteel and fair way. I never heard any criticism of him. Sadly the house was burnt down in the 1950s.

Right in the middle of the glen was the schoolhouse with a large dwelling house attached to the school, but surrounded by a good-sized garden. The school itself was two larger rooms with the early part from five to eight, and then the upper part from eight to twelve. Each room sat in lines according to your age. Outside there was a large playground with grey asphalt chips. The loos were sheds sited on the north side of the playground one for the girls from which the boys were mostly successfully excluded – and another for the boys. In the latter there was, I think, a trough and one or two seats. Visits were brief and hurried because of the smell and the chill, and then only if essential. They were pretty primitive.

There were two teachers, the Head being a Miss Macpherson, a formidably tough but fair lady who lived in the house with her father. She ruled the school with the aid of a swinging belt, which she was never slow to use. She expected high standards, and the ultimate threat was either to bring in your parents or that you would be destined to go to Newburgh. The school system was clear – if you passed the qualifying test you went to the Bell Baxter in Cupar. If you were thick or lazy, you went to the Junior Secondary at Newburgh. I did not make progress, though the teaching was very sound and my parents decided that it would be a benefit by going to Lathallan, a prep school about 20 miles to the southwest. I remember little of the local school apart from two things, the first being totally humiliating when I had just learnt to ride a bicycle and the parents forced me to tie L plates when I rode to school. I have a sly feeling that I removed them once I got round the corner. The second was painful, and I still carry the mark. I had made friends with one Bill Watson of Johnston farm, where we got our milk, and we sat side by side. I think that I once made some rude remark to Bill, and he promptly jabbed his pencil into the back of my left hand – where the blue mark still lies. Memento mori!

The main road ran through the parish bisecting it. The buses ran every two hours between Perth on the west side and St. Andrews on the east. The journey to Cupar took about twenty minutes, and for some reason we rarely went into Newburgh. Once the war broke out, everything was blacked out including the windows of the bus, so you had to judge arrival on a time basis. The road from the bus stop to the manse was frightening. It was pitch black and ran for over half a mile, including a journey under the railway bridge and, having far too vivid an imagination, I believed every ghoulie and ghostie in the kingdom of Fife would pounce on me. The journey meant quick dashes at top speed, except on moonlit nights when I only had to run under the bridge. Parallel to the road was the single track railway from Dundee to Perth. Trains only ran rarely, and not at all after war broke out. I remember only one journey on it to Dundee across the Tay Bridge, as usual worrying all the time about the weather as the bridge would join the stumps of the fateful earlier one and crash into the water. Despite there being no trains, Mr Currie, who lived near the line, was kept on as rail man.

Even though we did not often visit Newburgh, it had an important position. There was the telephone exchange, manned by ladies. No automatic in those days. They could be very helpful. "Oh, it's no use trying the doctor, I saw him going out a few minutes ago!" The doctor was vital, and dealt with all our childhood maladies. As Dad believed in the vile calomel and salts for every known pressure from headaches to constipation, we had instant domestic relief. The calomel, a small pink pill, was delivered the night before, and the Epsom

Salts first thing in the morning. The effects were instant and sometimes catastrophic. Mum did not suffer like us – she just had senna pods in a glass beside her bed for daily intake. Her teeth lay beside, and I often worried that she might take the wrong glass in the dark. The other regular visitor to the doctor was Jo on his return from Academical matches, to remove the blood from his swollen ears.

The manse was a huge stone building, with an equally enormous garden. The ground must have extended to at least an acre. There was a large stretch of grass at the front or north side, a wooded and a number of rhododendron bushes on the west, with the old steeple sitting nearby. On the front of the main window of the drawing room was a grey mark where some local parishioners had tried to blow up the minister for not joining the Free Church at the Disruption. Outside the wall was the orchard with swathes of daffodils, which were picked by me in the spring and toted round the doors of the farms to raise money to "buy spitfires". People were always very generous. The rest of the orchard was rough grass with plum and apple trees.

Round the main garden was a high stone wall. On the wall were more plum and apple trees with more growing in the centre. We never lacked for plums or apples! The rest of the garden was cultivated by Dad, Mum and us. It was some job, with all the digging, planting and cropping to be done. I don't think that they ever really stopped. Right at the start, Dad decided that we should have a grass tennis court and an area was ploughed, flattened and grassed. It was a good investment, and much used both by the parents and by visitors. Dad used to organise those ministers who were young enough and able enough round for tennis tournaments – quite fearsomely competitive!

Incidentally, I never managed to beat Dad. He was extremely competitive, and had an extraordinarily strong wrist. There were no motor mowers, so the grass was cut by hand and the lines marked with a small marker. The worst part was the measuring out afresh the comers at the start of summer. Dad was keen on strawberries, raspberries, gooseberries and blackcurrants, so the summer was filled with jamming and preserving. Nothing was to be wasted in wartime. The downside, apart from a fearsome amount of sweat was the dreaded berry bug. From the end of July until September, the itch began. At the ankles, round the waist, at the wrists and under the armpits, and in an even more uncomfortable place, the summer could be hell. Blisters, agonising red swelling, blebs (liquid filled blisters) and this all-pervasive itch, particularly at night when you went to bed. Never forgotten and only matched by the chilblains of winter when your fingers became swollen and looked like bluebottles and stank of wintergreen. I suppose in many ways we were lucky.

There was no real heating in the manse, and no electricity. The fires had to be lit, and coal brought in after cleaning out the ashes. The kitchen stove was only lit for four hours in the morning to allow cooking, and then went out to eke out the coal ration. Light was with candles and small hand lamps with glass globes that had to be cleaned. And for the sitting room, a large Aladdin lamp with a delicate cone mantle, which had to be allowed to warm before you could turn it to full light. Later there were the Tilley lamps, which gave a better light but needed to be pumped into action. Paraffin was important and had to be bought in Cupar and brought back in cars. The wireless was powered by an accumulator that needed to be recharged at regular intervals at the garage at the entrance to Cupar. The gramophone was operated with a winding handle.

What I remember most about the manse is the cold and its draughts with flickering candles, and the almost endless challenges that were presented to both parents. Mum had come from being a lady of leisure in Kenya with houseboys and cooks, to having to do everything herself. She was never a great cook, but she coped, and Dad faced the Herculean task of keeping the garden going and running a parish. To add to that, he became a county councillor. Mind, that gave him petrol at a time when there was great shortage, and our Austin 12 was a real workhorse. It also meant that at the mature age of 12 Dad got out of the car one day as we drove to Cupar – "it's time that you learnt to drive." So I used to drive him on many of his journeys, empty roads and no police. No wonder I could pass my driving test five weeks after my seventeenth birthday.

The war, apart from the shortages of almost everything and the continual bad news in the early years, hardly affected us. There were uniforms everywhere, concrete blocks appeared round all the beaches to prevent invasions; all signposts were removed so that the Germans would not know where they were; poles appeared in every field to prevent gliders landing; and there was the blackout. All headlights were masked, torches had their beams lowered, every window had thick curtains and there were sandbags outside important buildings. Dad was also an air-raid warden, so we had a stirrup pump, useful for washing the car. He received warnings over the phone about expected air raids. My parents must have had endless worries about Jo fighting in the Far East. We became very much news junkies, with the 9 o'clock news a no-no in timing. Maps of Burma and India and the news of the war were high on our personal agenda.

Occasionally you could hear German aircraft passing over. One of our aircraft crashed near Higham farm and a Polish airman baled out from his Spitfire over Aytonhill. Dad immediately rushed in his car to collect the shaken young man and rewarded him with a cup of tea, heavily sweetened with our sugar ration. I suspect that he would have welcomed something rather stronger, but ours was a teetotal house. My reward was a Polish eagle badge to wear in my jacket – much prized at school. The other worry was the endless problems of rationing – 1lb of sugar a month, no bananas, meat at so much a week, butter and so on. We were lucky living in an agricultural area – we had a lot of fruit and vegetables ourselves and kept hens, so we had endless eggs and chicken.

There were almighty sessions of jam making and fruit preserving with all sorts of methods – vacuum jars, eggs in a revolting liquid. How quickly one forgets the huge benefits of a deep freeze – we did not get one until 1965 when my glamorous assistant, Rose, persuaded us to spend our money.

The manse had two huge rooms at the front – one was the drawing room, and the other above was a bedroom for the parents. Dad had small study which was heavily used, there was a dining room and a good sized kitchen with a stove and then the awful back kitchen which became the base for all the hard work – evening meals, laundry and sundry other tasks. There were few carpets and much linoleum. Beds were freezing in winter, and you quickly learnt to undress and to jump at maximum speed, and then a big leap into a bed with freezing sheets, trying not to burn your toes on the hot water bottle. Beds were freezing cotton sheets which had to be washed every week with two or three blankets and a quilt.

Making them up each day meant squaring off the corners – hospital corners, as insisted upon by Dad. Bedtime was not good for my imagination with those candles flickering and going out at the slightest draught, the huge dark corners, too much reading of ghost tales – Scott, Edgar Allan Poe. Every shadow had to be tested and passed safe.

Winters at that time were tough, with heavy falls of snow, often above the car roof and hard frost. Frost was great, as it meant skating. Lindores loch froze every year, and the miracle of skating over black ice with the weeds waving gently below your feet was something magical. I learnt to skate at a high level, back turns, elegantly on one leg, figures of eight – nae bother! There were fierce battles at school when the pond froze, with ice hockey fought to the last drop of blood and endless bruises. Winter sport was for me a joy, apart from the chilblains!

Dad was a very dedicated minister and fulfilled all the duties of visits, sick calls, help in any way that he could – even with small sums of money to help tide over disasters.

He wasn't the world's most wonderful preacher, but he had a wonderful and much respected faith that could overcome all doubt. One of his specialities was his children's blackboard. The text and the examples were all drawn in colour, and then hidden under small bits of black paper. They were quite magical and much enjoyed by the children. He also gave lectures in the hall, slides or cine of Kenya, the work of the church, fishing trips, climbs up Kilimanjaro and Kenya. These were taken round all sorts of places – other parishes, the Royal Geographical, Kenya Missions and Ardeonaig.

I used to act as projectionist, and became quite skilled at working the film projector and the slide one. I got to know when to make the changes of slide at the right time and how to repair the 16mm film, which frequently broke.

Among other activities, Dad started first Life Boys and then the Boys Brigade. Mum was a cousin of Sir William Smith, the founder of BB, and Dad kept in touch with Stanley Smith. His son, Stanley, was a real Glaswegian, a big man with a lovely sense of humour who was General Secretary of the BB. He visited us once or twice. His younger brother, Douglas, was quite different, physically much smaller and very square, with the smoothest voice you have heard. He worked for the BBC. Douglas was a Lorettonian, and kept in close touch with the school. He always had a small coterie of boys whom he used to take out to tea at the Co-op. A big fry-up, as much bread and butter as you could eat, scones, cakes and tea, all for half a crown He was very good to me. There was a bit of tittle-tattle about him, but I think that he just genuinely liked younger men and their cheerful and noisy company.

Dad used to take on locum duties in the summer for George Grieve, who had been the head of Alliance High School in Kenya, and then went into the ministry and became parish minister at Ardeonaig on Tayside. It was a gorgeous situation, down a narrow road with an open sward, the manse and the church. Dad organised a BB camp with Cupar boys, and we all drove up in an open lorry one scorching July. The open part was half the fun but what would H & S say now? It was a great success, and I was welcomed into a very different culture, but I never found any difficulty in fitting in. Their language and jokes were not half as bad as at Loretto! Most of the boys, including myself, were persuaded to join the church.

At the west end of the parish was Blinkbonny Farm, with a Major Lawson. Major Lawson because he joined up at the start of the war event, though farming was a reserved occupation. He was a nice man, very gentle, and I have a feeling that he was killed at the end of the war, leaving a wife and young child. Coming into the centre were Higham with Mr and Mrs Stirrat, and then the oddly named Glenduckie, with the Arbuckles. Mr Arbuckle was a formidable man and was the Session Clerk.

Next door to us was the home farm of Dunbog, which belonged to a Mr Spence. Spence was also a butcher and was rarely at home and the farm was run by his son, who later turned it into a sort of zoo. The offload – all manner of offal – from Mr Spence's business was downed on the road over the hill. This was known as the "Stinks Road", for obvious reasons. It was a well-run farm with a very good grieve. The manse had two fields as our glebe and this was rented to Mr Spence for £10 pa, though they were rarely used except for ingathering. I used one as a sort of Murrayfield on which I played endless successful games of rugby as one of my heroes – Keith Geddes or W.I.D. Elliot, who were very kind and often let me score tries or convert goals, including one immense drop goal from halfway a la Jean Prat of France.

Imagination was my saving grace. The other field I occasionally used for hunting rabbits. Armed with Jo's 410 shotgun, I sallied out and practised my kitten or leopard crawl. Sadly it soon became clear that I would never make the commandoes. Whether the range of the shotgun was inadequate or I was a rotten shot. Anyway, the rabbits were safe.

On the way to the main road was Dunbog House. It was almost out of Dickens, huge and mysterious, but an almost complete ruin. The roof leaked, many windows were boarded up, the paintwork was peeling. Inside it was no better – rather like a film set for a vampire movie with cobwebs and candlelight. Miss Menzies, who lived there with an equally ancient cook/companion, was large, and she waddled, clothed in enormous cardigans and holey slippers. She was delightful and humorous but how she lived there none of us could understand. When you rang the bell it echoed cavernously and you waited an age for the arrival of one of them with a lamp, to be ushered down the dark corridor to their kitchen round which all life revolved. She had a brother – equally large – who was a GP in Portobello. In later days he kindly gave me a lunch at least on one Sunday a term on my out days from school. The real attraction, however, was his elder daughter, a gorgeous teenager named Rosemary, who came to stay with her aunt. What she thought of the house I dared not think. But for me it was a turning point, and I fell deeply in love. I fear it was vain, as Rosemary had a stream of admirers much nearer at home, and probably much more worldly wise than me. She even fell for Hamish Inglis, a large Academical who later played for Scotland. It was a sad affair as we hammered the Academy that year, and she eventually married a small fat Jew. I felt that that served her right.

Below the big house was a ramshackle cottage where dwelt the local poacher. He was a charming man, cap over his eyes, unshaven and with a long coat to which were attached rabbits, hares, etc. In one capacious pocket was his weasel, always available with a toothy snarl for display. He was easy-going and always happy to sell us rabbits when needed. I seem to remember that he had a pretty daughter, but sons of the manse had eyes far above poacher's daughters.

On the main road was a pretty little cottage which had a renowned well in the garden, a well-polished car, and a little sweet shop that died with the war, but occasionally was able to sell Highland Toffee. It was lovely, but must have done endless damage to my teeth. Mr Speed had been in service as a chauffeur and had been given the car – a Humber – as a reward for long service. His car was the local taxi service. Speed might have been his name, but dead slow was his driving. He often undertook to collect me and any other local boys from Lathallan, either for days out or at the end of term. It was a stranding joke in the school – was it Speedy coming to collect you? He also took us to the occasional party, usually at Kilmaron House, the home of the Lowe family of grocery fame. Speed did his reputation no good when he made silly comments to Carol on one trip.

Beyond the school and hall where we had our Sunday school and village parties, was the rail man's cottage. Here lived Mr Currie who also the beadle in the Church. A nice man. The next stop was the smithy, where there was always a heat. The fire blazed and the bellows blew, horses for shoeing, machines to be repaired – the day was never long enough. If you were lucky you were allowed to work the bellows. The smell of horses' hooves – how patiently they stood while the smith did unmentionable things to their feet – of dung, of oil. The smithy was a wonderful place for a small boy with never ending tasks. I soon learnt that farmers are the most casual people about their machinery. It could be left outside, it could rust, it could have broken down. Nae matter!

Above the smithy was a big farm with the Todds. The son went to Loretto, but was much older than me. Behind it was the main hill of the area – Normans Law. It had a prehistoric fort on the crest. It was a gentle hill ideal for Sunday afternoon walks, with a glorious view over the Tay to the North and to Dundee. For Dad it had memories of the real mountains – Kenya and Kilimanjaro – for him a hill of home but no real compensation for those distant snow covered peaks.

Dad always kept close touch with neighbouring ministers but he had a few particular cronies. Flisk was just over the hill overlooking the Tay, and the minister was Rev Dunnett, a delightful, quiet man with a sweet wife. He retired to Joppa Park and was always willing to give me lunch on a Sunday out from school. He had two sons – the younger went into the RAF and was killed, while the elder one, Alastair, worked as journalist, I think for the BBC – not to be confused with the more famous Alastair Dunnett, who became editor of *The Scotsman*. At the top of the hill on the way to Cupar was Moonzie, where the Rev Duncan preached, tall and rangy and father to the famous and charismatic George Duncan, who preached in the Episcopal church in Corstorphine, and the much disliked Jack Duncan. The latter was an odd man who had the knack of raising hackles whenever we met. He had been briefly in Kikuyu and came back to Earlston in the Borders. He managed to referee a match with Wanderers and Earlston, which he ensured that we lost 8-6. Mind, I am not wholly prepared to admit that I failed to kick two conversions from almost in front of the posts that would have given us victory. Then there was the large and fun loving minister of St.

John's in Cupar, John Macphail, whose bellowing laugh used to echo over the tennis court.

The other family with whom we had close connections were the Maitlands at Abdie. They cherished their grandfather, one Captain Maitland of the Bellerephon – a large ship of the line, which had taken Napoleon to his prison on St. Helena. There was a large painting of the embarkation of Bonaparte onto the ship hanging in their hall. Old Mrs Maitland was a sweet old lady with pink and white complexion and a lace mobcap. The son went to Lathallan, but was much younger. His father was a Naval Captain in the family tradition, though I never met him as he always seemed to be at sea.

So that is, or was, Dunbog, a big part of my childhood and of my growing up. I don't have all that many happy memories of it, though equally I don't have many bad memories. It taught me how to get on with people of all types and classes, and made me realise and enjoy the land and its people.

Life was very lonely – there were no boys of my own age, and where there were they were working on their farms. Both Mum and Dad were slaves to the parish, Dad as the minister with far fuller involvement than in the equivalent small parish today. There are, of course, no small parishes now. Then there was the County Council and the garden, and his links with the missions. Mum was little more than a drudge, as the house was full time with all the cooking responsibilities and the garden. She never stopped trying to be a good minister's wife. They had little time for their son, and that is not a criticism it was the reality of the day. They had a maid for about a year until the war got under way in late 1939 – from then on, it was all on their shoulders.

It meant that I was on my own for much of the holidays. Jo went off to the army in May 1941, and Carol to the Royal in Edinburgh in 1944. Loretto, oddly, did not lend itself to making close friends, as you were moved from house to house and room to room. I was in Newfield, then Linkfield and finally Holm House, and in different rooms all the time. I found myself heavily dependent on my own resources. The war was very inhibiting in that you were not encouraged to travel much, even in the locality. I did a lot of work in and around the garden and the house, but for the rest I was playing imaginary games on the tennis court or in the field, or reading. I was a voracious reader – we got boxes of books from Douglas & Foulis in Edinburgh, and I read most of Dickens, a lot of Scott and all of Thackeray, not to mention Biggles and Percy F. Westerman.

I suppose that this made me very self-contained, not as good as I might have been in making relationships, and totally reliant on myself in dealing with problems. Life could be very tough, whether at school or at home. We accepted that we would have hard knocks and have to get on with it. Counselling or support services were something that only the weak needed, and anyway did not exist. Odd then, that I spent my life with an organisation like the Samaritans – or maybe that was why!

Dunbog, looking back on it after almost fifty years, was an interesting place, but now it is long gone in terms of the twenty first century – farms are still the same size but run by many fewer people, often only two where there were up to a dozen. The role of the church in rural areas is quite different. There is no longer the isolation that there was when people were dependent on the bus, as they all have cars. Poverty as we knew it does not exist on that scale, and morality as laid down by the church and by local culture has lost its grip. Schools are happier and less brutal places, though not necessarily more effective. Quite simply it is, in 2005, a different world. The world for young people is quite literally now their oyster – good luck to them!

LORETTO: As Time Goes By

The trouble with an aging population is that the memories get larger and longer, and the changes that have happened appear that much greater. It's a horrifying thought that a simple lunch for the over 60's has brought on a torrent of recall, and strangely, that was within a situation where the physical surroundings were not so very different from the 1940's. The wall colourings of the old school are still that yellow ochre, an odd hue to one who has spent much of his life a long way from that East Lothian shade.

It's when time has passed and one has absorbed the differences and one begins to wonder whether there is much left of that school that absorbed you for those six/ten important years of your life. It should be remembered, too, that that was a time of unusual pressures, of restriction, of rationing, of wartime, and, of course death. For the school was no different from many others in the list of casualties of the 2nd World War.

I think that we were lucky in many ways with the extraordinarily efficient control of the meals. We never went hungry, the diet was never dull, though it was not exciting and there was the awful ships biscuit barrel outside the matron's door as exceptional backup. Rationing of clothes was no problem as Lorettonians could never be described as being the height of fashion – except on Sunday of course. It was a matter of pride that the tweed jacket had to have leather patches – but not too new nor too many.

Of course the school is different to-day, it is now the twenty-first century, academic demands play a huge part, there is no more Remove for those thickies who were also the backbone of the rugby XV. Entry to any university at that time was easy, simply a phone call from the Head, and there would be no demands for academic requirements, and you even had the choice of college to Oxbridge. Can you imagine a leaver to-day who would be happy to leave school without those requisite ever more demanding qualifications, particularly at the cost of the fees to-day. I seem to have a vague memory of my father paying out a cheque for £100 – but was that for a term or a year?

Then I noticed the car park recently was full of large cars – of course, at that time no car ever appeared, or rarely as there was no petrol, only rationing. For all of us it was the 1p (penny) tram from the GPO, or 3p after you were 16. Dare I mention that a lot of those from the Borders frequently came by car, but then farmers did get extra petrol. The tram was our main point of access, that wonderful front seat at the top, as we rolled down the hill, that was the prize on that shuggly journey – Abbeyhill, the open air pool at Portobello, Joppa. Trams were the most important means of transport – away rugby matches meant a convoy of trams loading up the school and a lengthy trip along Seafield to the Academy, or Fettes or Merchiston up at Colinton.

Of course the trunks for the new term had been packed and sent on ahead by rail at 1 shilling and 20 pence. We had to remember to send a post card to the Head to inform him of the time of our arrival, and that was checked as we queued in the corridor outside his room on the first night. I have to confess that I, as well as my parents, were so ingrained with that warning postcard that I even sent one to my CO at Catterick on joining up for national service – I'm sure that he must have it framed somewhere as an example of idiocy!

Wartime did not really impinge upon us. There were enemy air raids with that reverberating engine noise and the sirens and a rush to the shelter with your rug and not much else – freezing in winter. A quick prayer for the siren to end it all. VE Day was celebrated with a day off and an Expedition on our bikes – for some reason my travelling companion called off and I went off down the coast to North Berwick and Gullane, a bottle of lemonade (the luxury of peace) and a stop outside, yes, outside, the pub in Aberlady at 3 o'clock to listen to the radio and the voice of Winston Churchill announcing the end of the war in Europe. That night was a huge celebration with the pipe band marching through the Honest Toun and the whole school joining in with the all the other celebrators. All I remember was being allowed to mix with girls, with much kissing.

Now girls! Well there were not any in the school – the odd sister or the others (well checked if invited for the Senior dance) It was all very respectable and hot with country dancing and summer dresses for the girls. Why does one recall mainly sweat with a little perfume? The acme of excitement was the capture of the couple at the end of one of the dances – the Grand Old Duke of York, and the embarrassed hostage kiss! Wow! Now to go into Chapel to-day to the serried ranks of the Ladies of Loretto and the beautifully svelte Head Girl in her long skirt, and neat jacket is to bring up you up into reality and to stare out at a new world. Having been involved in joining girls and boys into a new school the shock for me was small, but the new appearances brings one up short on the return to a very old traditional boys school. That world of beatings and "whites" has gone, and for the better. Civilisation has broken through to LSM. Loretto was always an exception, it was not a smart school. When we were founded in the 1840's it was laid down that the whole purpose of clothes was to have freedom, no stiff collar, no ties, open to the winds, to the air, shorts, open necked shirts. We were forbidden scarves by the Doctor – "the neck is the warmest part of the body." There were two occasions that demanded a set type – returning to school or going up to Edinburgh. The former meant a shirt with collar, tie and plus fours- in a restrained tweed. Then Sunday, with the Eton Collar and the painful bite into the neck of starch, that is until you were in the 6th form. The tie was grey. I remember Douglas Smith (son of Sir William of BB fame), an OL, telling me that there was a terrible argument about the idea of an Old Boys tie – it was to be a garish green as Loretto was Italian! Douglas simply took our grey tie and daubed on red and white stripes – such it is to-day. That red and white tie, that mark of distinction – for 4 rugby 1st XV games or a prefecture, or 5

Distinctions at School Certificate – but the rugby one was the one to prize!

How would all that serried array of old-time staff get on to-day? Remember that at Loretto at that time teachers were allowed to play no part in the running of the school, it was all done by the Head and the Head Boy. It was said that on one occasion the Head and Vice Gerent were away and the school ran smoothly for two weeks with the Head Boy. The staff were very much old style teachers at that time, the war was still on and it wasn't until that ended that anyone under 60 appeared! There was Cutty Horton with his stammered speech teaching high above the Ash Court; the Prune – Mr Drury – of the large shape and the very accurate shot with blackboard dusters doing the classics; Donny Reid with the small moustache and the cleared throat ramming down those same classics; Dr Mosely he with the lovely tenor voice and total lack of control over boys – the ceiling bars of his room became a regular gym: then there was Dickie Dark, author of Sheep's Tales from Shakespeare, sitting at his desk teaching always with a cigarette in his mouth and wearing his dark hat and greatcoat. Dr Greenlees arrived one night and both the hat and the fag disappeared in record time. "Mr Dark, " the Doctor, remarked as he left, " I fear that your hat is on fire!" It was not unknown for chips to be cooked in tommy cookers at the back of that class, and even an ice from the famous De Lucas. And very nice too.

Newfield seemed to have the eccentric and, at times frightening Fred Morrison with the strong Irish accent and moustache, mathematician supreme and terror inspiring figure on the touchline as he galvanised the XV. Strangely, he gentled on his marriage to his lovely Irish wife His place was taken by the eccentric Mr Taylor, a superb rugby player and coach but who could be seen coaching the team from his bedroom window at Newfield while making calls to his bookie for the latest races.

Then across the way was the elongated shape of Eek Turner, a delightful enthusiast for his French. On one occasion I can remember him sitting in tears at his desk while reading to us of the death of his Gascon cavalier. Next door was the uncontrolled workshop. It would have been closed down to-day as a terrorist centre where experiments with gunpowder and bullets were carried out. There was no shortage of explosives with so many boys whose parents were dedicated country sportsmen.

As for the buildings Loretto had long offered far from comfortable accommodation. Without better boarding the school would have disappeared. No longer those huge 12 boy dormitories of Newfield with their fearsome rugby games across the beds. The red blankets and the unique tartan rugs across the base. The fully open windows at all times, the frost-like lino floors. Today there are as many day pupils as there are full-time boarders. Schoolhouse is still redolent of the old days – central hall where the letters were laid out, and the latest team photo was on show. The dining hall now enlarged, then long and narrow. There were the long oak tables with oak benches, that wonderful statue of the Loretto boy by Pilkington Jackson. Loretto was strictly hierarchical, one started at the midway on the table and progressed upwards to the final heaven of better choice and of size of helpings, and a glass of beer if an OL was visiting. Here were held the Head's Doubles – so called from the double peal of the bell. Here the Doctor banged his heel against the metal surround of the fireplace while he laid down the law on the world and Loretto in general, and of course his dedication to the value of trees. Here he recalled in memorable terms each of the old boys who had been killed during the war, with a vividness and genuine affection which I have never forgotten. And then the final thunderous invitation to the Lord's Prayer with the rumble of the desks and chairs going back followed by the very male glorious recitation.

Dr Greenlees was a remarkable man. A GP in Glasgow, a former 6' plus rugby international who had begun the Loretto tradition of the unorthodox selection of Heads. Here was a man of huge dignity and understanding of boys, a disciplinarian who had a genuine, unsentimental affection for his school and its members. Even with the weight of headship, while at war, he did a share of fire-watching and even a shift a week at Brunton's wireworks. I was lucky as my father and he had worked medically in Glasgow and played rugby at a high level together. That meant nothing in terms of being particular but I always got a big smile and a question as to why I did not have my older brother's grin, and how was he getting on in Burma? His teas were remarkable with a gigantic cup and saucer, filled to the brim, allied to scones with jam and cakes, and very one-sided conversations.

Above the Head's room was the 6th Form library which I regret to report was a bridge den, with cries of –Two spades, Four aces, and total exclusion of card illiterates. At the other end was the high cubby-hole of Letter A. I was horrified to make a call recently to find a small study room, beautifully clean and sparkling, and smelling fresh. Upon my request to ask if there was no slight hint of a century of nicotine smell, the reply was that there was none. Here was the ultimate reward for the weight of prefectural duties, with a pipe of tobacco on Wednesday and another on Saturday. Here too was the sleeping quarters of the Headboy. There was an apocryphal tradition that the first Headboy was married and thus allowed to have his wife stay in school. The first question, therefore, for each new Headboy on his appointment was in connection with the prospects for a wife!

Then there was the upstairs dining room brought into use on the Sunday after a 1st XV rugby victory when the successful team were allowed to sleep in late and arrive to a full breakfast of bacon, sausage and eggs. That, after the much enjoyed triumphal carry-out from the hall after a victory had been announced. It could also mean being dropped on the outside orchard, often painfully. Such were the small boys joys and some of the traditions of Loretto.

Much was made of filling the hours of a schoolboy's life and ensuring that he never had the time to get up to mischief. Saturday was the time for exercise, if not rugby then the runs. The short one to Forman's Inn- a doddle, then the Short Wally, about 3miles, the Long Wally – twice as long, the Carberry Tower – see the hand hole in the wall from generations of boys, Carberry Three Trees – all the way along the top of the ridge, and finally, Carberry Towers – about 13 miles. Wow! All far too dangerous in modern traffic. The final luxury in the summer term were the Expeditions, an extraordinary example of trust. From lunchtime till tea we had the right to make an entry in the book, simply saying where we were intending to go – Pencaitland, Aberlady, Gullane, Haddington -wherever. Off we went on our bicycles, our red blazers tied neatly round our waists, to enjoy that wonderful freedom. I never heard of it being abused and of only one fatal accident, that of a lad who went for a swim by himself in a reservoir – Gladsmuir? and got into difficulties and drowned. What school to-day can offer such trust and freedom. No wonder it bred individuals.

So were we different. Yes! As a school which prided itself on being egalitarian, on having an inborn sense of doubt, bred in that freezing East wind. We had a sense of individualism, of standing alone in a tough world, there was a pride in the toughness of life. We often claimed that prison had nothing on Loretto, and it could serve as a perfect preparation for it. Certainly National Service held no fears. We did have a sense of concern, practical if possible, for others. We learnt to stand up for ourselves. Of course we were not perfect, we could be the ultimate snobs in our little beliefs that we were a better school than any other. We expressed huge doubts about other schools – Fettes in particular, but also the day schools – Heriots, Stewarts, none were in the same class, even Watsons. It would have been unbelievable to play rugby or cricket against any other but those "top" schools. But that snobbery was really very shallow and bred in reality a very different boy who, while a strong individual, also felt genuine concern for others. We even shared with Fettes the support for a Boys Club in Edinburgh's High Street.

Whisper it not but a famous user of that club was a milk boy, one Sean Connery. He took much pride in that fact. It was an interesting school, very different, and proud of it in many ways, but then time has gone by!

I attended Loretto 1943-48.

STUDENT JOBS – 1948–1952

Dad had retired and I had left school and I had started my degree, so I was faced with earning money for the first time. This was a completely new experience as I had never had the chance to earn money before having lived in the country with no opportunities to look for a job, so it suddenly became very important.

So 1948 and 1949 – Christmas Post. Most students at that time did a Christmas Post round, something that is, of course unthinkable to-day as the unions would object and Health and Safety would find a reason to prevent such work. I was lucky for my round as I was handed mostly Woodburn Terrace and Nile Grove in Edinburgh, and as we lived in a flat at No 13 Woodburn Terrace I knew my way round. That last street was fine as they were mostly single houses, but Morningside Road and Woodburn were hard going as they were all three storey tenements and it always seemed that the only letter to be delivered – usually a pools form – was for the top flat. All the tenement stair doors, in those days, had a special lock half way up the door that you had to lift with your fingers/finger. This could be difficult when it was freezing and you had to take off your gloves and the lever had frozen. It was great that the official postmen were all very cheerful and helpful. I think that the enthusiasm of students – particularly for the money – was welcomed, it also meant a bit of laughter and new jokes. On the whole the customers were helpful and understanding even when you got it wrong and delivered the wrong letters to the wrong person.

The day started at 6am and the first post had to be finished by about 11am and then you had a break and the second post from about noon until 2 o'clock. For me it was a great job even though it was short lived, for the first time it meant money in hand. Sadly the use of students at Christmas to work in the Post Office came to an end soon after.

Summer 1949 – Fruit Factory in Evesham

I cannot remember where the chance possibility of going to work in the Vale of Evesham in the fruit industry came to me. I suspect that someone at University had done it the year before and had given me the contact name. I suggested the idea to both Willie Grassick and to David Kerr to see if they might be interested. These were two Scots from the Argentine. Their parents had had jobs which had taken them out there and both lads had been educated in Buenos Aires, but had done their National Service in the UK and thus were then entitled to a free degree course. Willie Grassick, with whom I had cycled round Scotland, was not interested, while David Kerr liked the idea though he warned me that, as a keen and excellent tennis player he might not be able to come for the whole time. In the event he won through into the later round of most of the top Scottish Championships and only spent a few days with me. David was a powerful guy with strong views – he was a very good games player, gaining his blue at both tennis and rugby. I lost touch with him later and never knew what happened to him. Willie was very laid back, went into the Bank and ended very high up as a senior executive.

The firm where I got the fruit job was Henry Idiens in Evesham, and they found digs for me with the local barber in Henry Street. That family were very kind and friendly, and I kept in touch for a few years with them. The job was good. The firm were into crushing apples and plums which were used in all sorts of ways in sweets and cakes. The boss was an elderly man who had no hair as he suffered from alopecia, but he was a good boss and, worse, he had a pretty blonde daughter who appeared regularly on the factory floor but, sadly, was kept well away from any predatory student. During the day I was on the factory floor, usually moving the tubs, boxes etc, and they were some weight, while in the evening I was sent out with another student in the lorry to collect from the various farms. I cannot remember the name of that student. He was a mature one who had been with the firm before, hence the driving job. He was married, though you would not always have thought so! It was an interesting introduction to adult life, and my education on a wide range of subjects was enlightening, sex, marriage, cider or scrumpy, as it is known in Evesham. The farms were very diverse and we had a lot of fun in the collection.

Spare time was filled with visits to the pubs where I soon learnt that scrumpy was a killer, particularly with only one pint. The cinema, which in those days changed three times a week was a godsend. It was a job that I enjoyed and it was in beautiful countryside. The money was reasonable but not terrific, but it was money.

I think that this was the year that Dad had his first heart attack, a small one, while Willie and I were cycling away round the Highlands. He was then diagnosed as having angina.

Summer 1950 – Aluminium Factory at Fort William

This was big time for big boys. I was told that the money was good, but it would be hard work. The British Aluminium Co. ran two factories, one at Kinlochleven and the other at Fort William, the alumina, however, came via Burntisland in Fife. The main factory was on a big scale on the shoulder of Ben Nevis with a seventeen mile tunnel bringing water for hydro power and leading back into the hills. It was said that they had started the tunnel at both ends and it was only a half an inch out when they joined! The company was accustomed to employing students in the summer to fill holidays and we were offered accommodation in a Nissan hut camp about a half mile away from the factory at 29 shillings all- in for the week – £1.40 in our money. I had to be fit and was expected to work all hours, and that for the princely wage of 2shillings and 2 ½ per hour or 12p if I worked on the furnaces, as I did. It would be a forty four hour week with enhanced wages, an extra £5. It was a good job with a great company. The furnaces were tough, being box shape, about 12 feet long and 8 inches wide with eight carbon blocks perched on steel rods. The carbon blocks were red hot and wore out and had to be replaced every ten days. This meant standing on the edge of the furnace – pretty hot – and then unscrewing the block and attaching it to a small crane, which then removed it. You then had to replace it with a new block. It was heavy work and scorching. Your boots wore out quickly!

The other students were a good bunch, much given to betting, which in those days was illegal. The betting shop was on the front of Fort William and well known to everyone, including the police. I remember muttering to one student who was going on his own to climb the circuit of the Cuillins that he was stupid, and it was dangerous. He smiled sweetly and three years later that George Band was one of Sir John Hunt's Everest group!

Summer 1951 – Navvy on the Hydro-Electric Dam at Mullardoch.

Mullardoch was one of the first and biggest projects of the new hydro-electric schemes and I got work for a month at Mullardoch near Glen Affric. It involved a train to Beauly and then a bus to Cannich, from where I was picked up by lorry for the 12 mile trip to the dam. The camp of wooden huts was comfortable and warm – necessary at that height – with food laid on at all hours and a bar. The latter was a problem for some of the navvies. These came from "all the airts", Glaswegians, highlanders, crofters, the lot. Most were friendly and helpful, we were all in it together to outfox the bosses and to make money. The topman was a devil, constantly trying to outwit us. He was known to take his car to Glen Affric and stumble through the half-completed tunnel from the other end just to catch anyone idling.

I began, for my first job, on the shutters of the top platform of the dam. The dam was completed in sections in a jigsaw fashion to give strength so that one segment fitted into the midway of the next one and so on. The shutter was filled with cement poured in, well mixed and filled with steel rods to reinforce it. Our job was to keep the mix going and clean the top, so as to be ready to accept the next layers. There was a wooden ladder to the top of the tower. My first task was to take the cans for the shift down for their morning tea break. The cans were simply old syrup or treacle cans with a wire through for carriage. Four cans filled with rich, sweet tea (mind I like six spoonfuls of sugar), up that two hundred foot ladder. Ugh!

The lads were great and spent their time pulling my leg and wondering how on God's earth such a stupid young man would ever make a success in real life! After a week I got transferred into the Tunnel Tigers, who were better paid but worked non-stop in shifts of eight hours, including nights. Thank goodness this was at ground level. It was non-stop shovelling, picking and cleaning, and I soon learnt why you see so many men, who do much physical work having to stop occasionally and lean on their shovels. It is very hard work and you just cannot keep on without a stop. The other problem was the "gelly" fumes. The rock was brought down with gelignite. For all the explosions, the tunnel was cleared of the workers and when you went back in, there was this strong sweet smell, and headaches. Interesting!

For Queen and Country

From 1939 onwards until 1960, there was conscription, and even by the end of the war it still applied with time limits to all men, unless there was some physical problem, such as very bad eyesight or flat feet! Conscription then went under the innocuous term of National Service. At the time of the medical, we all had the slight hope that there would be some minor problem that might save us. By my time in 1952 we faced two years. I had had the choice of doing it when I left school in 1948, but because Dad was going to Kenya, he had urged me to leave it until I had completed my degree. What made my time in the Army so much more difficult for me was that Mary and I had become engaged and that had to mean a two years separation.

When the time came for my call-up, I received notice to report to Catterick Camp to join the Royal Signals. I had no particular personal reason to join Signals but my cousin, Bill Stoddart, had been a Colonel in Royal Signals and he recommended it, and, indeed did a little gentle pushing of the military machine. Anyway, I sent off the necessary, well-trained school post card to the Commanding Officer of 7TR to tell him that I was arriving by train at 4 pm on the fourth of September 1954. So much for my long term school discipline! I think he must have had a real laugh, and probably had it framed and hung in the Mess. When I arrived, with my short back and sides haircut, my little brown attaché case with pyjamas and shaving kit, along with a few hundred other poor souls, all with the same attaché cases. To be loaded onto trucks and carted off to the camp – a grim large stone block with a huge parade ground.

The next hours were a nightmare. First, allocation of rooms and then to a platoon of other new arrivals, next the provision of kit, boots, belt, anklets, shirts, ties, beret, pyjamas, haversack, pack, cleaning kit. Then we were invited to clean that spotless barrack room. It was "filthy", the walls had to be scrubbed, the floor cleaned and polished, and that saw the end of all my razor blades to clean that floor. I don't think that we got to bed before midnight and were up at 6 am to the shouts of the corporal whose description of our stupidity and laziness was clearly phrased in a new language – mostly of four letter words. Breakfast, shave, wash, careful instruction on the exact layout of the bed, the cupboards and the unworn bits of the uniform. More shouting, onto the parade ground to be "welcomed" by the commanding officer to the service of the Queen and how lucky we were to have been so-chosen! Then the first marching – "left, right, left right.... all the regularly up-dated information as to our intelligence. It turned out that my squad consisted of twenty graduates, while the Corporal was an "ignorant" eighteen year old – "What are you?" – "Stupid, ignorant.......b's......, Corporal." Then off to the medical for the first injections. I have a definite fear of needles after that series that we had – sometimes with the same needle. And the Medical Officers were usually newly qualified doctors who had been immediately commissioned after graduation! No going through basic training for them. Why do I still look askance at doctors?

The next days went like wildfire – drills, education tests, my neighbour could not read or write! The only relief was when they found out that I played rugby. Signals were very rugby orientated, they won the Army Cup every year. Ken Scotland was in Signals and we had Ian Thompson, the Scotland full back and Trevor Brewer of Wales in our squad. As a result of the exhaustive tests a whole lot of us were transferred to 3 TR Signals as potential officers. They, the staff were no more polite but the huts were warmer and any excuse to play rugby under the CO – Major 'Egg' Rapsey – was gratefully received as light relief. We had our first pay parade – 28/- with 5/- off for barrack damages! Whose? Just enough to allow us to get to the NAAFI, or even better to the Church of Jocks canteen – what a marvellous place.

So time passed with endless drills, endless inspections, boots gleamed, brasses polished, weapon training, inspections, more drill. Brief moments of time to ourselves with long letters of love to Mary and the same in return. I did collect all her letters over those two years and so did she. At one point, later in time, we did look at them, and both sadly decided that we should destroy them. At that point, 1953-54, they provided us with the only time of warmth and love, and were cherished, but we agreed that they were just a bit too..............

We were now getting lined up for the visit to the WOSB – the War Office Selection Board – and the chance to get away from the awful boring drill, marches and training. Just as that time approached I heard that Dad had had a heart attack and I should have to come home. It was a strange dilemma If I went I might lose the companionship that we had built up in the group, I would be left behind for another four weeks and then..... For me there was no choice, and the Army proved to be fantastic and helpful. Leave and a pass were organised, travel tickets and reassurance that If I was not away too long I would be still with the group. I got home to see Dad in hospital and say goodbye – he was so strong and so quiet, and so dignified – " he had had his three score years and ten". This was his time and there were no regrets, and that was it. For me I was so lucky that that wonderful woman just took me over. I just could not think straight., My world was falling apart. I was in another dimension, she wasn't. Those strong arms, that common sense, that love. What more could one ask. The funeral was great and moving. Mum was her strong self. We had a hilarious journey back by train from burying Dad in the Western Necropolis in Glasgow, where the carriage had a character who regaled us with stories about the "black dug of Linlithgow". What it had to do with funerals, I do not know. Then it was back to the abnormal in Catterick, more drills but now off to WOSB, all with full kit, rifles and a night in the Union Jack Club in London and on to the camp. It was all very proper with various tests, checks on how we held our forks, and cleaned our teeth, and a pass. Whoopee – that little blue badge on the shoulder to show we were potentials. A quick journey across London. Why was it in all those times that the journey from Victoria always took us through Soho and the Ladies of the Night........ We even had a competition to find how many propositions we had had on our journey.

The weeks passed. The rugby was great and the pressure came off, we had endless games, and won them all. Then down to Aldershot for the next six weeks of learning how to be an officer with the full attention of Guards RSMs, and RSM Britten in particular. What a man, large upright, proud, little moustache, swagger stick, and upright everywhere he went. Always accompanied by a large bit of terror. The charges – idle while cleaning boots, idle while parading, idle while sleeping...... it was funny but, "get that smile off your face " we learnt. We even began to imitate, same shoulders back, same march, same pride. Now was the great advance, we could go out in civvies, and this meant a trip to London to get a proper hat, coat, jacket etc from Moss Bros. I do look back on Aldershot with a real sense of achievement. You could see why the Guards had pride, they were different, they were the best. It is odd to think back and to remember that time there was so much laughter. We had the reward of one week's leave over Christmas – fabulous.

After our six weeks at Aldershot we were back to Catterick – same journey with kit and rifles, from Victoria to Euston, past that Soho, the same ladies- always lots of soldiers in uniform – the whole of Britain in uniform. But on to Catterick, to 4TR and a better barracks, but still a large square, alongside a long nasty Assault Course, and 8 foot high wall that took Thomson and me as six footers at the back to get the rest over, and then ourselves, half-knackered with the effort of being dragged up by two others leaning over the wall, then a crawl under the barbed wire, with that b****** dog, which one of the officers used to send down, either to meet us face to face or to chivvy up from the rear. All to time and constant upgrading of the times, 10 mile marches back from the range- "shoulders up, swing your arms.." Cheerful Captain Charlie Clelland, the wee man with the moustache, always chasing us. Course 305 – the universally ever, and so proud of it the worst ever, we failed every pass-out parade, yet it was the funniest unit and we were the ones who sang everywhere. It helped that we had a number of Welshmen We were all a great bunch and at last to much loud discussion we all got promotion. Got rid of those white shoulder flashes. But worse or better was to follow. The army believed in leadership and every squad had to have its leader, and no question of democracy. So did I achieve power, the first as Senior Warrant Officer with a crown on my sleeve, and a Sam Browne with an odd hanging belt, and for the last six weeks – Senior Young Officer, or SYO, with a room of my own. Wow! My job was very demanding in that I had to march Course 305 around, usually to ribald remarks about "b***** Jocks, stuck up etc" And, of course to arrive on time and at the right destination It also meant that Stewart Hay became my SM, and his onerous job was to hold up the squad, at attention of course, outside the NAAFI while they prepared for the break. By leaving Stewart in command – thus ensuring that he had the opportunity of command – I could get in first for my chocolate snowball and coke and, of course buy one for Stewart before the rest were dismissed. The world for me was fine, and actually it made not the slightest difference to my relationships with the rest! I made a point, as I always did later as a Head of mixing with people. The choice in any situation of authority is to take the easy one of the loud mouthed bully, with continuous pressure and noise or a quiet and authorative show mixed with understanding. Then at last came the last Passing Out Parade – which we actually passed with Mary smiling sweetly from the stand, and a posting to 1 Corps in Germany at Herford with John Stirling. Our uniforms were immaculate our boots shone with the blanco spotless – from then on that would be the batman's job. A great trip back on the express from Darlington followed, a luxurious train with dinner in the dining car and my lovely lady opposite me, smiling with pride as she always did. Joy was unconfined.

We had a fortnight's leave and another massive pack, now with civvies and uniform, but, thankfully no rifle. The train was, of course Fist Class to London and then to Harwich and the troopship to Amsterdam, followed by a train across

Germany, all in great comfort. What a world of difference being an Officer, if only a very junior one. One became aware that, even after seven years of peace, Germany was still very much the occupied country. For a hundred metres beside the railway there was still much rubble, the result of the Allied bombing. German police had no right to stop and search or interfere with the British. We had won!

Herford was a day's journey across the North German plain. John and I were met by a Volkswagen with a civvy German driver and a truck for our kit. It was strange that, in conversation with these drivers none ever admitted to having supported Hitler. The barracks were some way out of town. It was a large area with trees, football pitches, tennis courts, a huge parade ground, neatly laid out huts and the Officers Mess at the foot. My room was very comfortable and a batman appeared to check my kit, then a meal and an introduction to the CO, one Colonel Peter Bradley. I got on well with Peter. He was tough, he had fought at Arnhem and was very proud of his Para badge. He expected things to go right but had a great sense of humour. His motto was "Go to it" – it headed every notice, and even appeared on the wedding telegram that he sent me. The Second in Command was a quiet nonentity, and my own company commander was Major Jimmy Romanes. A quiet, very tough guy, who had had a DCM awarded on the field of battle when he was promoted from the ranks. He was not easy, a disciplinarian but with no real understanding of his men. He was happily hated, and claimed never to sleep on exercise. My job was the running of the signal office, which was both a post office, with dispatch riders, wireless, telephones, teleprinters and was the centre of command. The wirelesses were in huge trucks with very slow and inefficient communication. Then there was the cipher office with a humourous Australian in command. Finally the cable laying squads under John – these were the toughies, in a world of their own – found on exercise with fishing rods outside a chicken farm, hoiking out the chickens with hooks baited with food!

The mess had only five officers – Sergeant Melia, the mess sergeant from Scotland and Major Leith, an old hand. He had fought in Russia at the end of the First World War and was as tough as barbed wire. He hated young officers, he said – but put up with them and ran the transport system. He authorised all trips, from the major journeys to our visits to the cinema in Herford – a regular weekly outing with a car to take us and to collect us! Apart from John with whom I had a close relationship as we had the same ideas and standards. He too had a girlfriend, though no formal engagement. He also played scrum half and I played stand off and that was the beginning of a very successful rugby team that won the Signals Cup. There was much opportunity for games and physical activity, I swam for the regiment, I ran for the regiment, I played hockey. Now, that was vicious, as the CO played and whacked everything and to blazes with "sticks" or any other rules. As most of the officers and NCO's had served in India where there was much emphasis on hockey and its skills we had some great games on that beautiful parade ground.

Finally there were two other young officers and we became a tight group – cinema, parties, Saturday nights at the various festivals – beer, hamburgers, wine, you name it. Then the trips in Peter Talbot's little car – off to the car races, or to fun at Hamlin with the piper, or to horse races, and even one a wild 5th of November when with a large amount of alcohol taken we dropped thunder flashes outside the senior officer's houses, including the Colonel's. He was not amused. In the 21st century can you see wild young officers even thinking about it? I think that there were a few extra Orderly Officer nights. The last was a rather innocuous character but a nice guy. We had fun.

So looking back on the fifteen months that I spent in Germany I do so with pleasure, it was a good regiment. The officers were good though the equipment dated. It had not moved on much since 1945. Communications by wireless were very poor and subject to endless problems – both technical and atmospheric. The Russians were always around and the plan to deal with them was to make an immediate retreat to the Rhine, followed by nuclear bombs on them. We still had gas masks and I was sent on a six week enjoyable gas course on Salisbury Plain in December 1953. There were endless exercises throughout the year across Westphalia or down the Rhine – Javelin 1, 2, 3....They were very keen for me to take on a short service commission with immediate appointment to Captain and a better income. It just did not appeal, I liked some of the army but I really did not want to find us being moved every three to four years, and the difficult times with Mary left at home and the kids at school. I knew that it was not for me, and I have no regrets.

Mary came across in July for two weeks in which she made her usual huge impression on them all – we even went on holiday to the Harz Mountains, during which my idiot Corporal jumped over the warning fence on the East German frontier to see what " life was like", and spent two months in prison. The regiment very decently gave me 3 weeks leave to get married and it's life brought me to my senses as I realised, during a scorching hot exercise, near Dusseldorf that I was not at my best in heat. So what about the Colonial Service now? Allan Arthur's grim warning – "David there is no empire, there is no future for you." I wrote to Hutch, headmaster at Larchfield and he offered me job at the School in Helensburgh, while Forbes Mackintosh, at Loretto, refused even to consider me, mad – he said – to get married "at your age."

So on the fourth of September 1954 I was demobbed at Newton Abbot and given my train fare back to Glasgow, with John as companion, to meet Mary at Central Station in Glasgow, ready to go to Helensburgh and start my real life. Looking back on those two years I feel that I learnt a lot about leadership. Though I think that those first six months were grim and unnecessarily grim, but perhaps it served to reinforce that survivor attitude.

MARY – THE WIFE OF MY LIFE

Alice Mary Frost was born in Joppa on the 15th of July 1927 at home in her parents flat in Joppa, but then of course at that time everyone was born at home. Her parents were both English though her father, Robert Frost, was born in Edinburgh and was proud to call himself a Scot. His family originally came from Suffolk, his grandfather being the head game keeper on the Somerleyton Estate near Ipswich, having come originally from Moreton Hampstead in Devon, where all his ancestors are buried in the churchyard, including one Mary Frost. Mary always enjoyed the fact that, on one holiday in the south, she had sat on her own gravestone. Her grandfather had a big family, the two eldest boys having disappeared to Australia with the suspicion that they might have been involved in a little poaching – embarrassing for their father! Both appear to have gone without any real trace, though we know that the elder became a doctor and died while riding out on horseback to see a patient while still only in his thirties. The younger kept a diary at sea but this lasted only as far as Perth in Western Australia. Then they disappeared, though we did try to find them in the 1990's Young Robert Frost (grandfather) was apprenticed to a furnisher in Ipswich, slept under the counter during the week, walked home on the Saturday with his washing, having locked up the shop, and walked to get back to Ipswich in the early hours of Monday so that he could open the shop. There was a rumour recounted at the Golden Jubilee of the firm that he had actually ridden a penny-farthing! After he had finished his apprenticeship he decided to travel up Edinburgh, having visited Inverness first to seek his fortune and then to work in a large West End shop called Maules, which later was to become Binns, and finally to Frasers. While he was there, he saw an opening for a soft furnisher in the city and opened a shop in Shandwick Place. He was lucky to marry a lady, Alice Miriam Underwood, born in Hackney in 1826, who had an eye for colour and whom he had met in Reading. Her Grand dad had met his Grandma through the mutual friendship of their parents. She had worked in a haberdashery and so had developed that eye for colour and design. She also had a good business brain. Robert developed a friendship with her when he was an apprentice in Manchester. The shop, Frosts, when it finally opened was a success and became a byword in the city for quality.

Grandfather Frost kept his interest in country sports and both shot and fished. He latterly rented a farmhouse near Gifford in East Lothian. Earlier he and his wife set up home at Joppa Road in Portobello, and later moved more permanently to Sandford Gardens. He had a very tough reputation, was much feared by the young Mrs Robert Frost, Mary's mother, and he had a reputation for being a hard man. Mary alone in the family had the gift of softening him up, and was able to twist him round her little finger.

Sadly, in later in the 1970's, the business ran into problems primarily because there was no access from the rear of the shop for deliveries and there was no hope of getting one. The city added to the problems with its ruthless parking restrictions in Shandwick Place. At the same time many family businesses, Little Forsyths, C & J Brown also faced difficulties and Frosts amalgamated with Martins which ran the business a great deal more ruthlessly. As in many current times none of the family wanted to go into the business, and all became very involved in their own personal lines – history, veterinary, flying, teaching and occupational therapy.

That original Frost family consisted of Gladys Mary the eldest, then Eadie and Dora, with the only boy, Robert George. I never knew any of them except Bob and Eadie. Eadie worked off and on in the shop and was a strong character but very kind to me. Mary was very much a favourite with her. Gladys Mary had married Archie Gray, who was a Scot and had joined the Army, fought in the First World War and stayed on in the Army. I suspect that he was one of the famous "Black and Tans", this was a part of the British Army serving in Ireland at the time of the Irish Revolt. He was, probably one of a much feared and hated Intelligence group, they were named after their black belts and khaki uniform. One grim night the IRA went down that street in Dublin where the officers were billeted, and shot each one, fourteen of them – the only survivor being Archie. The whole event is tied into the famous Irish stadium, Croke Park, and is a reminder of the massacre of a number of Irish bystanders following the massacre of the Brits. He, Archie, immediately resigned his commission and took up the offer of land in South Australia, where they successfully set up a vineyard. Sadly drought hit the area and the vineyard was wiped out by that and phylloxera and Archie never worked again until the outbreak of the Second World War when he was employed in the Australian Army on the supply side. I suspect that he was never a very happy man and resented the success of the Scottish business, and was always happy to accept any financial help that they could get. Certainly Alison had the reputation of getting everything that she could from her relatives in Scotland. G. Mary, as she was known, was a very talented painter. Her main claim to fame for the younger generation was the story of the billiard ball. She was challenged as, having such a big mouth, that she could swallow a billiard ball. She did so on one occasion and put one in her mouth, then she could not get it out – panic, but thankfully she did!

Dora was the youngest and, tragically, as was the custom in those days of home births, a nurse had come in to help who had previously nursed a TB patient. The result was that the baby had a hip that was affected by TB. I believe that Dora was a wonderful woman with a tremendous sense of humour and great energy. She died relatively young and sadly had not been given the chance to look at her Will which had been drawn up many years before. Her estate went to the Princess Margaret Hospital which was promptly nationalized into the NHS. A sore matter for Mary who had been told that she would be the principal beneficiary.

Mary's mother, Rose, came from New Brighton in the Wirral. Her grandfather had been General Gordon's Sergeant-Major in China and was one of the lamp carriers for Florence Nightingale in the Crimea. Rose's parents ran a pub, the Red Lion in Wallasey, and Mary's grand-mother was a formidable lady who lived to ninety one. Rose met Bob Frost when he was working in Manchester. It was a very happy marriage. Bob Frost was a lovely man, straight as a dye, a keen churchman, an able but gentle businessman, a good shot and a fisherman who spent much of his spare time as a Special Constable, rising to the rank of Superintendent. Rose was also a tough lady with a warm personality and enormous energy who really ran the family. It was not a joke that she made all the decisions. In her younger days she was a great hostess always with a wide assortment of young people around – Ian Blake, Derek Mackenzie, Alec Drysdale, (whom the family wanted Mary to marry – too boring in her words), and Pat Rodger, later a very superior churchman – Secretary of the World Council of Churches & Bishop of Manchester and later Oxford, and of course, David Arthur. When the latter was around the air was full of numerous cracks about "red meat" or " do laurels really have flowers? " These were quite unjustified references to the pair, and their regular innocent trips into the countryside to study "wild life", Mary had the use of the little business Austin car, and this served a useful purpose for all sorts of journeys. At 47, Braid Road there were parties, dances, regular suppers after Evensong in St. Johns with Robert and their gramophone and "Life gets tedious, don't it", and wonderful New Year parties with incredible games from Washing the Elephant to Rabbits.

Mary grew up with the handicap that she was not a boy. The Whites, Douglas and his mother, lived up above in Portobello. "Give us a knock to tell us it's a boy," said Auntie White. No knocks, so an anxious enquiry followed by two knocks and it was a girl – no champagne! She, Mary, grew up to be a lovely person with strong leanings to athletics, won the cups for tennis, a hockey blue at Moray House, tennis, golf and squash, all at a high level.

She and Noel Milne met in their respective prams, and went to Cranley School a long way into Edinburgh which required a return journey by bus for five and six year olds of half an hour.. Then Mary went to St Margaret's, which was closer, but meant evacuation to Strathtay in 1940, with the risk of invasion worrying many parents. The damp climate and unheated houses led to a mastoid in her ear which led to her withdrawal back to Edinburgh. Next they, the family, moved to Carlops, and she was sent to West Linton for 2 horrible terms and finally to her happiest time at Beacon School in Bridge of Allan. Despite her desire to be an accountant and join the business, her father – on the advice of his friends – decided that it was not an appropriate profession for a girl and she was sent to Moray House to learn to teach, A career much more appropriate for a girl! She went on to do an extra year with a Froebel Certificate at Roehampton in London for a year. Mary and her friends formed a terrible quartet Mary Roger, Doris Beattie and Christine Scott at Moray House that must have enlivened that place. Stories are told that she remarked to one of her lecturers, a relatively young man, that he would be in the next world by the time that she ever started to teach!

From there she went to teach at Pennywell, which nearly killed her with the stress of a new job and terrible teaching conditions in a room in a prefab council house, and up to thirty kids. The result of that was that she was sent to her bed for three months on medical instructions. At times the visitors to her room led her brothers commenting that it was a bit like an episode from "Forever Amber", the current favorite bodice ripper of the time. Luckily a vacancy came up and she then went to teach the entry class in George Watsons Ladies College in St Albans Road. This she enjoyed and blossomed as a teacher, though she was forced to resign when she married! Can you imagine that happening in the nineties? By this time her fate was sealed with the appearance of David whose charm and youthful zest quite captured her heart – at least that is what he says. The acquaintance grew out of a chance joke at Braid Tennis Club when Lee Cuthbertson and David were planning a visit to a "hop" (dance) at Craiglockhart. David was all set to ask the Club's glamorous blonde bombshell, Margaret Adams, but Lee got in first and cheered David up with the crack " Go on you take Snowie here." Engagement followed in September 1951, though not officially until 1952, so it was to be five years of knowing each other before marriage – quite common in those days. Mary proved a superb teacher – there are no blinkers on the writer – but she bitterly regretted that she did not go into business, Perhaps her happiest and most fulfilling years were spent working for Black Horse Relocation from 1987 to 1997. The business was one of taking over the houses of top managers who were being relocated, either for promotion or to a new job, and ensuring that the houses were sold, and that they were maintained in the meantime to a proper standard. She loved the interaction between estate agents and the firm. Her world covered from Carlisle to Berriedale in Sutherland, to Mull and Dundee. I think that she felt for once truly fulfilled in doing a worthwhile job.

Mary has always been a wonderful mother and wife, uncomplaining and always willing to follow that man as he went for jobs in all kinds of places. She never enjoyed the best of health with period pains of a vicious kind, then difficulties in becoming pregnant, stones and menopausal problems. She rarely complained and believed that life had to be fought and conquered.

One of her hobbies was music and she loved concerts and opera. She also sang with a small select group in Helensburgh under Roger Clegg. She was a very useful piano player and finished up to Grade 6, but for her slippage to a man she could well have gone on to her LRAM. The purchase of a grand piano was a highlight and the break of her wrist was a tragedy when she could no longer enjoy playing. She was a very skillful embroiderer and tapestry worker, with the dining room chairs showing off her skill. She taught all the daughters how to knit, using the Shetland Belt and happily darned all his socks. The skills were very much the Frosts, and have been inherited by Gillian, while her sharp business brain appears in Seonaid. Probably the mixture was in Catriona.

She was much respected by the family as the financier who kept her man off the rocks. She once made the mistake of letting him do the money only to bitterly regret it and quickly take it all back! She had a wonderful budgeting system that actually worked. She also introduced home banking on the computer.

Sadly, from about 2000 she began to suffer from memory loss. This deteriorated dramatically with Catriona' s death and then the onslaught of my own pneumonia in Autumn 2006 to an extent that she needed to have more or less permanent care, with Alzheimer's, which reduced a wonderful and vibrant personality. I would wish only to remember her at her wonderful best, the most marvellous companion that a man could have had for over fifty years.

She died peacefully on Wednesday 7th March 2007. A wonderful and colourful service with a packed congregation was a tribute to a remarkable lady.

5TH OF JUNE, 1954 – THAT WEDDING

The recent Royal Wedding celebrations brought back all sorts of memories – thankfully all happy. With the benefit of hindsight I do realise that our wedding was a little unusual as I had been away on National Service for two years and had hardly seen Mary for almost eighteen months. We, John Stirling and I, had to get back from Germany so as to arrive the night before the wedding, and so to make the best of our generously granted three week of leave. I say "we" because John Stirling was to be my best man and we both were serving with 1(BR) Corps Signal Regiment at Herford in Westphalia. John and I had gone through the whole of our training at Catterick and Mons without being close friends. We had both played a lot of rugby together and come home on leave by the same train, with John going on to Glasgow. He was a Glasgow graduate, I think in Economics, and intended to join the Inland Revenue when he was demobbed. He, too had a girlfriend in Glasgow and looked forward to marrying her in the future. We became very close in Germany. He had a Line troop, had the next room, we both loved rugby, he played scrumhalf and I was his stand off, and we both loved peanuts. He was good and very tough. We also played endless tennis, table tennis, went out on Saturday nights to the various fests – beer, wine, sausage and got into trouble with Peter Talbot and Henry when we "bombed" the houses of the CO and the Adjutant one famous 5th of November. That brought us all extra Duty Officer times. So it was only right that John should be my best man. John was a very "canny" man – he was solid, sensible, with a great west coast down-to-earth manner, more cautious than me, a great sense of humour. A rock! The journey back on the Thursday and Friday, 3 and 4th June was a long one by train across Germany to Zeebrugge and then to Harwich with the threat of a dock strike hanging over us. We arrived in Edinburgh late afternoon on the Friday and were met by Robert, and taken to spend the night at 13 Woodburn Terrace with Mum and Carol. A quick meeting with Mary and a rush down to St. John's, followed by supper at Braid Road and a warning of an early night to allow the bride to prepare.

It was amazing, and everything had been organised - present showings, photos, guest lists, all done. The Frosts had done a great job, and I was sternly warned that my darling wife had removed the word – "obey" from the promises in the Order of Service. She looked lovely but tired, and very excited. Saturday was a lovely day with sunshine and Keith was to take the Wedding film and saw us off in a taxi to St John's still, in those days, with that large well-kent policeman controlling the traffic at the West End. He stopped everything to allow our wedding car out from the church afterwards. I have tried to remember what the whole ceremony was like. I think that I was desperate to marry Mary. While National Service had been fun, in parts, I had had enough. I adored her, I needed her love, her laughter, her fun, her good sense, her toughness and our marriage was going to be like the best books, the best films, just like the imagination. I don't think that I had seen any really wonderful models to copy – my Dad and Mum were great but Dad was the boss, though Mum could be awkward though she was very restrained, very unphysical. The Frosts? She was the boss but he was the kindest, gentler, a real gentleman, with a fantastic sense of humour, and just to listen to those musical-hall songs. No – ours would be unique the best ever! You don't wait four years and then eighteen months separation, not to be desperate.......I do not remember anything of the service –it was so wonderful just to be back in Edinburgh, to be in long remembered St. John's, the smiling faces, the remembered colours, the windows, and the expectation. This was it – at last. Then she came in with Father Frost – a small veil, a lovely dress and that smile. The bridesmaids – my sister Carol, Sheena, Mary Rodger.......

After that was the Reception in the George. I had a major worry, why there was this very nice, well-dressed lady who insisted on coming with us in the bridal car? Who was she? Eventually, I had the courage to ask if she was coming on the honeymoon. Howls of laughter-this was the dresser for the bridal gown! I knew that I had to do a speech but I have small memory of it. It would have been brilliant – maybe. There were so many people to talk to and to meet. There were old friends, relatives, new friends, new relatives – some even from the Land of OZ, and Mary's old friend, Charles Batts, inimitable as ever. There was a lot of champagne and a beautiful cake, the top layer packed for the first birthday. (I think that ever practical Mary decided that we should eat it as there was no chance that we could have kids for a year or so) I do remember Father Frost's amazement, as he stood at the back of the crowd and a waitress came up and filled his glass – "Come on drink up I have to get rid of this stuff!" John enjoyed himself, a little too much with Mary Rodger, instead of his fiancée. Then the off and the crowds. The rotten lot were all going at the Frost expense to the Caley for dinner while we flew south. Off to the airport and we had carefully kept quiet that that was where we were going. Yet the whole family amazingly appeared out at Turnhouse to wish us well. It was lovely and bright and it all looked great until we got into the old lounge to hear the announcement – "Sorry we have had to cancel the flight to London, the haar (mist) has caused the flight not to come in. Never mind, Glasgow is open." So onto a bus and off to Glasgow to Abbotsinch – an old military airport and the excitement, a chocolate for me and a Marmite for the beautiful bride. It was freezing in the old hangar. Then the flight to Hendon and a taxi in to London to the Waldorf and straight to bed, as we had missed the gorgeous dinner that I had ordered. So why bed.........? We woke next morning to breakfast in bed – joy unconfined – until we discovered that Mary's tennis racquet had been left in the taxi. Now just don't ask. Why do you bring a tennis racquet on your honeymoon. Now the flights to Jersey were all set for the afternoon, so all we wanted was a quiet restful morning. Well it was interesting as we had no idea of what taxi we had used, so off to the police. We were careful not to explain that we were on our honeymoon or why we had lost that piece of equipment. There was even a quiet suggestion of preparations for Wimbledon. Still no racquet, so off we flew to lovely Jersey and St Brelade's Bay, in Jersey and a bit of luxury. Now, we had been clever. Only the parents knew where we had gone but Ronnie, our future brother-in-law, had an aunt who lived in Jersey and we knew he was coming for a holiday the next day, so.......... Now how do you explain to anyone why you had brought a tennis....... and why you wanted him to bring one with him when he came? He must have dined out for years....

THE CHILDREN

When Catriona first read the family autobiography, she pointed out that there was nothing or very little about our children. She was, of course, quite right, though I am not quite sure why I left it out, as in so many ways they have been and still are the most important part of our lives. When we first married we knew that it would be difficult, and financially almost impossible, to start a family until Mary could stop work. In the first two years of our marriage both of us were teaching at Larchfield, in Helensburgh, and there was absolutely no question that we could afford a family on £575 per annum £330 for me, and £275 for Mary, as she did not have a degree, though a qualified teacher ! And I think that our big fear was that an unexpected pregnancy would have all sorts of repercussions. Mary's gynaecological problems did not make it any easier. This was a time before the pill.

It was not until the summer of 1956 when I left Helensburgh and was accepted on the Special Recruitment Scheme to go to Moray House for a year, with the sole purpose of getting a teaching certificate and so becoming qualified to teach in any Scottish, or English school, state or independent. My fees were paid and we got a small grant – enough to keep us with the savings that we had made. Oddly enough our time in Helensburgh, on £575 pa, was the one time in our lives that we were able to put some money aside. We were also lucky that Auntie Eadie had decided to go Australia at that time and so that allowed us to use her flat in Heriot Row for three months – Fancy having a Heriot Row address, as a student in Edinburgh! That is if I succeeded at Moray House – did anyone ever fail (?)

I would then be formally offered by Graeme Richardson, the Headmaster, a job at Melville College. Meantime, I would get some small payment for refereeing the boys rugby on a

Wednesday at the school. Life that year in1956/7 was very busy with games, school work and getting the house and garden right at our lovely new bungalow in 9 Swanston Drive, which we had acquired in December 1957.

Mary had always had problems with her periods and she went into the Elsie Inglis Hospital for two small ops, one for a D & C, and another one for the removal of a small cyst – benign, thank goodness. We both then went for other tests and at all times we were guided by Donald Cruickshanks, a wonderful model for any GP, and an enthusiast for babies and mothers. I was tested and proved OK. And he was sure that Mary would overcome her problems.

It was made more difficult for us as Robert & Anne moved into 3 Swanston Grove after us – a bigger house, of course, as befitted the elder son, and they had a son almost immediately, and Anne faced difficulties and had to spend time in hospital with depression. This meant that Granny Frost had to come and take over for long periods. She, Grannie, was then too busy to spare much time or thought for Mary. Grannie also changed character dramatically, had less sense of humour, became more dour and somehow lost that lovely sparkle she had always had. Looking after a baby, a son and a husband explained that.

Finally, we succeeded in our hopes, having tried all the tricks mentioned in all the magazines and books. That bit of exercise was fun anyway! It was a wonderful moment after many disappointments and endless tests that came to nothing, when Donald at last told us that we were expecting. He was as excited as us! Just previously we had been to the Guild of Service to ask about the possibility of adoption and had been accepted – perhaps that was the nod for success.

Anyway, for an exciting nine months we awaited Gillian or JOG – John or… Mr Rodger, the milkman, from Hunters Tryst, shook Mary's hand when we handed him that magic book that gave us additional pregnancy milk or something or other. Our milk was delivered by horse and cart, and Mr Rodger was the epitome of a carrier with gaiters and bright red cheeks.

We had a lovely week of clear blue skies at Oban in April, with Mary resting and hoping that all was well. That summer was a scorcher, with hot sun until late October. The garden was super with a new patio of cobbles, or setts in Edinburgh speak, that we had bought as they were removed off the Edinburgh streets. The birth was slow in coming. So we took time to redo the bathroom the week before, and Mary had permanent heartburn. She took so much Colantyl that we decided that the baby would come out covered in white powder from the antacid. At last it started, and off we shot to the Queen Mary in, I think, Keith's car, as Agatha – our proud Baby Austin, was not working. The target was the annexe to the Simpson Hospital with Dr Alastair on duty as Dr Donald was on holiday. I remember we were watching an exciting American TV film – Surf 11 or something, and sadly I never did know the outcome.

I was allowed in for the early part, but then kicked out when the serious stuff began. We did not – or Mary didn't – have the easiest of births, but at last there she was, the long awaited girl – bright and cheerful with a touch of red hair and a wonderful black eye. "Did the coalman call recently?" asked the nurse. She, Gillian, maybe was not beautiful but she was adorable, and how. I blotted my copybook when admiring at the cot-side. "They really are not very beautiful at this stage – are they?" I remarked to another father. "Well," he said, "That may be true of yours, but mine's perfect!"

At last Gillian and Mum came home, or to Braid Road first.

"Now you will have to keep her quiet, your Dad is working." said Grannie Frost. Some hope, she howled most of that night, poor wee soul, she had bad wind for weeks. So it was a rapid return up to Swanston and home. Like both Seonaid and herself, they were not the easiest of babies with real wind problems that made sleep difficult. But she suffered badly from adoration by both parents. She was just wonderful and it was just magical that we had her. Even at this time I can look back and think what a miracle, perhaps why I have never been able to understand baby battering or murder. Gillian inherited her mother's obstinate nature and her father's outbursts. We had an interesting lunch one day when she, first, did not want to say grace and then she did, but would not say it. That was thirty minutes of screaming hell and tears. She was a character and how!

By this time we had a prefabricated garage for Ssshh….A Morris 8 Series 8 which cost us £ 200 and a half hour interview with the manager in the bank who wrote it all out in long hand with a scratchy dip pen! Were we sure that the car was worth it? Was the garage, in Colinton reputable? Could we really afford it? By this time I was paying £ 4 a month to Aitken & Niven, the tailors, this meant that I could then spend up to £ 24 on clothes. I bought an overcoat and a suit. We also bought a fridge to replace the OSO Cool which you filled with water to keep the milk cool. We even got a Hoover washing machine – single tub.

So that was one. How could we have enough love to give to another? Funny, love is not like a cake where you cut off a bit and only so much is left. Our first was just so important. She grew up and kept young Robert down the road lively and was adored by her Grannie, Gran, Granddad and all the aunts and uncles, well the ones in Inverleith who were close at hand.

She was so admired with her gorgeous red hair and cheeky face – not much change? She made a hit with Mr Hughson next door and life was perfect. She was introduced to Loch Tay from the age of one and her nappies were washed in the freezing cold of the loch, and she picked up tummy troubles from the milk next door. She was a very competent young lady and good with her hands and she had verbal diarrhoea….. she never stopped talking. She also developed the habit of being a quizzy lizzie. If we had people in at night, without fail, there was a shuffling at the door and a little head would pop round with that engaging smile. Of course it meant further adoration., a thoroughly bad habit.

So to number two, and back to all the same wind problems as with Gillian, added to looking already after one lively small child. I think that we both wondered whether we would have enough love for another. Once again, Donald was so supportive and encouraging. Life was very busy, Mary was very involved with St. John's Church Young Wives and we saw a lot of Keith Arnold. David was up to his eyes with Samaritans, not just the Edinburgh branch, but spreading the word with others all over the country. He also taught! At last the word came through that we were expecting again. Whoopee! More antacid, more worries over a name. Finally decided on Seonaid at Mary's insistence that it would be the Gaelic spelling – so JOS. I seem to remember seeing a boat in the West Highlands with Seonaid correctly spelt. The summer of 1962 was not so good and David was looking for promotion, with not much success in Edinburgh, so an application to Robert Gordons in Aberdeen was successful. All sorts of problems followed as I had to start on the 1st June and live in Aberdeen in digs, near to Jimmy Shearer. I was welcomed with open arms by the Aberdeen Samaritans. It was hard going and I bought the house, got it all organised for August, decorations, heating, furnishing, etc on my own. Poor Mary had to cope without any real idea of what was going to hit her. All the money problems – the house cost £3, 100, we had offered £ 3,000 and George Lawrence suggested another hundred and we would have it. Then redecoration, coke boiler and central heating, carpets etc. It was a lovely semi-detached house on 3 floors. The drawing room and our bedroom were just masterpieces of artistic design – mine! An outside loo, an extra, with a swing over the door, and a sideways leaning main stair. Apparently there had been subsidence on that side of the street. It was great.

Seonaid's birth was tricky, like the other, and the family, less Mary, spent the day drinking fizzy and picnicking on the beach at Dunbar. Ronnie had his leg in plaster and Gillian and Bobby had a wonderful time sliding up and down the sand dunes.

Mary, plus sister Carol, travelled to Aberdeen by train – first class! I think that she was too tired to appreciate 95, but she settled in quickly. Seonaid was like Gillian a bad sleeper, with tummy problems, added to that the first year was not easy in a new city. I was fine with school, the Samaritans and hockey. I even went onto the National Executive of the Sams and flew to London every 6 weeks, so I did not suffer from boredom – lucky dog. Mary was, as always, wonderful.

Seonaid did not have an easy life, she had problems reading which turned out to be dyslexia, which she did a wonderful job of conquering. Number two is always a hard place for a child. Gillian was a strong character and very aware of being the first for almost three years and was the centre of attention. One can always find deep psychological problems. How else would psychologists survive?

We still loved that lovely little devil who decided that she was going to be herself and live life as she wanted – And why not?

Number three was a surprise. Mary had a new doctor in Aberdeen – Dr Forbes, another wonderful GP, an ex Jap POW. A lovely man for whom nothing was too much. trouble. No wonder none of our successive doctors matched up to Dr Donald and Dr Forbes. She, Mary, was under Prof. McGregor who was endlessly patient and kind, and all sorts of pills were prescribed. Once again conception was not easy. It may have been fun but it was not easy. We had occasional week-ends up at Fort

Augustus to enable me to play hockey for Ruthrieston against the Abbey school. This last visit, for Mary, was a bit of a nightmare as she had been put on water pills as she had put on weight. It was agreed by the experts that it was all the menopause – some menopause!

We all went riding that day, but not her, as it would be sore. Some pain – it was Catriona Cor! – another 6 months of putting on weight and antacid! Eventually she came – even more difficult than the others. Somewhere Mary had a bend inside that she should not have had. But she, Catriona that is, came plump and smiling as she ever was. This time statistics came into play as Forrester hill was meticulous. "Would Dad come and be weighed and measured?" – "Certainly." – "Should I take my shoes off for measuring height?" – "Don't bother." – "You do realise that I do not go to bed in my shoes!" Collapse of statistical survey.

We have been so lucky with our daughters which is why the loss of Catriona has hit us so badly and always will. Gillian has done a remarkable job. She was always determined to be doctor and blew her top at anaesthetist Archie when he chattily advised that she would make a good nurse. When she did not get her expected A in physics at Higher she went up to Aberdeen and bearded the Dean who finally agreed that if she got an A next year in physics he would take her. Her wonderful agility with her fingers has stood her in good stead as a surgeon and spells at the Vale, Ham Green, Bristol, Birmingham and Great Ormond Street and finally to Sweden and Upssalla have seen her reach her target, and now she is a Senior Consultant in Paediatric Urology –wow!. She married a scientific expert, Chris Barker, who has taken her away to Sweden but has brought her happiness and fulfilment, not to mention two lovely daughters –Ruth and Deborah.

For Seonaid, life has been much more tricky. She had a spell in the Bank and then a lawyer's office, time with Enable, and then at the Base. The last was not a success but she has now come into her own with a firm engaged in producing and selling motor additives, building an empire in Scotland from nothing to over 180 outlets. When that came to an end she worked first for Mercedes Benz and then after a horrendously long interview, which she conquered brilliantly, she became Scottish Manager for Ring Automotives – a car electrics firm. It has been a measure of her determination and hard work. Her marriage to Ian Brown was a success at first but Ian had a sailor's eye for the girls and it did not last, but at least gave her a giant in Colin. She has proved to be a wonderful daughter, tough on the outside, soft inside, an eye for marketing and getting on with the garages. She has been a godsend at a very difficult time in our lives. We could not have managed without her.

Catriona – our lost darling – had health problems all her life. At Highers time, she was suffering from one of those adolescent difficulties and did not get the grades she wanted so she went to Glasgow College of Technology which was immediately upgraded to Glasgow Caledonian to do Business Studies which was great. There was a wonderful year at the University of Georgia at Athens, and then a job with Insight Tours that had to cut back with the first Iraq war. Finally she worked at the Royal Masonic and on to the St Marys where she transferred from personnel then to IT and found her niche. She was an outstanding success. Her marriage was a great one to John Bowker, an IT whiz with a passion for Grand Prix cars, and the result a gorgeous ginger – Max. What more is there to add.

We have been blessed with our children. I don't suppose that we were perfect parents, and nor were they perfect children, but they have all turned out so well. They had much of their mother, honesty, toughness and caring. What more could we have asked?

CATRIONA – THE DEATH OF A BELOVED DAUGHTER

This was a tribute that I gave to commemorate Catriona at the Opening of the IT Centre in St Mary's Hospital, which was named after her.

She died from breast cancer in 2002 having filled a number of highly successful roles at St Mary's.

"I would like to say, first, that Mary and I, together with the whole family – though Gillian has no option but to remain cutting and chopping in Sweden as surgeons do. Seonaid is beside us, and of course very important John and Max -that is the "wee man" as he is known in the North, or the Gingun the Ginger Boy. We all feel so privileged to be here today. Privileged that we are part of a great idea on your part but in an even more important sense that it is to commemorate what our youngest daughter achieved for St Mary's in her short life. It also gives us the chance to recognise the tremendous kindness and support that we have had from St Mary's staff over the years.

"It was wonderfully exciting to hear of your intention to set up a training centre for IT and to name it after Catriona with the explanation of why you all felt that it was so appropriate. You know why you loved her and I thought that in turn I would say a little, very briefly, about what she meant to us – her parents and her family. Now I have to add a personal note of caution. Because I have a default on my Y chromosome Mary and I had three daughters. This major fault line has meant that I have lived a large part of my life in a minority of four to one. Now, we did have a lovely Labrador, Dylan, but they, that is the Famous Four, swiftly ensured his neutral status. I have always had a nasty suspicion that that operation was carried out simply as a gentle warning.

Consequently whatever I dare to say today is said under the watchful eye of a three to one plus, of course, one up there.

"Catriona was our youngest by five years and because the other two, as they grew up, went their own adult ways, for much of her later years she was in some ways an only child to us and we probably got to know her more intimately than we did the other two at that adult stage of her life.

"I am only too aware that this may not be the occasion for honesty, but I do have to start by saying that Catriona had her problems – that is apart from her two older sisters both of whom are strong characters, and her traditional parents, one of whom, tragedy of tragedies, happened also to be her Headmaster. Being a kindly lass, that was a fact that she occasionally forgave me – "Big Boy" she once addressed me in one of her early IT communications. Apart from those handicaps I do have to reveal that Catriona was accident prone – if we went near water she went over her wellies, and if there was a bug to be caught Catriona caught it. Indeed, as for water she was returned to us, aged four, one day at Loch Tay, having fallen into the deep end of the loch by a nice young lad of about ten. The situation so resembled a Tom and Jerry cartoon with him handing her over and asking if this belonged to us. Later she fell in the classroom and smashed her beautiful new front teeth. Later she slipped on the pavilion steps before a hockey match and hurt her shoulder. She fell through a window at a late night party – surprise, surprise – and severed a muscle and part of a nerve, and, of course, she had that famous motor-bike accident. Need I go on? All I want you to ask yourselves, in part cautionary, are you really sure, with this heritage, that you want to endanger the odd million pounds worth of all this wonderful IT equipment that you have invested and put her name to it?

"Nina also had a dangerous determination to be different, with an accompanying charm that could knock the birds out of the trees. Who else but her would be given a large stirrup cup, a heady mix of Drambuie and whisky – a gimlet no less – at a rugby match at Murrayfield simply because she had a seat beside a handsome young man? Who else could get away with her steely grandmother while helping herself to a whisky and Crabbie's green ginger – a Whisky Mac – all the while smiling serenely and explaining "It's only a ginger cordial, Granny!" At one point, and I do apologise for these revelations, she went through a bad period as a Goth, this time again saved by her mother as she left for the pub one night, and dressed in the blackest of the black, and when Grannie asked – "You are surely not letting her go out looking like that are you?" "Well," replied Mary – you can see the genetic resemblance – "She is much safer looking like that, isn't she?" And what about her return at Christmas from her Rotary Scholarship year in Georgia? A year, incidentally that her tutor vigorously opposed on the grounds that she was far too pretty and she would never come back. That return to the loving bosom of her family was marked by scarlet and green hair! Now I ask you, need I go on?

But with all that there was a wonderful saving attribute – her winsome ways. There was that famous gift aged about fifteen, that she exercised on an infuriated French father as she and Valerie returned rather late after a visit to the Ganguette night club in the Dordogne only to have her produce that inimitable charm and smile, which was guaranteed to turn away wrath and reduced poor Guy to smouldering silence. There's no doubt she had a something in terms of the ability to recover lost ground.

There was too the hard work and a willingness always to go that extra mile. There was her ability to get on with people, whether it was the Chairman or the Chief Executive, or the cleaner or the girl in the office. She loved a challenge and she and her beloved John revelled in thinking of new ways of making a better life, and more cash. Wines on the Internet, buying and turning Taymouth Castle, by her adored Loch Tay, into a seven star hotel. That is, incidentally, now happening at a cost of some seventy million pounds.

"You never really know your daughter. This lass who could sing in a way that brought tears to your eyes – that chocolate rich mezzo soprano voice soaring to the rafters in the

Messiah. Those dimples, with that smile. Young Max has inherited those as well as her impish grin and quick wit. She was never at a loss for a word or even words, yet with a sweetness and genuine niceness of nature. I think that her early battles with ill-health gave her an empathy for problems and for other people's difficulties, allied to a determination that she was not going to be beaten by difficulties, whether in life or in her work. She had that gift of defusing situations, whether at work or in the family. Once again that twinkling smile and those eyes – "Oh Dad for goodness sake, " or if it was more difficult – "Oh, father, why don't you think again…" With three daughters, all with something wonderful and special, Nina had her own unique and special gifts which Mary and I are just so proud to have honoured to-day.

"I said at the beginning how appropriate it was that you should want to mark her life and her contribution to St. Mary's Hospital with this Learning Centre. I found on my desk almost the last e-mail that I sent to her. It must have been near the end, and she was very down. It was a simple couple of lines that I had found – "Courage is not freedom from fear. It is being afraid and going on." As one who has spent his life in education, that is not bad advice for us all when facing difficulties and dangers, and is perhaps fitting for this Learning Centre.

"I think that even more appropriate of her are the words engraved on the wall in that lovely little church at Loch Tay, where she was so happily married and where she now lies buried –

To have done whatever had to be done
To have turned the face of your soul to the sun
To have made life better and brighter for one
That is to have lived."

Church Window in Kenmore Church

MEMORY – 41 YEARS WITH THE SAMARITANS

Memory is a funny part of our brain. Sometimes something jogs it – a word, a voice, a smell. We do tuck away an enormous amount of material in that small area, which can suddenly reappear from those tiny cells. Often it is about a beginning, or sometimes an end, the first being usually better than the last. It might be that first day at school – en route for Turi, in the old Kenya – on the old KUR, after a disaster with a pineapple pudding; or that small cup of tea while meeting with Dr Greenlees, that giant of a Head, with his equally giant cup of tea, while trying for a bursary at Loretto; or the vision of that young lady in 1948 as I walked into the Old Quad to register at Edinburgh University with her ankle length New Look skirt; the scent of jasmine on the road up to Braid Road to tell Mary for the first time that I loved her. Later memories are much more mundane – jumping onto the stage at Greenfaulds High School, because they had not got round to put up steps, for the first assembly of the new school; or the look on the faces of the staff at St. Bride's as I arrived for an interval coffee, unheard of in the days of headmistresses, they being much like the Dowager in Downton Abbey, and I asked for sugar. "Heavens – we don't have any sugar, we'll have to get some!" Would this odd man really want a coffee?

Recently reading in a book by Susan Howatch about a healing centre at St. Benet's in London set my mind wandering back to the time of our return to Edinburgh from Helensburgh in 1956, so that I could go to Moray House and then to a job at Melville College in the heart of the City's West End.

We soon discovered that it is dangerous to sit over breakfast while on holiday, with no children at that point, and to read *The Scotsman*, and then to find your mind caught by an article from Wilfred Taylor in the Scotsman's Log about his conversation with one Chad Varah, who had started a suicide service in London and was looking for anyone interested in Scotland to contact him. Mary and I had been listening only recently to Radio Luxemburg, as you did in the days of no TV, about that very man and his work. A brief, tentative letter from me to him followed, and then in reply a phone call from that very man to say that someone who had been a "client" of the London branch had committed suicide and it was his wife's wish for him to be buried in his home town of Edinburgh. Now, in those days suicide in England was still a crime and no one could be buried in consecrated ground. In Scotland it was only a breach of the peace!

So, where was I to start in a completely new world? Keith Arnold had just become Rector of St John's, and we had met him and his wife, so it seemed sensible to go and talk to him. For Keith there was no problem – he would be happy to organise the funeral if I would set up arrangements with Warrender Crematorium. A phone call to St. Stephen's and we were to meet the widow in the Royal British Hotel on Princes Street the night before the funeral. I have little memory of that meeting, except that I felt very inadequate with a small talent or experience in dealing with such situations, but it went well.

So that was it, except that Chad arrived in Edinburgh a month or so later and a meeting was set up with the RSPCC in Melville Street, just across from the College. Of course, I was invited, as the only one with personal experience of this work. Oddly, the rugby club were organising a film night on the recent Lions Tour to South Africa on that same night. One does naturally have one's priorities, and I could manage both with a quick jump. That was the night that changed my world.

Now, I had a picture of Chad as an elderly cleric, benign, yet with an interesting vision and with that name, probably a Chinese connection. When I went into the room here was a youngish man, in full flow – as Chad always was, a chain smoker, multi-talented, vigorous and practical. He had just been given a tour of Edinburgh, had seen the Chaplaincy Centre in Forrest Road, and he was quite convinced that that would be ideal for his purpose, and that Jim Blackie, the

University Chaplain, was the perfect man to lead. That at once brought a scream from the back from Nancy Blackie, Jim's wife, to say that he was already over committed and Chad could forget it. An interesting start.

We went then for a drink – and a smoke in Chad's case – to Richard Baxendine's, he being a GP in the Polmont area and who was to prove a very important figure at the start in getting things going. The discussion was interesting and positive but I cannot remember that I contributed much. After all, I was only twenty eight!

So began an extraordinary nine months – September to June 1959. It saw, in very fresh circumstances, a very different and worthwhile development of the Samaritan movement. At that point, only St. Stephen's was working, and it was very much in Chad's image – a city church, well funded and supported by a very wealthy and ancient city guild. Now, by that I do not mean that it was not effective or well run, but it was at a time when most voluntary bodies were still serviced by the middle classes. In St. Stephen's case, it was run by Chad and his close friends, and there was little input in terms of organisation from the laity. The controlling body were the Companions. We, in Scotland, were the first to move to a basically democratic movement. Of course, how very Scottish – complete with a committee, a secretary and a treasurer. This was a new control system, and would lead to a gradual diminution of the role played by the church, and one much more adapted to modern life. For many clergy in the 1960s, as they often admitted to me, Samaritans was the obvious way out for old churches and old thinking. Then I went down to London for my first meeting of the Council in Peter Palumbo's mansion. There were nineteen present, and, apart from me, they were all clergy. Today the Samaritans is a recognised way – it is accepted, it has dozens of branches, it is worldwide. This is the biggest volunteer group in the world, with over twenty two thousand volunteers. Chad was the way, but perhaps with the way that we in Edinburgh began – we were a glimmer of light for a new future.

I might add that Liverpool might well have been first but, as Chad sarcastically put it, Christopher Pepys was too busy praying! Now, there was another lovely man, a gem of a Bishop with a heart of gold, for whom communion ought to be treated like a cocktail party! He also played a pivotal role at national level over the years.

It is impossible to remember all that had to be done over that nine month period, but it did get done by someone, or all of us, and that is a tribute to all who were determined to make it work. There was a meeting of the four clergy who had agreed that they would run with a committee and saw themselves as leaders who would take control for one in four weeks overlooking casework. There had to be a proper front in Edinburgh of course, so they agreed that Rev Harry Whitely of St. Giles' would be that as Chair – another lovely man with a great sense of humour. These four were Jim Blackie, solid and sensible and very hard working; Keith Arnold, cheerful and willing to try anything; Hamish Smith from the Congregational Church, again a quiet and sensible man; and that highlander Campbell Maclean from Cramond, cheerful and chatty. It was a year before we had a Roman Catholic – Father Anthony Ross, the University Chaplain – now, there was charisma and a power. It was also agreed that each would take over the service after 11pm on their week when the phone was transferred at night. During the day, the duty would run 9am to 11pm, with two on at all times. I cannot remember how long each duty was to be.

Would I be the secretary? Me? I could not type, had no shorthand, and I had never taken a minute in my life. I had never even sat on a committee. My only experience of life was in the Army and as a leader of a boys' club on the High Street. Mind, that Club did have an unusual ex-boy in Sean Connery. I think that, while I recognised that it was an honour, I was both stunned and petrified. I already had a full time job just teaching at Melville. I was running the rugby and cricket, so I was involved at weekends. I was a captain in the TA – only five years to go for a TD! I discussed it with all the family. My Mum was delighted – for her it was time I did something churchy. Father and Mother Frost kept quiet, while Keith kindly said that he would be treasurer. My darling Mary just smiled sweetly and then got down to discussing all the pros and cons, and she agreed that it was all in line with a somewhat mad husband. For herself, she had better things to do, like getting pregnant.

So, for the detail. We had no money, bar that one cheque for £100 from Professor Dover Wilson, but money rolled in, and it was never a problem. That delightful millionaire, Calouste Gulbenkian, who ran round London in a taxi cab, handed over a large sum as a result of a letter from me. I had then a huge service of visits to make – the Presbytery of Edinburgh were very polite and listened and gave me some cash. Miss Coverdale, the Director of the Council of Social Service, was a power of strength. We set up a Council as, of course, all good Edinburgh bodies did, with Social Work, the Council with gloves, the Law, also with gloves, the Council for Marriage Guidance, and others that we thought might help. I went to see the Director of Social Services in his council offices in Castle Terrace. I parked outside, as one could in those days, in my little baby Austin 7, and saw a man with his hands behind his back at a window staring out to the Castle. He was the Director, happy to help in any way but he was, of course, a very busy man.

Then the phone. What about 9000? Sorry, but we could only have CAL3333, and there was a problem in changing from one district to another for the night calls, but they would sort it, and they did. An odd visit next that I made was to The Samaritans, a dying voluntary body in those days in Edinburgh, started in the days of Florence Nightingale for Almoners – they were the social workers of the time. It was an interesting meeting, very Edinburgh, with a fellow TA officer, Henry Cook, as their lawyer. We had already agreed that we would be the Telephone Samaritans, so that was all right.

Premises St. George's in George Street had a spare hall in Queen Street, and we could have it but it would need a clean. And how! There was a dingy entrance hall, down steps with one or two smaller rooms for the "clients" and a kitchen. So the week before opening on the 2nd of June the volunteers arrived in old clothes and set too cleaning, polishing, finding desks, chairs, anything to make it look homely and friendly, and they did. I might add that I had a letter a few weeks on from the session clerk, sadly writing that we seemed to be attracting the wrong kind of persons, so they would not be continuing the lease. For me, God bless Jean Watt, a fount of all knowledge who had experience with Marriage Guidance and whose husband was minister of St. Columba's. She did the awful job of rota, and it worked.

Now, we had all to get training in this totally new concept of "befriending" from the Edinburgh University Social Work Department, who turned up trumps – they provided the accommodation and the lecturers, all in their free time. The subjects were very brief – how to befriend a person with money problems, how to befriend a person with marriage problems, how to befriend a person with mental problems, how to answer the telephone. Simple but practical, and everyone turned up and there was a lot of discussion. Because the leaders all had evening meetings, I seemed to become the centre round which all the questions were asked and, of course, with my "huge" practical experience I was the acknowledged expert and guide.

I was very lucky with Graeme Richardson as Head. He was involved with Marriage Guidance himself and thought it good for me and the school, so I could go ahead. I will not repeat what the staff felt – they were all sure that I would finish up on the other side of the service.

By this time, Keith Arnold and I had been summoned to London to learn how to do it. It was an eye-opener, as we did night duty in the Tower of St. Stephen's. I finished up taking a homeless family from St Stephen's to Liverpool Street Station, and Keith was up for four hours with a phone call. We were a couple of rather exhausted parties at early morning communion, and all with a Chad homily.

The other odd feature that began to emerge was the number of phone calls and letters to me from interested parties all wishing to start up branches, and as we gained success, so that number grew. What it is to be an expert – I even learned to type.

So, the 2nd of June 1959 saw me rushing out of the College at 8.30 with the key to open the office and running along Ainslie Place and Queen Street to get it all going. As I opened the door, the phone was ringing and I had to answer it.

"Happy Birthday Samaritans. Look, I have a big problem."

So it all began. The line hardly stopped that first day and from that day on. It was all a bit chaotic at times but it worked, and we had begun...

As the pressure on the leaders grew, I found myself promoted/demoted to be a leader with the week's overnight calls. As I had to leave home at 8.15, that meant Mary, with an exuberant young lady in tow, was left to become a fully-fledged Samaritan. Inadvertently she answered one call with our address in Fairmilehead, and because she could not help an angry lady, she was threatened with "coming up from Morningside to sort you out." I found myself on a number of call-outs in the middle of the night – Blackford Pond and the Braids in freezing rain were memorable moments – while an escape from the bedroom of a distressed titled lady was an even more interesting situation.

Life only got more hectic as the calls seemed to shoot up and all kinds of administrative devices had to be introduced that we had never considered, records, back-up reports – even a brief lexicon of problems in a list on the office wall and how to think about them – the most memorable being a one liner from me that was headed "Marriage – see Divorce."

So, that was a day that changed my life, from which there followed forty one years of endless journeys to London and to Slough, as the head office and round numerous branches as the first lay Chair – to Israel, to Geneva, to the States. Letters and suggestions on how to start a branch and how to run it. I was so lucky with Mary, who backed me all the way, and with all those friends that I made. Looking back for me, it was the inspiration that came from the dedication of so many ordinary people to do that job of helping others.

Lucky me.

THE SAMARITANS

"In Praise of some who should be Famous Men and Women"

A recent meeting with the current hierarchy of the movement brought home to me just how far we the Samaritans have come, from being virtually unknown, to being a byword today. Since those first days of the early fifties when the movement consisted of one branch in London and others in Scotland, it was very fragmented and there was little real overall control. Time passes and there is not much that remains in the present memory of the Samaritans about those remarkable men and women who were in at the beginning, and without whose efforts there would be no Samaritans as we know them today. It is accepted that the organisation was the creation of one man, Chad. While in one sense that is true, it is but only to a limited extent. What should be recognised is that in the beginning the organisation could have nose-dived and disappeared, in the same way that a number of other similar efforts had gone. That that did not happen was due to the calm practicality, the organisational skills and the good commonsense of a number of people. To pick but one important moment, at one of the early Councils at Durham in 1963, the movement were on the verge of falling into disarray and the whole organisation was almost driven apart because Chad tried to force through his views of making all branch structures based on that of St. Stephen's, it was one of clergy driven with a strictly hierarchical system. The Scots, who by that time had built a close-knit regional structure, backed by all the chairmen of Edinburgh, Aberdeen, Glasgow and Dundee, were very angry at Chad's attitude and considered the possibility of declaring the possibility of a breakaway. Fortunately, solutions were found thanks to the good sense and cool heads of Christopher Pepys in England, Bill Thomson in Ireland and even myself as the Chairman in Scotland.

Christopher Pepys

It is natural for memories to fade or progress stops, time moves on, but it is still worth remembering and "praising famous men." This record is a very personal memoir, written probably as the result of ageing, but also with the wish not to forget. Hilary has done such an excellent account with her book, placing the story in its historical perspective while providing a wonderfully human element to that record. Mine is an attempt to bring to life some of those characters and some of the events in my time of working with the Samaritans that helped to make it what it is today. One of the myths about us is that our work was frozen in time, that there were rarely problems and that change never happened. I cannot remember a single moment in all those years when we did not face enormous challenges and constant problems, and the need to make sometimes dramatic changes to meet those challenges.

It is important in writing about the Samaritans to put it into the context of the world of the 1950s. Suicide in England and Wales at that time was still a crime, and acts of attempted suicide were regarded equally as crimes. Scotland, as usual, was different, in that suicide was a matter of a breach of the peace. In both countries the church would still refuse to hold a service for the suicide, and often refuse to allow the body to be buried in consecrated ground. Throughout the UK nationally, the church still played a central role in life. There was a church in every parish and a church hall, even if often run down, both of which were to play a crucial part in the housing and manning of the early branches. It is hard to believe today, with the central role played by that department, of the then secondary importance of social work departments. Yet it has become an increasingly important, almost central part of our social fabric, but in those days, most of the work was carried out by probation officers. When I first arranged a visit in 1956 to the Director of Social Work in Edinburgh, he was standing in the window of his Castle Terrace office looking out towards the Castle, his hands behind his back with nothing to do.

Telephones, never mind mobiles, were not available in many houses, though there were public phones in their red boxes in most areas – but were too often not working. Public mention of suicide or use of the word was forbidden, and any attempt to use those terms in publicity ran into immense obstacles, particularly on or round the railways. All our early attempts to get publicity on any of these sites ran into a blank wall of resistance. The domestic gas supply was not only dangerous but lethal, and together with the railways, offered the main avenues to suicide. Over the years, there had been various earlier attempts to establish suicide rescue services, but all had failed. Society was still very hierarchical so a service which offered the concept that the final decision, indeed any decision, might lie with the caller – or client, as they were then known – was ground breaking. Sex, of course, had not yet been invented and the pill was only just beginning to play a major role in human relationships. Knowledge about sex, which is a rather different kettle of fish, was grossly inadequate with consequent major problems particularly for young people. I remember showing a film on contraception to Sixth formers in the late 60s, but being forbidden by the local authority to explain or expand, even though – as one boy remarked – the film was sponsored by the London Rubber Company! Contraception or abortion – certainly not!

It is true that Chad's efforts, therefore, were not new but the 1950s were a point in time in which he caught a "tide in the lives of men". His ideas were different in that while church based there was a total ban on any attempt at proselytising, the service was readily accessible, it offered a genuine system of befriending, and it tapped into the desire of ordinary people to do something constructive to help. There was, at that time, a very strong ethos of service and a wish to offer commitment. It has also to be said that Chad was a brilliant publicist – and that is not a criticism – and because of his journalistic connections he was able easily to tap into the media. His earliest efforts were a short dramatised series on Radio Luxemburg, I think on a Sunday evening, which is where I first heard of him.

Chad

Chad is a towering figure in the life of the Samaritans, a most complex character, loveable at times, intolerable at others. A mind that was brilliant in so many ways, a polymath being the best description, linguist, writer, scientist and psychologist. A powerful character who brooked no opposition on deeply held principles. He had little sympathy for anyone who opposes him, with an elephantine memory for any differences of opinion or apparent slights, and oddly little time for any human frailties in normal situations. He had few management skills and little interest in them. He can be implacable, as his views on Scandinavian help lines or Lifeline proved. Sadly it ultimately included IFOTES, a body with which he had worked, and of which indeed he was a Chairman at one time. He has a wonderful gift for communicating his ideas to people, he has an almost mesmeric ability to set a scene and put over an idea in a novel and fresh way, and in particular about the Samaritans. He spoke once of "Bison, Buffaloes and Men" at a Scottish conference, which brilliantly expressed his thoughts on suicide – could you get a more memorable opening? He had financial support in the early days from an M. Martin – head of the Samaritaine store in Paris.

However difficult Chad could be, and few Chairs escaped major problems with him, it has to be said that he was a giant figure of the twentieth century. In the early days we were supported by a tiny administrative body, which consisted of Daphne Morriss, who had been his secretary. She was a sweet person with severe arthritis in both her hands, which made it almost impossible for her to hold things. She and Leslie Kentish, the Bursar, lived in the same village in the south, where all the minutes were kept under her bed. Daphne had a will of iron and was totally devoted to Chad. She was an excellent organiser and prepared all the arrangements for the early School for Directors, which was held in a retreat in Hertfordshire. Leslie was the epitome of the accountant – tall, moustached, grey-haired. He counted every penny. He could never understand why I had been invited to join the Executive, as that involved the expense of an overnight sleeper and a flight back to Aberdeen. He always made me feel that I should have walked, or at least tried a bicycle.

Executives, if you could call them that, were held occasionally, either in the crypt of St. Stephen's, but more usually in Church House at Westminster from 11am until about 4pm. This meant having an exciting lunch for a small coterie of us – Mike, D.M.J., Richard and myself in the St. Stephen's Grill opposite to Parliament. The original idea was that there would be present the officials, Chad, John Eldrid (I think came at a later date), Christopher Pepys, and one clergyman from each of Scotland and Ireland,

John Eldrid

Sadly, it could not be a clergyman from Scotland as Jim Blackie declined and landed me into it, the Hon Psychiatrist, and any others approved by Chad. My first experience of the Executive, when both Richard Fox and I joined together on the same day, turned into an unholy inquisition, where Tony Fryer of Reading, complete with "friend", was arraigned for some remark that he had made about Chad's ideas. I think that Tony was "released on bail with a caution" and a black mark on his record.

Tony later became a stalwart in the movement, though he could be very different – his branch had an elaborate entry process of being blindfolded and led by the hand round an obstacle course. It certainly taught you the importance of trusting others!

The early meetings tended to be rather long winded and mostly involved a lengthy report from Chad. He was not a good chairman and was quite unconcerned about any admin matters. Once Chad had decided that he was not really interested in carrying on as chair, the meetings became not just more lively, but better run and more purposive. One aspect of all Samaritan meetings, whether Executive, Council or branch, was to me the all-pervasive humour and sense of fun. The other feature that I recall was the smoke filled fug of the meeting rooms – Basil's pipe, Jean and George's cigarettes. Perhaps it ensured a long immunity for us non-smokers! I am sure that dealing with matters of life and death required humour as a necessary counterbalance. Incidentally, my first experience of the ways of the Samaritans was a visit with Keith Arnold, later Bishop of Warwick, to St. Stephen's. We, on arrival, were handed the overnight duty and slept – well, lay down – in the tower. Keith finished with a three hour stint on the phone. I was sent to collect a homeless family and deliver them to Liverpool Station. Neither got much sleep, and we were up all the next day on duty in the vestry until the evening meeting with Chad and a number of his clients when he did a counselling session en masse! It was very Anglican and public school!

I found myself expected to be the fount of all wisdom and of guidance for setting up new branches which were springing up all over the country. I wrote numerous letters and I found myself expected to have all the answers on such diverse matters as selection, preparation courses, rotas, publicity, structures, and where was the finance to come from. Chad's St. Stephen's was not the right system for many of the hopefuls, all desperate to make an early start while their enthusiasm was still there. Chad was all for starting Samaritans, but did not wish to waste time giving any details on the management or administration of a branch. Next I was "invited" to represent Scotland, as well as becoming the first layman on the Executive, and finally I became the first lay Chairman of Samaritans.

David Arthur

Once the Executive was up and running, Chad decided on a system of visits to ensure that all was well – actually to enforce his authority. The first of these was a visit to Guildford branch, who had dared once again to make comments on Chad's methods and views, and implied that they might be willing do their own thing.

Richard Fox and I were delegated for this onerous task, with instructions that if all was not well to close the branch down at once.

We arrived to a great welcome. I had not revealed that two of the leading lights had come from Edinburgh – John Cotter, a lovely Ulsterman, and I think George Brown. The visit went a bomb, and it turned out that all they wanted to do was to have a committee and a chairman. After our report, Chad reluctantly agreed to allow them to continue.

In my time there appeared the dreaded Branches of Special Concern, which always took an inordinate amount of time to cover. I think the earliest troubled branch was Worcester, who had had their visit from Elizabeth Salisbury, who was only allowed inside on the production of her visa card as evidence of her identity. Many others followed until that awful Council where Blackpool, who had failed in all sorts of ways to offer a service, and had resolutely refused offers of help or advice, were finally shut. There followed a motion, proposed by me, to the Council to close it down. Poor Cecil had to drive to the branch and collect their funds. It was most unpleasant, but it proved a salutary lesson to any other recalcitrant branch. "Just remember Blackpool" was usually sufficient.

The Executive met six times a year in alternate months, the Council twice in the year and once at the Annual Conference in September. A unique feature of the Annual Council was the approval of all the appointments of the Directors and Chairmen, a very useful power that should never be lost. The Executive also had a Retreat, I have no idea why it was so named, it met at Swanwick in October – it also gave Chad a chance to behead the dead dahlias in the gardens! This weekend was always a very pleasant, relaxed affair when we got through a great deal of work and planning for the next year, and Richard and I took each other on at table tennis, much to the amusement of the others. The "Befrienders" had its first rehearsal here, using Chad's script for the first episode. I was the young "star", and Christine Hamilton, a gentle and very capable psychiatrist from Glasgow, whom Richard had brought in, was the female lead. Sadly, Christine died early from cancer. She was a great loss. Writing of the "Befrienders", I remember the appearance at the Executive of the producer and author, a Canadian whose name I cannot remember. He was the very picture of the TV producer, large and theatrical, and complete with cigar. He started by asking us all to introduce ourselves and tell him what we did. Surprisingly, none of us had much knowledge of what the others did for a living – they felt quite shocked to learn that I was a teacher, and of course the majority of the body was clerical, as were the great majority of branch Directors at the time. His introduction ended with an impassioned plea for us to approve the production with the memorable sentence that "this was our chance to cast one small stone of hope into the vast pool of despair." We approved it, much to Chad's joy, as he did a great deal of the writing. It proved a great success and really made the Samaritans a household name.

Bill Thomson

John Eldrid, when he joined the Executive, was a tower of strength and common sense. He was Chad's sidekick in St. Stephen's and could always be relied upon to give a sensible view on all matters. It cannot have been always easy with Chad as his boss.

Bill Thomson from Belfast was a gem – he later became the first Chair after Chad. He was a quiet Ulsterman with a sharp wit, great patience and considerable administrative skills. He laid down the first rules for visits with a checklist of what to look for and what to ask. He followed Chad as Chairman, and brought a quiet authority and delightful Irish charm to the task and a determination to avoid confrontation.

This was a vital time for the movement, as there was a widespread tide of discontent and a feeling that all was not well. There had been annual conferences – I think the first was in Oxford followed by Cambridge, Glasgow and then Durham in 1963. Durham was where the first Articles and Memorandum were agreed, but I remember a very angry group of Scots, aided and abetted by others, returning home ready to declare UDI. Basically the problem was Chad's dictatorial approach in which he laid down the law and was quite unwilling either to listen or to compromise. The idea of moving the annual conferences, at that time from one place to another was to attract publicity and it was not until 1977 that it finally settled in York. For my conferences, I am not quite sure why, we always had the Secretary of State, Keith Joseph, whom we met with at least three times and he agreed to give us the first government money; Barbara Castle, with her wig and blunt refusal to meet the members from Rhodesia as they had just declared UDI; and David Ennals, who got up Richard's nose for some reason.

The Scots, because they had almost a national coverage with branches in Edinburgh, Glasgow, Aberdeen and Dundee, had already set up a regional committee with close communication between the branches and a willingness to work together. I got landed with being the first Chairman. Each branch was very different in set up. Edinburgh at first was very much church based, on Chad's instructions that we must have the leadership of the national church. The Chairman being Harry Whitely of St. Giles', a delightfully puckish figure who enjoyed baiting the establishment, Richard Baxendine, a GP, steady and solid, and Rev Jim Blackie who was Professor of Clinical Theology. Rev Campbell Maclean was a parish minister who enjoyed the appearance of being delightfully highland and vague, and Rev Hamish Smith, a congregationalist. Only later did we entice the charismatic and formidable Father Anthony Ross, a Benedictine monk who was the muscular Chaplain at Edinburgh University. Father Antony came from a highland Wee Free family who himself had converted to Catholicism. As a result his family never spoke to him again. A truly saintly and wonderful man. We were at that time entitled the Telephone Samaritans, as there was already a Samaritan Charity – an almoners group. We were very formal, with everyone known by their surnames.

Glasgow had Rev Tom Allan, with the backing of Lord George Macleod of the Iona Community, but was really dependent on the enthusiasm and hard work of the Macmillans, while Aberdeen was quite different, with Dr Charles Strachan, a physicist, and Jimmy Shearer. Charles was very deaf, very down to earth and completely dedicated to Samaritans. He had an extremely salty sense of humour and was very unhappy about confidentiality. "What?" he said, "If a client tells me that he has put radioactive isotopes into the reservoir, do I just sit and smile?". Then Rev Ian Begg, later

Bishop of Aberdeen, who always arrived in a filthy old raincoat and was once directed to the interview room as a prospective client, as they were called then. Jimmy Shearer was a gem. He was an enormous worker, down to earth, a genuinely lovely man who became a Regional Rep. Then there was the Dundee branch which was churchy, with Rev Roy Hogg, a charming and incompetent man who was made Citizen of the Year, but whom I had to sack only a month later, because his branch was neither manned nor ever open on a regular basis! The Scots had decided to have Chairs, not Directors and a Committee of Management – all to Chad's horror and threats that his companions would not see their way to recognising us!

Chad had come up to a Scottish Conference in Dundee and did his usual on sex. That fairly woke up the old gentlemen and ladies who were sleeping at the front. We also started our own regional conferences at Carberry House. Chad came up on one occasion to Gorebridge and delivered his extraordinary "Bison and…"

I attended my first Council of Management in London at Peter Palumbo's house in 1962, next to St. Stephen's. I think Peter was another of Chad's sponsors. All I remember of that meeting was that there were nineteen of us and all but me were aged clergy. Talk of "old f***s". I do remember leaving, feeling very depressed that it was in the hands of these old men and that most of the conversation was ecclesiastical – a typical response from a young thirty two-year-old! The Council also met in different towns. Once it settled in London it met first in a hotel in Paddington, and then later in Church House. The Council gradually changed complexion with more and more laymen, but it still tended to be dominated by the clerical Directors.

Of all the clergy, two were memorable because of what they did for Samaritans. First was Chris Pepys, who was the first Director of Liverpool and who was cynically accused by Chad of holding up the opening of the branch with too many prayer meetings! Chris was great – a real "gas and gaiters" Bishop, who presented a picture of genial bonhomie in true

Anglican tradition. "Ducky," he used to say, "Cocktail parties are really a form of communion." Really, Chris, and what would the Archbishop say to that? Underneath he had a sharp mind, a clear vision of what we should be doing and a willingness to stand up to Chad – Bishop versus rector – Chad was very hierarchical and normally gave way. Chris Pepys did an immense amount for us and had so much common sense. No one could not but love Chris.

Basil Higginson

Basil Higginson was so different. Small, hair hanging around his face, prominent teeth, with either a pipe or cigarette in his mouth. Basil was the common man in the nicest possible sense, kindness itself, and he would do anything for anyone. He understood what made people tick, and he was nobody's fool. He had been the Director at Manchester and was much loved as a parish priest. There was a very down-to-earth north country way to him. Sadly his last years were badly affected, first by the death of his son, Rosser, and then by a brain tumour that ultimately killed him. That caused a major crisis as he started to ring up branches in the middle of the night. He was the first General Secretary, and set up the first administrative HQ in that tiny house in Slough. He had a lovely sense of humour, which appeared at the most unlikely moments. He nearly gave me hysterics when I was about to deliver a keynote address on Befriending at the Manchester Conference, by making some crude comment on my conference dress of the kilt.

Jean Burt

Jean Burt took on the task of Assistant General Secretary. It was not a good appointment with Basil's illness, and it was the wrong job for her. It was sad, as she was a very gracious lady and a good worker. She had worked in the Cabinet Office and had been one of the early Samaritans in St. Stephen's and was a huge supporter of Chad, which did not make life easy when there was a bust-up with our Founder – not too unusual at any time!

David Evans

Basil's successor was the inimitable David Evans. David had been the successful director in Birmingham, and proved the ideal man. He has a natural charm, allied to a wickedly subtle wit, all with that smile alternating with a civil service po-face which completely allays opposition. Having been a volunteer himself, he never lost his understanding of the dangers of the full-time professional taking control. A very smooth operator, but in the best sense of the word and the interests of the Samaritans.

Another formidable clergyman was Father Aidan Rossiter, who was Bursar of St George's school and Director of Weybridge. Cheerful, red-faced and large, but capable of cutting through all the verbiage of meetings. His common sense support carried me, as might be expected, carried much weight. There were, of course, others – John Williams a tower of strength, and the odd man out, Theo Westow. I think that Theo was a Quaker and one of the awkward squad, a quality which was a useful antidote to an easy consensus.

Doris Odlum

Samaritans were blessed with their psychiatric support in an exceptional character, Dr Doris Odlum. Dear Doris, she was such a tower of strength, small, slightly rotund, immaculately turned out, and no one could ever doubt that here was a powerful character. She had immense resilience and strength. One very hot Council meeting at Church House, when the temperature must have been close to the nineties, she was asked to speak at the end, a task she carried out with her usual acuity and good sense. She was very deaf, a blessing when in earshot of one of Mike Charman's parties, but always a cause of worries to all the ladies in case she did not hear fire alarms.

She attracted almost mystical adoration from everyone, yet retained a wonderful humility. She had a remarkable mind that could penetrate the most confused situation, and an ability to win arguments with sharp logic. She alone could persuade Chad of a wrong course, she made him cool his ardour in the famous Brenda sex calls, when he was about to attract universal fury from the Church and the Archbishop in particular She had incredible energy. I once asked her, at the age of at least ninety, if she would speak at a conference in Dundee in November.

"Sorry, dear, I can't," she said.

"That's all right, Doris, I know it's a long journey in winter."

"Oh, no, dear," she said, "I'm lecturing in Newfoundland."

She used to ask me how long she should speak, whether it was in the course of discussion or at that wonderful end to conference. She always finished dead on time, she never hesitated, and she never made a grammatical mistake. She was a truly great lady who touched us all with some of her greatness. She once told me about her father, who owned the Ritz Hotel in Bournemouth. She swam every day in the sea, summer or winter, and he did not approve of women doctors so she went to Oxford to read Classics, and then took her medical degree. She was a suffragette, but "dear, I never had the courage to chain myself to the railings!" I remember her in Geneva when we had been invited to visit a mental hospital, as the Director believed in locks and keys. Doris was furious, and demanded that he unlock us and allow us out.

Richard Fox

Richard Fox was quite different – urbane, smooth, a marvellous communicator, at ease with ordinary members and the rest of his profession. His mane of hair with the falling lock, a beautifully modulated voice, and an inexhaustible gift of words he was meat and drink to the media. He had his doubters in the profession, but he had a charisma and a charm that carried him through. He was the seventh or eighth member of his family to be a doctor and traced his ancestry back to the famous Quaker Foxes.

He was dreadfully upset when his son refused to be a doctor. His wife was or still is a faithful Samaritan in her branch. Richard divorced her, married an American, worked in a run-down downtown Bronx hospital, nursed his second wife through cancer until her death, then returned to the UK and remarried his first wife.

A remarkable person, who did so much for the Samaritans. He was a delightful character – charming, he could be occasionally bitchy when he felt that there was a bit of hypocrisy, but he was always well worth his contribution to the movement. He had that necessary touch of common sense and was able to express the good sense of ordinary members. He would go anywhere in our support, and gave us a genuinely recognised place in the helping and professional world.

George Day

A third in the world of medicine was Dr George Day, a real country GP complete with his Hawks tie, his pipe, his tweed jacket, carefully thought out opinions, and later carpet slippers. He was a doctor to whom anyone would turn with confidence for in-growing toenails, coughs, etc. George had a special place in the hearts of all Samaritans, and rightly so. Warm, humorous and a wise old owl, he would deliver judgements with such aplomb often with particularly caustic additions. He was well up with medical matters, and had the time and the gift of communication. Mind you, he was a rogue at times. He produced a wonderful new concept of the R factor – repeat clients/callers. I remember his whole statistical basis being destroyed at a conference in Birmingham. George sat quietly puffing at his pipe in a corner, and totally ignored the careful build-up of evidence against him. The R Factor, of course, continued to play a part in his thoughts.

He was a cornerstone for us because of that quiet sense of confidence that what we were doing was right. He, Basil and Jean once went by car to Helsinki for a conference, and stopped off in Copenhagen for a break. George told the other two, "Off you go, my children, I am going to stop and sleep in this quiet square." A gentleman sat down beside him and started a conversation. It turned out that he was a doctor in Hungary. "I have always wished that I could meet one of your

English doctors," he said. "A Doctor Day who wrote a wonderful article that changed my whole approach to medicine!" I think that was so true of the George that so many of us knew.

The international scene was always difficult because of Chad's paranoia about professionals and evangelising. The first meeting was at the Chateau Bossey on Lake Geneva in 1960. Chad was there, Chris Pepys and myself, together with an odd couple, an elderly Methodist minister from Manchester who must have been their first director, and a Rev Evans from Bournemouth, who was very high church and very pompous. The group was high-powered in an academic sense, as most of the European groups were run by professionals – the Berlin one, for example, was run entirely by men and women with at least two degrees – so the concept of lay volunteers was a hard one for them to swallow. It was a very hard working two days, after which it was agreed that we set up an international body, IFOTES (International Federation of Telephone Emergency Services). Chad made a big contribution, stressing the need to offer uncomplicated help without any religious connotations. I do not remember any great opposition. The first president was a Swiss, Pastor Enrst Schwyn. I remember him standing up and explaining what an unexpected honour this was and pulling out his twenty minute acceptance speech in three languages. Chad later became President!

At this point, there were the Samaritans, IFOTES, Lifeline, and the IASP (International Association of Suicide Prevention) and the AAS (American Association of Suicidology). Chad fell out with IASP and AAS, or they fell out with him, as they were none too happy with his approach to sex, particularly with his very personal approach to nubile young ladies. Richard and I were sent to the meeting in St. Louis in 1975 to try to convince the Americans that the Samaritans were normal human beings who were not obsessed with sex. As a result, I suffered badly at the hands of my education committee who gave me two weeks off to go to the States, but added frequent references to sex and kidology!

BI did not appear for a long time, and until that time the Executive had to approve overseas branches, which was plain stupid, and it was a considerable relief to see that responsibility pass to BI. For some reason, Chad got it into his head that I opposed this. I suspect that it was his way of getting back at me for backing Cecil over the money affair, so in his book he totally misrepresented everything that I had done or said in any connection with BI. But that is Chad. It's sometimes a great help to have a one-eyed look at anything.

Mike Charman

There were a host of others who contributed to the work. On the straight and narrow aspect of the law, there was the formidable figure of Mike Charman. Mike was the classic Englishman – be-piped, hearty, loud of voice and the producer of instant opinions, most of which were, surprisingly right. If it was wrong, it made no difference. Underneath the slightly brutish surface Mike was a gem – he genuinely felt for people in distress, he would go the proverbial extra mile to help anyone.

Fools, he hated them and was not prepared to give them space or time. When he wanted he could be an extraordinarily gentle chairman, and his parties at any conference were legendary for their sheer noise and fun. He was a godsend, actually. Samaritans did not need a legal eagle who would never give an opinion. We were not that kind of organisation.

Cecil Barber as Bursar was very different. The perfect example of the accountant, except that he drove an MG sports car and frequented racecourses. Was the success of Samaritan finance really due to Cecil's unique skill in picking winners? Cecil knew his monies, and the law related to them. It was most fun when he and Mike disagreed. Cecil was usually right. Cecil was blunt, and if he disagreed he said so, and why. He kept a tight grip on our money. If not always liked, particularly if a branch was fiddling to avoid their contribution, but he was widely respected. The classic confrontation was when Chad had wheedled a large sum of money from a certain wealthy donor which would be given to Samaritans, presumably for tax purposes, and then handed over to Befrienders International. Cecil absolutely refused to have anything to do with it on the grounds that one charity could not give to another. Cecil won, and assured Chad in an immensely vitriolic exchange at Council that Chad's elephantine memory for insults was more than matched by that of Cecil's.

David Merrit-Jackson

Then there was publicity, and who better than David Merrit Jackson, larger than life, with a booming husky voice and a determination that Samaritans should get the best publicity, and the best service at the lowest cost? Who could forget that emphasis on brown, brown and brown again as the only colour for the movement. He always had his collage of publicity material laid out on his desk, and huge blackboards. He had no time for anyone who was not prepared to give his or her all. He always had his little coterie of his wife, the Archers and Elisabeth Salisbury, who were the backbone of the reception group at conferences. The picture that remains of D.M.J. was the large figure, cigarette in hand – very common in those incorrect days – to the Samaritans, seated at a desk with his husky voice laying down the law.

The early days saw mostly men, but the ladies soon made their impact. The largest, if she would forgive the phrase, was Audrey O'Dell, a formidable lady from Hull. She had a wide experience of the social work world and a gift of putting forward her case.

She would do anything for the movement, and had a most delightful giggle which would give the lie to her appearance of dominatrix. She liked the conferences to finish on a high note with the Northern Choir, whose appearance was always greeted with a chorus of kindly boos. Nancy Kerr from Liverpool was a total contrast, with a sweet charm and reasonableness that belied a quiet determination to ensure that everything was treated in a Samaritan way.

Perhaps one of the most important contributions to the ways in which the organisation worked to a common purpose and a common rhythm was that little booklet 'The Samaritan', edited by Elizabeth Salisbury. Elizabeth first came to prominence at conferences when she manned reception. Basil used to send out A4 yellow information sheets from Slough, but these were soon superseded by the magazine. It was a remarkably fresh production that combined information, suggestions, disagreements with almost everything from individual Samaritans. It showed neither fear nor favour, and was always a good read. It was unique, and while it gave an impression of being a chatty contribution, it was anything but. The green monstrosity that passes for a read today for volunteers is symptomatic of something dire. Come back the paper that Elizabeth and I prepared for the Executive on communication!

Over time the Samaritans have been very fortunate in the calibre of people who felt drawn to work for them. Part of our success was due to the fact that all of us in leadership had to work in the frontline, even when we were at the "top". This gave us a really balanced sense of perspective, and a sense of responsibility as all the rules that were laid down applied to us as well. The talents that we all had were very disparate, but seemed to coalesce into a whole. We were blessed that there were no great egos – even if Anthony Lawton, now of Centre Point thought so! One has to recognise that Chad's great contribution was to back off from the control side at an early date. The problem that faces all movements like the Samaritans is that they have to grow and develop or they die. There is, of course, the need to create structures and fresh lines of control, but in so doing there is the real danger that we may lose that excitement, that spontaneity, that idealism with which we started. That is the challenge for the next generation of leaders.

I do not know whether all this will be of interest to the "old ex-chairs". You can always have fun recalling your moments and your memories. Perhaps we should put them all together as an archive for the future?

David Arthur – February 2005

SHENLARICH – PARADISE ON LOCH TAY

The huts with Mary, Gillian and father Frost
The Famous Huts

I am not sure whether I have got the name right, as we always thought that the croft house of the Keddies, which was originally down where the Martins built their house, was called Kepranich. The Keddies were the owners of the croft, and she had inherited it under crofting law through her parents and Mr Keddie, her husband, had been a builder in Dundee. Their son, Alastair, was a very bright lad who went on to Glasgow University and got a First class degree, I think in Astronomy or Astro-Physics. He later went down to London and finished at the top of the civil service tree in the DTI and is now retired and lives at Dall. He married Marjorie Masterton, whose father, the local vet, created those extraordinary Cluny Gardens. When we first knew Alastair he was at Breadalbane Academy in Aberfeldy and with the lack of transport he boarded in Aberfeldy during the week and only came home at week-ends.

The story of the huts is about fishing. That was a very common practice at that time, and still is, that fishermen, from all over Scotland, go to camp out for the weekend on the loch side, usually with a little refreshment. We understood that this particular fisherman, a master joiner, who lived in Falkirk had fished down on the lochside for a number of years, had finally approached Mr Keddie to ask if he could build a hut on the alp below the Keddies. This was on the site of an old croft which was surrounded by drystane dykes.

We believe that the steamer on the loch used to call in at Shenlarich. As you will know there is deep water – six hundred feet close to the shore.

The first hut that he built was so successful that the joiner went back to the Keddies and asked whether he could build another one with a covered area in between. This he did and "lived happily ever after…." well not quite. For he collapsed, and had to be taken up to the road on Stewart Keddie's tractor. I think that he must have gone home and died at home, because his family inherited the huts and arrived to have a noisy party in the huts, much to the Keddies' disgust who immediately invited them to leave and the huts were given to two elderly sisters, ladies from Balqhuidder, called I think the Misses McGregors. They did enjoy the peace and quiet.

Enter the Frost/Arthur connection. The Frosts were furnishers who ran an upmarket family soft furnishing firm – Frosts of Shandwick Place in Edinburgh. Father Frost had taken over from his father, and had three children _ Mary, my wife being the eldest – Robert who worked in the family firm and Keith who was an accountant and later joined with Frosts. Both Robert and Keith were keen scouts and Keith ran the St John's Church scout camp group. He was responsible for the summer camp in summer 1960 and went searching for a suitable site, trying to find a flat piece of ground by tracking along the north side of Loch Tay searching for such an area. He thought he had found one on the opposite south side and drove down to Kepranich to ask Mr Keddie for permission to use the ground for a camp. There had apparently been such a camp previously, and permission was readily given.

Keith was a charmer and, during the week, had been asked in to the huts for a cup of tea by the Misses McGregor. In the course of which they admitted that they were getting old, and were finding the steep track down to the huts more and more difficult. They were right – that track, about half a mile long was steep, rutted and very wet at times. The two ladies asked Keith if he would be interested in taking over the huts. Keith, was unmarried at the time, just out of the navy and penniless, but thought that his family could well be interested. They asked initially for £80 but on sight of Keith's face, reduced the price to £40. I was the one the Arthur side – had married Mary Frost and by that time we had had our first child – a daughter Gillian – and Robert had a son – another Robert. Mary and I were on holiday in the New Forest and received a phone call from Keith to ask us about the possibility of taking on the huts with Father Frost, Robert and himself. We were wildly enthusiastic, particularly me, as I had spent times at nearby Ardeonaig Manse, when my Dad did a summer fill-in for the Rev. George Grieve in, I think about 1942. I had camped there in1945 with Dad's BB troop, at a camp below the Manse. The Frost/Arthur family were summoned by the Keddies in August 1960 to have tea with them and perhaps to be approved! On passing that test we agreed to buy an interest in the huts for £40 – that was a tenner each for each family – and then to pay a £1 a year in rent. (That was later converted to a bottle of whisky!) The building of the huts had incidentally been approved by the Duke of Breadlbane as the chief landowner.

I think that we all spent time in the huts that autumn and winter of 1961 and Father Frost certainly fished there. I do recall that Mary and I spent a freezing week round Christmas of that year. We all agreed that work needed to be done in the spring, and a rowing boat, as well as a small sailing one – named Dilly – was purchased. Along with that went 4 kapok life jackets.

The sailing boat was yellow, it had a mast, it could sail and it could be rowed, all equally badly, and tipped very easily.

Father had a more conventional boat which was kept on the shore, while Dilly lay up by the huts. Officially we were only allowed one boat on the loch side.

The path down to the huts was between a third of a mile to a half. At the top was a strong wooden gate, which we always tried, with little success, to stop the kids swinging on. The next was rough track across a small burn (very wet when it rained), followed by a relatively easy bit, and then a long straight downhill part with kind of rough drystone dyke on the west side, followed by route to the slight corner, and a second path leading off to the right, This was a short cut to the huts, used by those who enjoyed racing and a challenge to get down quickest. Finally, or almost, finally, a kind of shallow gully to a small clump of trees with a short descent at right angles to the huts. Those trees were a godsend, if carrying trunks, canisters, or kids, as one could swing adroitly, or less so, down to the refuge of the huts.

The huts themselves were in two areas surrounded by stone dykes. The top, or larger one, had a small higher area, ending in a steep bank down to a path round the top hut which led to the loo at the back. Below the second hut was a an open area where you could sit and there were daffodils in the spring. Entrance to the huts was by a fence with a wooden gate, There were always things – hats, coats etc – hanging on that fence. Below this part was a small area, probably there had been a house, with a rounded end bounded with a rough wall of stone. The whole area was bounded by dry stone dykes – essential to keep out the cows or sheep which munched away on the fields.

That Spring Holiday, Victoria Day, at the end of May of 1961 was the target for a rebuild of the huts – an additional area for a kitchen was to be added at the east end. Mary and I were entrusted with the Frost van to carry up the wood and equipment. To make it payable on the firm, Mary and I had to deliver chairs to a house in Alloa. As I was a teaching and had that Spring Friday afternoon off while the others – poor souls – had to work, Mary and I were able to leave at lunchtime. I think that Granny Frost looked after Gillian, and Anne stayed with young Robert. Being adventurous souls, Mary and I chose to drive the van – not the most modern – over the Loch Quaich road, arriving at Kepranich as the sun went down. It would be a long carry to bring the wood down the track, so we decided to drive down to the old Kepranich steading. That was fine, the road was a bit rutted and difficult but I was able to find a park further into the field, so we only had a short carry across the dyke to the huts. Unfortunately, the road was a bit steep and the van ancient, so when we came to try get the van back up the old road, it refused the task. Thus Frost's, a prestigious firm as it was, had its van stuck down near the loch and it led to the indignity of being towed up the hill by Mr Keddie with his tractor. Father Frost was not amused. Mr Keddie thought it howlingly funny and I had lost what few points I had gained in seven years of marriage.

That was a glorious warm week-end, and we laboured away. Well the older Frosts, being skilled joiners, did the specialist work while Mary and I did the labouring. I suffered the further indignity of offering to do some small job of nailing bits together, only to find that Robert had later taken it to bits and redone it properly. It all made a tremendous difference to the huts and it meant that we now had two habitable huts and a very useful little kitchen. The front hut had two set-up beds and a very good paraffin heater. It was the main area for sitting, with comfortable folding chairs, and a table and chairs at one end for eating.

The kitchen had a gas stove. We had to carry up and down the gas canister, and that was some carry, whether it was full or not. I later added an Ascot water heater with a foot pump – taken off a boat, which proved a godsend, for it meant that we had hot water on tap, so to speak. We also had a collapsible tent arrangement with a small pump shower for when we there for longer than a weekend. The "tweenie", or the little hut in the middle, housed everything, fishing rods, spades, life jackets etc.

The back hut had two single iron bedsteads with a double bunk at the far end. We could and did sleep six and it was where the kids slept. At the back was the Loo with a View. Enjoyed by the adults for peace and quiet, and hated by some of the children for being so primitive. The contents went to improve the Keddies' fields! Below the huts was a small henhouse that was the centre for all the kids games, and next door to that a stone circle for the barbecues, while just beyond hanging from the tree was a swing that was used for all kinds of activities. All the water had to be carried from the burn to the west, or in a drought, up from the loch.

The track down could be horrendous if wet and even in the dry was a devilish carry. The trunk with all the clothes was sometimes brought down by Mr Keddie but more usually on the male backs. The kids aged two to four, were carried down on the shoulders, though a Carrymore proved a godsend at a later date. The path required regular attention to drain it and make it passable. As they, the children, grew it became a challenge to get down first and to see paradise first. The Frost boys and Arthur girls soon developed a venomous game for the car journey from Kenmore involving sighting of the broom nets and sticks for fire prevention. There were actually six of these from Kenmore to Kepranich and each was furiously argued over as to who had seen it first. It often required me to drive very slowly as I came up to a possible sighting so that I could get my claim in first. It also meant driving with two to four kids hanging over my shoulder, shouting in my ears. The other challenge started by Father Frost, was to see whether we could free wheel over the bridge at Acharn from the top of the hill at the point from which you could first see Kenmore.

I think that the Keddies loved having us. It was company for them, and the children were devoted to Mrs Keddie and there was nothing better for them than to be taken to collect the eggs, and to feed the hens or to walk the dogs. Their kitchen was always redolent of hen food cooking on the stove, and the smell of the dogs. Stewart Keddie was small with a permanent flat cap. He had a very sharp and sardonic sense of humour, and once he started on tales about the local folk, he had some wonderful stories. The best being of a burial across the loch at which all the men were required to dig the grave. Unfortunately as it grew late, they had to stop, probably for a long top up. The result was that on their return next morning, the dogs had broken into the coffin and a collection of body parts was necessary before the committal. He liked his fags, and pan drops, the former of these were hidden by Mrs Keddie. She never admitted that she knew that he also kept another supply at the fank, the shed, along the road. He loved his peppermint drops, and drove his car or the old Fordson tractor almost as badly as her. Ethel was a lovely lady, all hustle and bustle, always in a hurry – to feed the hens, to find the eggs, to prepare the meals. Sometimes the meal did not look all that different to that for the hens. It was permanently on the hob in a big black pot. Alastair was the quiet, well behaved son who worked like a galley slave on the farm when he was at home.

We were always invited up for tea when we were in residence, this meant that the children were cleaned up and told to behave.

All our food and milk had to be collected. At first, the milk was from along the road but a vicious episode of food poisoning sent us into Kenmore, where we bought it from a grim old man, Mr Menzies. Paraffin could be purchased – it was the only thing she sold – at the shop in Acharn. Acharn was also the site of the smiddy, or black smith, which was much loved by the kids when horses were being shod. At one point the large house at the bridge was bought and developed by the Targe maker, who sadly moved away. He did the shield for Greenfaulds School.

So what did we do? There was always so much to do. Getting the place tidy each morning, collecting the milk, and checking the water. If there were young kids the nappies were washed in the Loch – freezing even in summer, but it did keep them beautifully clean.. Shopping, sometimes from the travelling butcher or the baker. The endless fascination of the Loch – throwing stones, falling in if it was Catriona, sitting enjoying the view; taking out the boat and later the canoe, and the late night fishing in the hope that we would have fresh trout with bacon for breakfast. Incidentally the kids had to clean their own fish if they caught one – not enjoyed by some! The future surgeon enjoyed that bit! If there had been rain we went up the burn to Ardtalnig – there was the old lady who always remarked on Gillian's red hair – "just like the good Queen, Mary, Queen of Scots." We often caught up to twenty little fish, if there had been a spate.

What else? There always seemed lots to do – climb Ben Lawers, visit the waterfall at Acharn, go for high tea to the Aileen Creggan and talk to Mrs McGlespie, as she was known to the children, and eat their lovely ham and pineapple with that magic sauce. As the clipping season arrived there was work to be done carrying the fleeces to the shed, and, even once they were old enough, for the two older girls to go "beating" and earn some money. That was the task of beating with sticks so that the grouse rose up to be shot.

There were always jobs to be done round the hut, painting and repairs, though they were remarkably warm and watertight. Peter Frost was able to get experience of the veterinary trade with Mr Masterton. When it was hot, and it could get very hot, we even swam. The loch depths dropped rapidly off the piers – one pier was below the huts, the other further east. It was said that the depth off our area was six hundred feet. Even at its hottest, the only warmth was in the top 6 inches and below that it was freezing. Gillian kept swearing that she would swim the whole width of the loch. She never did!

I, and my brother-in-law Ronnie, who was no spring chicken, once went sailing in Dilly and we capsized. I went in to support Ronnie and could not get him back on board so the situation was a bit grim. Mr Keddie, who liked to watch through his binoculars called out to Ethel – "They are in, I knew it......." He then rang the fire brigade in Perth, the nearest rescue service that he could think of. Mary, who had seen what had happened, jumped into the car and drove like a crazy round the loch. By this time Borg, the mad Dane who lived on the other side, had seen what had happened and rushed down to the shore, and launched his boat with the help of a schoolboy from Rannoch School. They pulled us both out of the water and we then were fed hot soup, and I was violently sick, and at that moment the fire brigade arrived swinging grappling irons!

All good things come to an end. The huts were well used by all the families and friends. Even the older Frosts used it, indeed Granny and Granpa decorated the front hut. We had two camps there, apart from another Scout one. I remember a young Chinese lad singing – the first time I had heard it – “Where have all the flowers gone” at a Sunday service. There were camps for Melville boys to get them fit and then a group from Lomond attempting to climb all the hills. I even had a week’s “deep think” to give me time to plan while St. Brides and Larchfield were amalgamating.

The day came in 1991 when we learned that the Board of Agriculture had been instructed to sell off as much land as they could, and we were warned that we might lose Kepranich. I formed a small consortium of ourselves, Peter Frost, Alastair Keddie, the Martins and two others who had small local interests. I took advice from Finlayson Hughes, and they thought that a figure of about £ 37, 000 would be a sensible offer, so we put it up to £42, 000. The lower area of the farm actually went for £70, 000, with a similar sum for the top ground to the infamous Norfolk builder. I realised afterwards that we ought to have used Alastair Keddie and invoked crofting inheritance. We didn’t…. so it was sold over us, and we were given pretty brusque notice to quit – and Elysium was gone, but not the memories.

The Old Henhouse – Bobbie

A Loon In The Northeast

We moved to Aberdeen in April 1962, or at least I did. Mary was pregnant and expecting number two in July, so we did not consider it sensible for both of us to make the move at that point – also we had nowhere to go. This meant that I moved into digs on the South side of Aberdeen, not far from the lovely Shearers, who were at that time the backbone of Aberdeen Samaritans.

I had begun, in 1961, to start looking for promotion. There were no prospects of this at Melville College. I had made a mark there with the Cairngorm Club, the Duke of Edinburgh Award Scheme, the Summer Lectures and was doing my coaching of both rugby and cricket, and playing both against the boys – in the tradition of young masters of the time. No way is that involvement possible now, with Health and Safety rules. I also did my stint with the CCF, going to camps etc. Graham Richardson, the Head, was keen that I should move on and was very supportive, he himself would move not long after as Rector of Dollar and remained a good friend. Melville was too small a school and I suspect that Graham knew that the wind of merging toward Stewarts was blowing. The school had no departmental heads as such. I would be sad to move on as I was very happy there with good friends, the busy bee in Bob Fleming, the PE man, and Ronnie Chisholm, the happy-go-lucky cricketer from Aberdeen. But it was time to move on, Melville was too enclosed and it was not long before it amalgamated with Stewarts. Added to all this, I was not getting the satisfaction and challenge, Here I was just a jack of all trades, teaching history, maths and geography, as my class was heard to sing, following a recent song –"Arthur in the morning, Arthur at lunchtime, Arthur in the evening."

One thing that you cannot compare to-day is salaries. We started at Larchfield on £300 pa, paid in 6 instalments. Mary only got £275 as a non-graduate. Never mind that she had taught for at least 4 years and I had not. But then she was a woman. Our salaries were not pensionable though they did pay for the flat in East Princes Street, and we got some food, if Mrs Hutch remembered. When I started at Melville I was in the pension scheme – 1/80 per year with a maximum of retirement at 65. The scheme for me was a reduction as we would not get a full OAP pension. Crazy! I was allowed two increments to the salary for two years in national service, one for Moray House and two for Larchfield, a grand total of seven. It was not until 1960 that my salary reached £1000.

Robert Gordons had advertised for a Senior History Master at half responsibility allowance of about £250 but it had an excellent reputation so I applied though with very little hope. I got an interview and arrived in sunshine and had what appeared a good interview. I really was amazed to be offered the job, but I liked the school, it was very old and traditional, and the new Head – Jack Marshall – who had recently arrived from North Berwick High School. There was for me also, a joyous reunion at lunch afterwards with Jimmy Shearer and Charles Strachan from the Samaritans whom I had met and got on with at various regional meetings. They seemed delighted that I was coming to Aberdeen and, of course I would come into the setup in the branch. But first, a house, and thinking properly of the move – 150 miles north and no bridge. Gillian was only three and Seonaid now more than a thought but it would mean leaving home, both sets of parents and all the relatives and Mary's whole set up. As usual she was very supportive and looking forward, though with some doubts, to the move.

Our little house in Swanston went just like that, at a price of £ 3,300, so we had a little profit from £1,700 though not a lot. Out of the blue came a phone call from Jack Marshall to say that there was a house, just opposite them at 95 Hamilton Place coming up for sale.

It would need work but if I contacted his solicitor, George Lawrence, also a Governor of RGC, he was sure that we would get it. I went round to see this big semi-detached house and was taken with it. We offered £3,000 and George rang to say that, if we upped our offer, by a couple of hundred he was sure that we would get it. We did, and we got it. Mary was over the moon, but had to rely still, only on my description and some photos. Next we had to get estimates. Thanks to Jimmy, we got all these from local tradesmen, painting and decorating, a coke boiler and central heating. Mind the boiler was the devil to clear of the cinders and we had to wait for the Welsh coke to arrive at Newburgh! Wow! We'd never known anything like that, for the first time in our lives, we would be warm. Though I did invest in thick woollen combinations – very acceptable until we moved to the climatic sophistication of Bridge of Allan. Frosts, the firm, came up trumps with the furnishings and somehow we paid for everything, though with a little help from our friends! Incidentally, I found the Aberdeen firms were wonderful – "Och, ye dinnae need to spend that much, why not do it this way."

The house was wonderful. It lurched to the West as there had been some sand on which it was built, so the side door leaned drunkenly and the main stairs went at an angle. There was a gorgeous fireplace with Edwardian couples prancing round the side and the main bedroom was a delight. There was a lounge on the ground floor with a bow window to the front, a huge dining room at the back with room, for the girls, a cycle track round the dining table and a door into the small back garden which had a gate into the Aberdeen back alley. We parked the car in the lane to the west in a small garage which we rented. There were very few cars, we had a small Standard 10 estate. There was a kitchen with cooker and fridge and a table and chairs, and the new dishwasher. Then there was a back passage with the door to the outside, a back kitchen with the washing machine and a wooden box that housed the poor dog – Sable. Then at the back of this a coal cellar and the coke stove for the central heating and the hot water. It was great, except that it had to be cleaned of the clinkers every three days, and we had to wait for the Welsh coke to come to the harbour in the North-East. Outside there was a shed and a loo with a sky- light. Thank goodness for that, as Gillian got stuck in it, and I had to climb down from that window and release the door catch. There was a small sloping garden, and that was fine to sit in and with a few flower beds. There was a small front garden with a path and some sad roses.

On the first floor was our lovely bedroom looking to the street, which was very quiet, a small bedroom beside looking in the same direction, then a large spare room looking to the back with a loo and a bathroom opposite. The last room was enough for the two girls at the back. Finally, upstairs, a winding one, there were two attic rooms, a small study looking over the back to Queens Cross and where I escaped every night to do preparation and correction. No interruptions! Next door was a large floored room which we converted eventually into a very good playroom for the kids and their friends. A very comfortable and accommodating house. Dear 95.It was not a beautiful house at the rear, but we thought so!

Looking back, this was another world, oil had not yet been found in the North Sea, and Aberdeen prided itself on being different. It boasted of being an island and that "twelve mile around."

I enjoyed that first summer term at RGC, it was hard work, these were tough young men, and they were not impressed until I had proved myself. It was a fascinating old school. At assembly in the morning Jack Marshall would say "Good morning boys." And they would all touch their forelocks – surely we were not in mediaeval times? My predecessor had been the famous Johnny Mac who taught by rote but had a fearsome reputation as an eccentric bachelor and character, so it was a hard road to follow, how to change history into something real. The text books were out of this world, well not the twentieth century. However, we did it. By the time that I left the classroom was moved upstairs, and was a haven of light, with original texts and bright material scattered everywhere.

At a different level, I think that I played a prominent part in the staff cricket match, so that was a start. There were now other young men on the staff – Jim Rennie and John Jermieson, and Sandy Monro and this seemed to form a semi-rebellious group, but very much semi, but at least it was young and shared the same sense of humour. It was a table away, in the staff room, from the seniors and the more aged, at coffee time. It was still a school where staff remained, often throughout their teaching career, for that reason they were characters in a way that modern schools do not see.

George Donald, later of "Scotland the What Fame" joined the group occasionally, that is if we were not too noisy. There were some formidable senior staff in the school – Dr Forrest, very learned, sat in his seat at the foot of the senior table and read the Guardian. He was a considerable ally at first, and his son did well at history. We dined at their house and they at ours. But, sadly, something went wrong, I never understood what upset him. I had made some comment about Rhodesia which, at that point in time, had just declared UDI. I made some comment as the he got out of my car to go home at lunchtime. I think that I must have expressed some sympathy with Ian Smith and that was that. Doctor Forrest never forgot or forgave.

There were many interesting others, the Deputy Head. Mr. Hugelshofer who had a wonderfully dry sense of humour, he had a little moustache and a funny guttural to his speech. Then there was Davie Donald, renowned as the biggest belt in the north-east and the maths king. He also played cricket as had his dad before him. That is until the latter retired and became an umpire. The pair were weel-kent in the North-East – "How's that, Dad?" – "Out, son." There was Heckie Donaldson, of Head of Chemistry – a real charmer; and Hooter Gibson of classics – there was a legend – "Mr Gibson will you take an extra class this afternoon?" – I'm so sorry. Headmaster, this is my afternoon for gardening." One of my closest member of staff was Ralph Broadley, of geography with whom I forged a bond. Except that was in March when the 2nd year boys had to choose between geography and history for their certificate year. Usually we ended evens. Ralph was very good to us, and he and his wife had a lovely house out at Bieldside and we saw a lot of them. There was Douglas Tees from music who was a breath of light in the quiet of the school, and a very good musician. It was a very interesting staff room.

The Old Building of Robert Gordons College

The school under Jack Marshall was changing. A new science block appeared outside my room, with all the new ideas, except computers, not even thought of at that time. I actually had a tape recorder, which I occasionally took into school and I played LPs – the equivalent of today's DVD's, among them were the excellent BBC's 1914, 1940 and 1945. The boys were very able and very ambitious, and for the school the Bursary Competition for entry to the University, was the academic highlight of the year. This was a time far more important than the results of Highers, and RGC always tried to outdo the Grammar School.

I, personally, had a very good rapport with the Grammar, I made close friends with Attie McCombie, their Head of History and Douglas Maclean of Spanish with two boys and a wonderfully friendly wife. We usually came to share the festival of the 5th November and enjoyed fireworks in their garden. That is until his poor wife got up one morning and fell dead with a stroke. A tragedy.

We soon developed a small coterie of friends – Mary joined a Keep Fit group with George Lawrence's wife, and there were the Patons who had come from Edinburgh – he was an agricultural biologist with some way-out ideas – such as lettuces in the Sahara. Now that was an interesting thought. Next was the were the university group – the History man, John Hargreaves and Andrew Rutherford of English who went on to Goldsmiths in London. They were a challenging and lively group – we were never short of different interests or friends. Aberdeen was good at sharing school and university.

Our neighbours were different too. The Cockburns, at 97, never said a word to us at first except to incline their heads in greeting, that is until their grand-daughter was stuck in the loo, and as we had the painters in, they rushed round to us to beg for a ladder. From then on we were lifelong friends and they proved to be such worthwhile people. George was Head of Northfield School, and a very sharp old cookie with a caustic sense of humour. I only discovered later that he himself had been a pupil at Gordons and had actually been an Otaki Scholar. That scholarship was an award made annually to the top pupils at the school. Their son, Gordon, was a GP and their daughter-in-law a nurse. Their children got on well with ours.

On the other side of our house were a grim pair who never acknowledged us, even with a wave. Thankfully they sold up at the end of that year. Mary met her shopping a month later, and was to be greeted with a hug and an exclamation of how much she missed their wonderfully friendly neighbours! We were lucky, as their house was bought by the Flanns. She was a real buddy to us and her husband ran a little corner shop round the corner. They were a delightful pair whose children matched ours and with whom we ran a baby-sitting system by means of a microphone slung out of the windows! Seonaid ran home once to Mary to ask soulfully "I's not a bloody baby, Mummy, am I?"A phrase picked up from the painters next door.

My first classroom was next to the staffroom, very nice for coffee but noisy. When the building for the new science block started I was moved upstairs to a block of two. My first assistant was Clark Geddes, himself a loon from Angus, with an accent you could cut with a knife. He had a 1stclass degree from Aberdeen and was delightful, but not too quick. He did everything that he was asked of him, but I was never sure that he really understood what was going on. I liked Clark and he did well, but he was not in the first flush of youth and was ambitious to move upwards. After two years at Gordons, he was appointed Director of Extra-Curricular Studies at St Andrews. I was delighted for him and he went away rejoicing. There was a gap on his departure, which was eventually filled by Lorna Fraser. Lorna's husband had been Director of Transport in Aberdeen but had died a couple of years before we arrived. The family had house on Carden Place and I had often passed them having breakfast as Gillian and I walked down the street, – she to go to St. Margaret's School. Lorna was a great addition to the department in every way, but very much out of the top drawer of Aberdeen society – Chair of St. Margaret's Board of Governors, and she was an important part of the National Trust etc. She was very nervous about teaching, as she had never done any. But, none the less she did a great job, though without any teaching or academic background apart from a degree. The family became close friends, Caroline, the youngest, took over walking Gillian and Seonaid to school and the other sisters, one of whom married a Glasgow solicitor and lived near Kippen and got our swinging cot!. Oddly Caroline married an RAF officer who finished away at very senior level and they had sent their eldest son to Loretto. Mary and I went to the 80th anniversary of the 1918 armistice in Ypres, and her son was then the Pipe Major of the Loretto band. She, Caroline, stood next to Mary as they processed down the main street and she asked Mary what was her connection to the event! Surprise for both of us to find our guardian angel of 20 years before, standing next to us in a Flanders Field! Real Aberdeen!

Then there was John Petrie who arrived, a good solid, softly spoken Scot, very quiet and very competent. So quiet, yet he got the boys to do what he wanted and there was no trouble with discipline. Sadly, he became very deaf, and when he moved to Strathclyde University he finally had to give up teaching.

We were doing well in History in the school so Jack Marshall reluctantly agreed to another teacher, whom we would share with English. As a reward we got a stunner – Rose Souter. What a lovely girl. She wowed the boys but horrified the strictly male senior staff room. There was even a moment of horror when she was tempted to enter that staff room in to discuss some history teaching matters with me. It did not worry me! She was also a first rate cook – nothing to do with history, but she persuaded Mary to buy a deep freeze and from that we have never looked back. Perhaps she thought that it would keep me cool.

Among the group were the Maclachlan family, she did the Keep Fit class, and he taught. We had also had cousins in Belvedere Street. He was a psychiatrist and she was very sweet, but sadly they fell apart and the family went to New Zealand. Hamilton Place was full of intellectuals –as already described. The godsend in that purchase of the house had been the Lawrences.

Aberdeen was full of people to whom we felt very close. A fact that we regretted when we had to make the move, and we were sad to leave. This was of course long before oil was even thought of, much less found. Aberdeen was still very much as it always had been – "the toun and twal mile around." Stonehaven was a foreign land and as for Edinburgh, that was where all the trouble in the world came from. Oddly there was a very strong connection with Glasgow, particularly with graduates, found in a strong graduate association. The city was very proud of its academic standing and the wide flung numbers of Aberdeen loons who held big posts in the great world. At that point there was the Grammar and the High School for girls run as more or less as independent bodies. On the independent side were Robert Gordons, grant-aided, and St. Margarets and Albyn School for girls. It was not long before the left wing won over the Council and the Grammar became Rubislaw Academy and the High to be Harlaw Academy. (That was unfortunate as Harlaw was too easily adapted in rude terms). RGC offered bursaries, to reduce fees, for boys who were successful in the "qually" (12+ test (and the best teachers at Mile End were known as the Qualie Queens).

Rugby was important and was coached by John Dow, while I was handed the hockey at Seafield on a Wednesday afternoon. I thoroughly enjoyed that opportunity and it was soon suggested that I join the Gordonians hockey team. But for me, with teaching there I felt that would be sensible to join the only open club – Ruthrieston – who played at the beach. Anyway Seafield – the famed Gordons pitches – were always a sea of mud and the beach fields were fantastic. We even used to play on a moveable pitch on the beach in winter because of the frost. This was headlined with piccies in the press as the only hockey played in the UK at that time of the year. This also meant I came under the influence of the great Charlie Bisset, a Gordonian, but also the life and soul of Aberdeen hockey – Mr Hockey himself. We had a lot of fun and some success. The team were a great bunch who played to enjoy themselves and the beach pitches were excellent, though the dugout in the side of the dunes was not the best of changing areas. Matches with Gordonians were always good humoured, with a great many cracks about the incompetent coach who was supposed to work with the school team.

What were Gordon's boys like? They were very well mannered and came from a wide cross section of society. It is an element that I recall vividly for there was no way to tell from what group a boy came. Their accents were difficult, for they were all bi-lingual – there was the Doric, the local dialect, in the playground and standard English in class. They could be devils and boisterous but never evil. Those backgrounds covered every class, from Footdee or Fittee to Cults or Milltimber. Here were the grocer's son, the butcher's, the lawyer's, there was no obvious differences. In those days a few still wore kilts, while the main elevens refreshments were pies with a potato topping. A large number of the boys were bursars on the well-funded RGC Trust, possibly as many as one in eight, which is a large percentage. But all wanted to do well and achieve something. There was no doubt why the North-

Easter does well in life. While it was difficult to sway them from geography to history, I did manage to change the ethos of history and we seemed to have lot of interest, but reached a high standard and covered a lot of ground. History then was very much the story of the huge area of British/English history, with the emphasis in Years 1 & 2 on Scottish and then British. The boys then had a choice of areas looking towards their Higher exams, and surprisingly it was the Tudors and Stewarts that they picked, with the 19th century for the later part of the course. We also did include a coverage of local history with a very good booklet by another local teacher, Jim Buchan, who taught in Cults.

History was still very much tied in to dates and events. I know that dates are important, as they give a foundation to the time span, but they do need to be filled in and developed and given colour. I was very happy in this new world and felt completely at home. The school had a major Inspection and I was fortunate to achieve a high rating with the new history. I was also lucky as there was so much new and interesting material coming onto the market. It did mean a great deal of work, with all the usual preparation and correction, with an essay every fortnight for every boy in the Highers set. Notes had to be to be written and prepared and brought up to date. Interestingly Mary and I had a night out in Edinburgh at a later date, as we had made a special booking at the old NB, now the Balmoral Hotel, with dinner and tickets for the "Phantom of the Opera" included. We were sat in the main area of the hotel, having tea, and Mary remarked that there was a man sitting nearby with his family who obviously knew me. "Never seen him in my life", I replied, and went off to the loo. I returned to find him sitting beside Mary and claiming that I had taught him at Gordons! I suddenly recognised him, though he had been much younger and with a great deal more hair. He even sang my praises, he thought that my method of note taking was great and he even used it himself and was training his sons to do follow my example. "What are you doing now?" I asked. "Well, I am the Auditor General for Scotland!" Collapse of one not so stout party.

One of those areas Jack Marshall wanted me to deal with was the CEWC. That stood for the Council in Education for World Citizenship and the group met after 4 pm once a week. I cannot say that I found it enthralling, but it was interesting, and led to an interesting experiment.

That Council also led to two other schemes that involved me. The first was a summer term series of talks and discussions for 6th year, after the Highers were finished. These were along the lines of what I had started at Melville, with prominent locals coming in to talk on Politics, Education, Religion, Sex etc. These proved a great success, though I sometimes found it difficult to get the boys to open up and join in the discussion. There was a very Aberdonian reluctance to talk in public. I recall two memorable afternoons, one was on religion with Father Anthony Ross, a Dominican priest, who had been involved with me in the Samaritans. He came from Dingwall and from a Free Church family. On his conversion to Roman Catholicism his family at once refused ever to talk to him again. He was a remarkable and great man, and on that occasion he laid it on the line to the boys, most of whom probably had never seen or heard a Catholic. The other topic was sex, where I managed to persuade a local gynaecological consultant, Dr Gordon, to do the session. What made it worse for the boys, who had never "heard" of sex was that her son was in 6th year at the time. She was great success, and was successful in getting a fierce discussion going – to my astonishment.

The other idea that I tried out was the War Game. I offered the boys that I would run the Game for the last two days of the summer term. I would allocate roles to about 60 boys – prime minister, president, members of the government etc, and some other posts in a number of countries. At that time the war in Vietnam was at its height. We arranged some preliminary briefings, saw the film on the Atomic Bomb which shook the boys rigid, with its powerful portrayal of its effects. The big day dawned, to my considerable anxiety. I had organised a series of crises, and for these I had taped some BBC news items. I had prepared numerous sheets to cover all the events;

there was a 24 hour clock for each day, and off we went. The boys were totally immersed from the start. The Vietcong group even came in wearing black pyjamas with packets of Ambrosia Creamed Rice for lunch. The Chinese had researched the whole area of the grades of petrol, to the extent of identifying the best for the military. I could not have believed that it would go so well. A number of staff were so intrigued that they came over to the Macrobert Hall to watch. Mind, it saved them those awful last boring lessons in summer! Davie Donald came in deepest gloom but even admitted finally that it went well though it was still a waste of good maths time!

With the pressure we could not have kept going for more than two days, and even then many of the events took over and seemed to develop a life of their own. At the end the boys were shattered. Most admitted that they went home, but could not stay awake, they were so tired. All of them agreed that life for a politician was an incredible challenge, the media and the 24 hour clock had so changed the world and the individual pressures that they brought. Even the real BBC arrived to interview me and to make a piece for the Scottish news. Wow! Fame at last!

What of the girls. Gillian was 3 when we moved and she settled in well, and loved Aberdeen, indeed she returned there to do 5 years of a medical course. She went to St. Margaret's nursery and then into the Junior School where she was very happy. She had many friends. The girls were both very happy, there and were none too pleased to leave and to go to the Beacon school in Bridge of Allan.

It was 1968 and sadly, the time came to look for another job and Jack Marshall, as ever was supportive and anxious on my behalf. So I became the Depute Head of the High School of Stirling as Jack suggested that competition for the full Headship was tough and I would be better to try for the lower rungs first.

Aberdeen was/is unique, with a very different culture and sense of belonging. I know that oil has changed it, but for me I can only hope that it does not lose that wonderful sense of locality and determination.

TO TEACH AND SO TO EARN

"If you are going to teach, for goodness sake, try to get them to read, write and add up." So was I encouraged by my father-in-law, a successful business man in Edinburgh, on hearing of my intentions.

Having decided to go into teaching, as second best from that glamorous objective of wearing the Governor's Plumed Helmet, this meant that I had to do a very careful assessment of what I could do to earn some money, and how best to make use of what I had prepared myself. Our first knowledge of teaching is very much confined to our experience of those who had taught us. Some were good, some were excellent, and some were poor. I was lucky in one way at Loretto, with Peter Wood, who taught English and had come in after the war and so inspired me, to go up to University to read English. But then I was to suffer intense disappointment, under a sadly unappealing Professor in that subject at Edinburgh. That experience led to a switch to history and so to satisfy my desire to learn more of the past, and particularly of Africa. At that point there was no intention of going on to teach.

Larchfield, in Helensburgh, where I was offered a job when I left the army, was a very typical preparatory school for boys from age seven up to fourteen, This was my first teaching experience and, in this case, to teach mathematics. For one who had barely gone beyond arithmetic and with little interest in the world of numbers, it was an interesting experience. I know I took a very basic approach, and perhaps, because I myself had had difficulty, that approach was sympathetic. I quickly learnt, as I did in all schools, that discipline, and the control of the class was the first essential. I was to take a hard line and expected high standards in every aspect – dress, work, behaviour.

When I went to Melville College in Edinburgh, it was to be as an old-time teacher, mathematics, history and geography, and involvement in school sports and activities, and that included playing the games with the boys – that could be painful! Again I learnt that teaching alone was not always as satisfying as I hoped. I was lucky in that Robert and Keith Frost who were very involved in the Rover Scouts of St. Johns. They had started a number of treks in the Highlands and so had attracted the interest of Sir John Hunt, he of Everest fame. I was invited to dinner with him, and he suggested that I should look into the newly formed Duke of Edinburgh Award scheme. As I had already set up the Cairngorm Club, for boys who wanted to climb and walk. This idea met with instant success. It was an important lesson that teaching is as much about being in touch with young people through their everyday activities and interests.

On the academic side of teaching, history as a subject was going through a revolution. My predecessor at Gordons was a much loved teacher but, to him, it seemed to be all about dates and events. For me history is about people, about how events affect them, and so how they influence those events. While the examination system inevitably forced certain limitations – dates, accuracy in detailing the story, it also allows the exploration of deeper aspects of the lives of people, and of the various movements of that period.

To me history is never merely the account of the past. I think it was summed up recently at a lecture by a young professor that, to her, "history is about the three S's – smells, sounds, and sweat." Sadly, we may rarely learn from it, but that cannot prevent us wanting to change the world to a better place. At Melville and again at Gordons I was so lucky in having Heads who were willing to let me experiment and to be creative. One area that always worried me was the need to give boys, particularly the older one, an insight into what was going on in the world outside. The summer term could be difficult, Higher examinations were over by April or early May and there often followed a time of boredom and frustration for the senior pupils who were often leaving at the end of the year. I was allowed in both schools to organise a series of lectures on the world outside. I was also lucky to be able to attract outside speakers of quality. I was anxious that these meetings should be more than mere lectures, but to give the opportunity for some discussion. After all these were seventeen and eighteen year olds going out into the real world.

The topics I chose at both schools were – Politics with either an MP or a councillor; the Church in the widest sense, and in the latter I was fortunate to have in Aberdeen, Father Anthony Ross. Then there was the Press, with a local editor; Crime and Punishment with a Professor of Criminology; The Trade Unions; and Colour. And, of course the "War Game".

I think that my experience of teaching, while I doubt if it ever made any difference to that great hope of Mr Frost and of most business leaders, it led me to an approach that saw education as the centre of whole life growth. It was t not just be the central area of your own subject but should incorporate life in all its aspects.

GREENFAULDS HIGH SCHOOL – 1971-77

Oh happy days! It is easy to look back on those first few years at Greenfaulds as idyllic, and in many ways they were. Everyone was excited by that new concept of comprehensive education, and the raising of the leaving age for youngsters to sixteen was near. This was to be one of the new mega schools in the New Town of Cumbernauld. We would have a roll of 1700, and no expense had been spared. We were to be new school in a new town in a new era – change was in the air.

My first sight of the school was in late December 1970, having just been appointed and was desperate to see it. At that time entry to the area was from the south and there was not a building in sight. Condorrat was just a village, and access to Cumbernauld was off the main Airdrie road. At that point the new building looked like and aircraft carrier, at one end was the huge smoke stack, and the rest of it was just a building site, a tip full of wires, bricks and general mess. To my untrained eye I could not believe that it would be ready in eight months, but Mr Lochrie, the architect and soon to be remembered by the smoke stack at the end as Lochrie's Lum, assured me that it would be alright in the end.

I started in April 1971 with that grandiose, old Scots term of Rector, with one room at the northern end of the school, my office plus toilet and a janitor, the extrovert Pete Murray, who made me numerous cups of tea or coffee and regaled me with endless stories of his time as a stoker in the Royal Navy. This first appointment was followed by that of school secretary, Nancy Baker, who proved a godsend.

Most of the summer was committed to the appointment of staff, trying to answer all sorts of technical problems to do with the building, the equipment, and the layout of the rooms, all which would have an impact on the way in which we would develop. It all seemed to involve huge blocks of concrete, thinking of the shape of the timetable and having meetings with A.B. Cameron, the Director of Education in Dumbarton. We were, of course, still a part of West Dunbartonshire. They were on the whole, very helpful, and the appointments proved to be different and far-sighted. I did a lot of reading and research. I had completed a course in the new comprehensive scheme, which had been introduced in Sweden while I was at Robert Gordons. I had a good look at a number of old style and new schools, but in particular to Summerhill in Aberdeen with its innovatory Head. I actually used his assembly technique for future assemblies – the presentation of a simple proposition as the basis of any talk.

We held our first meeting with potential parents in Cumbernauld High, who were very helpful. The Heads of department were a good bunch, young, enthusiastic – it was a great group, and very contrasting. At the top was David Smart from Stirling, a mathematician who had just completed a Course Work syllabus on the new Mathematics. (Naturally, of course we used that, equally naturally without any financial connection) He was my Depute Rector. Then came Hugh Mathie, a good, solid and sensible choice. He was a quiet classicist and very much into the Baptist Church. I could not have had a better group with which to start.

It also meant that we started by setting up the first Management Group. This met every Monday after school to agree on where we were going. This group then included Annette Gibbs, a powerful character, who had been appointed the business manager. The group was to expand over the years as the Deputies were appointed. I think that we also added one Head of Department and a Guidance Teacher. I soon found that it proved its worth and I did the same when I went to Lomond.

The new staff came from a wide range of experience – Paddy Orr to English straight from Loretto School, who was later to go on to the inspectorate; Bill Reid to History after an interesting period of taxi driving; Bob Kay and Bob Graham to

Geography and Maths; Bill Warnock, Campbell Hannah, and Jo Sands to Technical, Physics and Chemistry; and perhaps the most original in her own quiet and determined way – Marion Mitchell to Head of Art; while Donald Macfarlane was head of PE, it was Bill Griffin with his enthusiasm for gymnastics that later had a huge impact; and finally Bob Morson – the drama producer supreme. I could not have asked for any better support.

Crisis hit the day even before we opened with a strike by the council workers, and I was faced the possibility that there would be no opening as all the desks and chairs still lay in the car park. My whole family –wife and all three daughters, aged from twelve to three – rallied together with the janitors and their families and we laid out the class rooms. An almost unbelievable scenario in a state school! We had then taken another different step with all the staff invited for a lunch two days before the start, with a little wine to oil the process. This worked well, and we repeated it until after 1974 when the unions decided that this could not be part of the two hundred paid official days! It was not just lunch though because most teachers always stayed on to prepare for the first day. A sad reflection that on the unions that can work diametrically against real education.

The same sad action happened again in the 1974 upheaval when the unions complained of over work and advised all staff not to be involved on any out of school activities. This action was to kill school Games, but oddly neither Drama or Music. It has meant that the independent sector which offered what most teachers would agree as an all-round school, it was the death of extra-curricular work in the state. For this reason many parents are prepared to pay big fees to get that full educational life.

School opened on time with the first assembly in one of the dining halls as the wonderful new theatre was not yet completed. There were four hundred in first and second Years. This roll was to rise to 1700 by 1976. That first year was a great encouragement to us all, staff and pupils genuinely worked together to create a good school with a real sense of involvement. We had sales for charity, we helped in setting up the wolf reserve up the hill, we planted thousands of trees to cover bare patches at Palace Riggs. We tried all the new ideas with mixed ability classes, though that changed as the difficulties emerged, but results were good and generally behaviour and discipline was good. I recall few removals from school, and all temporary. We had good support from parents. I remember pupils appearing in the early days with buckets and mops to remove graffiti.

The school was popular for meetings of the local Development Council, and we held the County Sports in the school sports field. We were blessed with the talented McCrackens, husband and wife, who put on their first Christmas Jazz in the new theatre, and Bill Griffen set off on a series of successful triumphs in the National Gymnastics. I still recall the horror on the face of the Director of Education who saw only the awful prospect of legal claims for injury as the children swung and jumped seemingly impossible tumbles and turns.

Bill Reid took the new school minibus, which he then almost lost, together with the pupils on a first trip to Hungary. While Andrew Reid took another group to the glory of Rome, only to be horrified by the sly nips and smirks of the residents at the sight of pretty girls. Bob Morson began a series of successful plays, first with the "Doctors", and later in the culmination of "Fiddler on the Roof".

I look back on six great years of successful work in a New Town with a new school. Of course it changed with its growth to 1700 pupils, with all the attendant problems of size, but it did retain its description as the friendly school. What it did lose was a levelling down of the staff as the Rector lost much of his control over the appointment of senior staff and the continuing interference of the unions in attempting to restrict involvement in the wider life of a school. The London Olympics was to raise that very question of the apparent differing levels of input into sport between the state sector of education and the independent schools. Having taught in both the difference is clear, changes in attitude, union pressure, particularly in 1974, have encouraged the modern teacher not to be involved in extra-curricular activities. This highlights the attitude of staff in the old senior secondary schools of pre-comprehensive days, who fully involved themselves in sport and school affairs.

This new attitude contrasts with that in the independent school where it is implicit in the appointment of staff which requires a commitment to the whole life of that school. The ethos of the independent school is to offer youngsters the chance to take part in life as a complete whole experience. This has an impact in the decision making process of parents who must find that extra money to pay the fees. It should also be remembered that it is those parents who save the state a very large considerable sum of money, but for their financial input the local authority would be required to find considerable money to cover the cost of those extra numbers to be taught in local schools.

After more than forty years, I understand that that new school that was Greenfaulds is to be replaced with a new building in the latest building plans. How different will those first years be from mine in 1971?

THE CREATION OF LOMOND SCHOOL

With the passage of time the formation of a new school, or the merging of two older ones, provides an interesting example of the way in which such a task was completed. Over the last fifty years, a number of all boys schools have become co-educational. To my knowledge, no girls school has done the opposite. The first group of schools, which were basically male, had to face up to financial problems, as well as a change in culture, which saw the need for the integration of the sexes. In the case of Lomond there were undoubtedly financial problems, on both sides, but this was the integration of a small junior boys school into an all-through girls school. Both St. Brides school for girls and Larchfield for boys date back to the middle of the nineteenth century. St. Brides opened in 1895, while Larchfield went back to 1860's.

This record cannot be entirely accurate as I kept no notes at the time. I have tried to keep it as honest as I can, and therefore my comments on individuals are as I saw them. I am the only one who saw the whole story, both from the educational side and the management one.

The Old St. Brides School

It is a story probably unique in Scotland – for this was the amalgamation of two very different animals, a small boys preparatory school geared to the needs of the older style public schools – Loretto, Glenalmond, Fettes and Merchiston. On the other hand St. Brides was an all-through girls school from five to eighteen, with a much more Scottish curriculum. It is important also to a record this successful process at a time when there was considerable political antagonism in Scotland to any kind of private school, and during a time of considerable economic depression in the West of Scotland. This is essentially the story of the hard work and dedication of many good people.

At Cumbernauld I found myself despairing of the state system for schools as being very bureaucratic and rigid. I could change little and the process of appointing the most senior staff was often blocked. I had no say in any such appointment, beyond that of choosing who would go for the final selection at Council level. Sadly this was the time of the great hopes for the comprehensive ideal. Life seemed to have become a constant battle of running just to stand still or even going backwards, and I began to look around.

The tale of the Lomond plan started in the early spring of 1976. The various newspapers carried adverts for a Principal for the new school, which would combine Larchfield and St Brides. It requested details of my CV, with an essay on how I believed that the school could be put together! This took a lot of thought and advice – most people whom I contacted considered that I was mad, that I was jumping into the fire, and that there was little realistic future for private schools. Graeme Richardson, at Dollar, in particular warned me against it – there would be no hope of money, no future. There were dark political clouds in the 1970's. This would be a small school in a small community. So I wrote my essay, though I really cannot remember what I wrote. I think that I stressed that I wanted a kindly school, a happy one where children would learn within clearly defined structures and boundaries, a disciplined structure, and where there would be great stress laid on children being encouraged to develop and to grow as individuals. I also mentioned that I had already started one new school, that I had been instrumental in starting Samaritans and that I was coming to the end of four years as national Chairman. I would be happy to have a go!

The next step was a letter inviting Mary and me to visit St Brides and go over the school. Now, that was a day to forget as it was a typical Helensburgh downpour, Miss Orr, the temporary Head, rather pessimistically took me over the grounds and nothing more depressing could have happened. By this time I had discovered that Miss Campbell, the Head of St. Brides, was going to Aberdeen to Albyn School and John Widdowson, Head at Larchfield was to be the new Head at Keil. Looking back I still must have been mad!

There followed an invitation to attend a two day interview including a night to be spent with a local governor's family in early July. At the family conference Mary was, as usual, totally behind whatever I wanted, Gillian was in her 6th year at Dollar, and having failed to get that vital B in Physics decided to confront the Dean at Aberdeen. However she had worked her charm on him, to be told that, if she upgraded it to an A she would get in to medicine. She wanted to stay for the spring term in Bridge of Allan with that term at Dollar. She did get her A, and later came as Under Matron at Lansdowne, the school boarding house for the summer term. Seonaid was totally in favour of moving. She was going through hell at Wallace High and offered to go to St. Bride's for the winter term as a boarder – a spy? Actually she was great and so loyal she never gave me any secret information on either staff or pupils. Unfortunately for my invitation, I had undertaken to do a visit for the Samaritans in Nottingham on the first day of the interview – this had been long arranged with an old friend and I felt that I could not renege. I rang Adam Bergius, the Chair of the new Lomond Board, to apologise and to be told that it was no problem and could I come to the second day. Oddly, the same happened when I had previously applied for Dollar, to be told that no way could they allow me that time! I recall that the Rev James Brodie, a Governor at Dollar had been appalled, and told me later that he had accused the others of a failure of honour! Why does that name of the Rev James Brodie keep appearing?

I arrived at St. Brides on that second day. Mary was due to be present for lunch and the girls were delivered to the Bear Park with brother Jo. The first interview, and I now discovered that there were six candidates, and that they had all been to stay with Governors the previous night. I think by this time that at least two had been dispatched as having failed. The first interview was very long and very detailed. Lunch followed at the Royal Northern Club. Was I holding my fork and knife correctly? Mary was a wow.

Another wife who had been there later remarked to me that she knew her man had lost as soon as she saw Mary. A very perceptive woman. There was a further cull of two, done while Mary and I stood nearby in the hall. Adam Bergius was brutal, "Thank you very much, I don't think that we should detain you!" Then there was another long interview, two more applicants went, to be followed by a last one with only two of us left. The whole process did not finish until 6pm. Mary had to go to collect the children but Al Macbeth would take me back to Bridge of Allan.

The interviewing panel were the new Governors of Lomond plus Al Macbeth.

Adam Bergius was the chair. He was a small neat man, an ex-submariner, superficially a typical navy man and an aristocrat, but sharp as nails and tough as befitted the Chair of Teachers, distillers, who stood no nonsense and never wasted a minute. He was a straight man who admitted that he knew little of schools but understood people. Then there was Rab Pender, ex-Larchfield, – a lawyer and a toughie. He always seemed to want to turn everything into an inquisition on every occasion in a nasty way. He was very much into the art world. Later I came to find him a very difficult man who did not really understand people but thought that he did. In contrast there was Teddy Boyd, also ex-Larchfield, an accountant and a charmer. I got on well with Teddy even though to him everything came down to hard cash. What was the point of a library, very costly? But he was a great support. Next, Bill Ingleby, also an accountant and much the best of the lot. He was perceptive, extremely bright, absolutely straight, and spoke his mind but nicely. I always remember him saying when some parents objected to long holidays –"of course, nothing will satisfy those and they haven't a clue about the strain of schools." The real tragedy for Lomond was that Bill contracted liver cancer very soon after, and died. He was destined to take over from Adam as Chair but too late. The last member was Miss Rachel Drever-Smith who had been Head of St. Brides. She was extremely sharp, very much the old style Headmistress, but now without that responsibility had turned into a moderniser. She would have been unrecognisable to any of her pupils who, I later learned, either loathed or tolerated her! The last was a lawyer Duncan McKichan. A small very quiet man with a very quiet approach and only very carefully thought-out answers. His wife was a formidable lady whose pigtails I had pulled as a small boy when she was at school with my sister. Finally, my driver after the interview, Al Macbeth. He was the educational advisor. He had been a Head in the Solomon Island for 2 years and was a lecturer in Education at Glasgow University. Very bright and a good interviewer, he knew his stuff. His trouble in retrospect was that I think he would have liked to have been the Principal or certainly the power behind the Board. (he actually asked to be a governor later on). There were two others who came on to the Board but were not at the interview – John Harper a local GP. John was a charmer and always admitted, with a big smile, that he hadn't a clue about schools or education but he had a warmth and was a real support. Finally Ronnie Kinloch, a local estate agent, came much later. He was very much into local politics and really played little part at the beginning. The statutory lady was Campbell Reynolds from Cove. She knew nothing of school but was a great support and very practical – the final, successful presentation of the new uniform was entirely hers.

The interviews were easily the best that I had come across, being professional, informed, very much in depth and covered every possible angle, except – very uniquely – never asked me a single question about my views on religion. I was assured that I would have complete control of things educational, that I could pick my staff – sadly with political changes this turned out not to be true. I would have a short term contract, be provided with a house and a salary of £ 9,000 pa. Slightly less than I was getting but the perks were better.

The interviews were over about 6.30pm. I was knackered and they must have been. I went home in Al's car and we talked most of the way about education and were much in accord – perhaps that was the final interview? But no indication of the outcome, except that there were only two of us left. I was offered the job first thing next morning by Adam. I agreed to accept subject to agreement on terms and we met in Glasgow at Teachers in St Enoch Square. I refused the house, that was on offer – Taybank, opposite the school. Unfortunately it was in absolutely filthy condition as left by John Widdowson, so they agreed to me buying in my own in Helensburgh and they would pay the rates and taxes. Everyone seemed delighted, and we went off on holiday to Studland for two weeks sunshine.

The next four months were hectic with numerous meetings at 8am or 6pm in Miss D-S's house for breakfast or supper, this to be followed by the drive back to Cumbernauld to complete my term as Rector. There were meetings most Saturdays, at least once a week in Helensburgh with a late night journey back to Bridge of Allan. I had a first meeting in St Bride's gym with parents which went a bomb and apart from Mrs Watson complaining that she had just bought four pairs of green knickers for her four daughters and was I going to change all that? I met the staff in Larchfield and that went well, though there was much anxiety about jobs which I could not completely allay. A second meeting with the parents was less good. I think that there had been a bit of a whispering campaign from certain Larchfield parents and some of their staff who feared the appearance of girls. They were sure that standards would drop, and that the ethos would be just a state version of a private school. Actually we did a simple test of

English and Arithmetic in the spring across the two schools. Only I and Eileen Shepherd, who became a Deputy and Dorothy Barbour, Head of English, saw the results There proved to be was a considerable difference in standard between the two schools, with the girls winning easily. Those results have never been revealed. Duncan McKinchan, had earlier dropped a bit of a bombshell to me. Having assured me that I would not have to take any staff that I did not want. With a characteristic quiet cough, he admitted that he thought that employment law might make for difficulties! Consequently when I was asked about staff at the meeting I could not give a proper answer. Apart from anything, I had had no time as yet to even see individual staff. The meetings continued at an even more hectic pace.

The Governors were a great support, as most had day jobs but they proved to be heroic. Each one had some child connection – Adam decided to take his son away from Millfield, Peter Paisley wanted Christopher to join, John Harper already had a son at St. Brides, one of the four boys at the time. Duncan had two girls there and Bill and Teddy had boys already there, though both warned that these were going to Glenalmond, whatever happened. My own two girls were to go to Lomond, so there was plenty of evidence that those who mattered were putting their money where it mattered.

I became the last Headmistress of St Brides in January 1977. Sugar, oddly appeared for the first time, in the staff room for my coffee. It was a very pressurised period but enormously encouraging. The pace was unrelenting. I did have time off to go South to Millfield and Atlantic College to look at the Baccalaureate which, in the end, did not really fit either with the Scottish curriculum or with Scottish Universities. I also visited Oxford and Cambridge to make my name known.

So to the problems and their solutions:

1. Staff.

To me, this was the key. I interviewed all the existing staff, though I found the process at Larchfield always filled with obstacles. A few said that they were not interested – Anthony

Creery-Hill (Unfortunately known as Creepy-Hill) made it abundantly clear that he did not approve of the merger, and that he certainly would have no part in it. I don't think that he did us much good with parents. Mrs Morrice in English did not want to teach boys and sadly Mr & Mrs Macleod, the janitor and his wife at St. Brides felt that it was time to retire. A lovely pair. I had only one real anxiety – Miss Robertson who taught science or at least stood at the front of the class – wanted to stay on. I had a long heart-to-heart with her and raised for her terrible fears of what boys were like, and that life could be a terrible burden with older ones. She sweetly agreed that the new school would not be for her. She never held it against me, and always smiled when we met. I have a feeling that she died not long ago, worth a few millions so she was not pecuniarily embarrassed. Miss Bruce in Music also did not want to go on, as did the Art teacher, whose name I cannot remember.

We agreed on the senior staff – Michael Howard would be Head of Middle School in Larchfield with considerable freedom. Michael I found a strange man. He was a madman for squash both for himself and for his squad. He could be charming and was much in demand with the ladies, why I never understood – mothering perhaps? He always seemed loyal. He was a good teacher and loved by those he liked and loathed or feared by others. A tough disciplinarian. Elizabeth Leitch would be head of Junior School in Clarendon. Elizabeth was a good teacher but found pressure at times difficult to take. She did a good job. Eileen Shepherd, Head of Maths, became Senior Mistress and a good one who grew into the job and could, rightly be very obstinate if she felt something was wrong in practice or principle. I had wanted a Sheila Mowat from Greenfaulds for this job. She had been interested and would have brought gravitas and a bit of weight. Unfortunately Rachel D.S absolutely refused to countenance it. I think that she was wrong and I think we would have got a good teacher with experience. The one vacancy was my deputy. This was advertised and got a big response, among was one, Chris Higgs, from Brentwood school. Chris and Hilary flew up and stayed with us in Bridge of Allan for the interview. The others were good, but I have little memory of any of them as Chris was outstanding. This was a key appointment and of vital importance, as we learned to our cost when Chris went and Will was chosen. Chris was great, not just as an excellent teacher, good with boarding, but his warm, infectious enthusiasm set a high level to all the others. He was much loved by all.

The various Heads of Department were chosen – Eileen Shepherd to Maths, Dorothy Barbour to English (she was an excellent teacher who went on to Loretto) and Caroleen Clark to PE, Mrs Baird to Science, William Mackenzie (later a tower of strength) to Modern Languages, Edith Kinnear to History, Miss Harris to Geography and Hugh Scott came in to Art.

It was a good team. We brought a number of new ones in – Nigel Penny and Alastair Hayton-Williams from the Marines. These were both enthusiasts. Alastair took over Lansdowne and could be seen stalking round the house after dark with his shotgun over his shoulder. We had no trouble with peeping toms and, of course, he was only clearing the area of squirrels and rabbits! Denny Hooper and Judith arrived to go as House Master at Burnbrae. The last appointment was Roger Ball as Bursar. Roger came from the navy and later became Clerk to the Governors. He was very much a Jekyll and Hyde character who could be extremely helpful and sensible and then absolutely bloody minded at others. He did not make life easy unless with a gin in his hand at a party. His man/woman management skills were too often abysmal.

2. School Buildings.

We had 9 buildings which kept me healthy, but involved major maintenance and headaches. We had a roll or 530 with 107 boarders. St. Brides House was easy, as the Senior School housing S3 upwards. I think that the St. Brides book got this wrong. Larchfield had junior boarders and had Transitus (Primary 6), then Senior 1 and Senior 2. Clarendon had Junior 1-6. At the top of Clarendon House was the Lomond Association shop, for second hand uniform. Larchfield gym became the dining room with kitchens attached. Boarders had breakfast and supper there. We appointed a Catering Supervisor – Agnes Pritty. who proved to be a tower of strength. The cottage in Burnbrae grounds became the nursery, and the Bursar's office and the doctor's surgery and sick bay. Burnbrae and Lansdowne housed the girl boarders and Ashmount became both home to the Higgs and the house for senior girl boarders. Taybank was upgraded for the senior boarders. We had to build a boys changing rooms next to the gym in St Brides while Larchfield kept the changing rooms for rugby and the old fashioned tub for baths. Those were much loved by the boys and admired by visiting teams!

3. Curriculum

We stuck by a fairly traditional curriculum with "O" levels followed by Highers in the 5th year with GCE "A" level in the 6th year. Larchfield was prepared to offer Common Entrance, where required, and we started French in T1 and German in S1. The Home Economics department was maintained. End of term reports were issued and read and signed by me. I always personally saw the better and the poor pupils in each class. After those reports was the opportunity to bless and "curse" appropriately. The day began with a traditional assembly in each school, which I believed to be of gr eat importance. I was in St. Brides on Monday and Thursday and Friday, and in Larchfield for Tuesday, and Clarendon for Wednesday. We made a point of trying to make these relevant and I think that we were reasonably successful. The chaplain, David Reid, came in once a month. At first, the girl boarders went to St. Brides Church and the boys to West Kirk. But eventually both groups went to West Kirk, much to the disgust of St. Brides Church. Later, we changed it all and the Sunday service was provided in school. The choice of curriculum never proved a problem and was understood by most parents.

4. The School Day.

This proved a headache. Larchfield went on until 6pm and St Brides to 4 o'clock. We compromised by finishing at 5 pm!

To introduce this we instituted “tea or milk and stickies” at 4pm. “The Stickies” being a scone or biscuit. This was in held St. Brides hall for seniors and Larchfield for juniors. I thought it was a success and was good for socialising as staff joined in. There was then a three quarters of an hour prep or games activity period. While it was an attempt to find a compromise which I thought would work because so many parents explained that both worked and it would make life easy for them. It was not a long term success. Oddly enough I also tried an extended nursery but got no takers. Do many wives work in Helensburgh? The time-table followed a traditional forty minute period with doubles and singles. I did try my old trick of the twenty minute unit but Chris was not having any of that.

5. Boarding

With a hundred plus boarders, we decided to stick with five houses. The staffing was good, with a family in each. The Higgs in Ashmount, Michael Howard, Colin MacGeorge and Alec Hope in the boys area, the Hayton-Williams in Lansdowne and Hoopers in Burnbrae. All the boarders were British, some traditionally from the Campbelltown area, then the children of ex-pats and service families. The days of searching the world and Chinese were still long in the future. Colin Macgeorge was a hang-over from Larchfield and acted both as an auxiliary Bursar and gave value. Alec Hope, proved a very helpful member of the boarding staff.

Both were relics of the old prep school, a worthwhile attachment that we felt that we had to keep to keep those parents on side who thought that we were destroying everything that they held dear in the old small school

6. Uniform

Despite Mrs Watson’s worries, we did decide on a radical change. The old uniforms could be worn for a year. Campbell came up with excellent ideas. We had a dress rehearsal at one Board meeting – rather more light hearted than usual. (The Board incidentally met in my house at first, as it saved having to open up St. Brides)

We had a choice between what we have now and the grey uniform with a piping which we all felt was grim. The vote was unanimous, and went a bomb with pupils and parents. We talked long about kilts for girls, and for boarders, but felt that kilts were too costly at that point in time, and we were already asking a lot of parents and felt that we could not burden parents any more. The badge was essentially Rab Pender's, both the design and the motto were his and were excellent.

7. Parents

We tried to accommodate Al Macbeth's ideas on a Parents Association. This had Mr Gilbert Porteous of Kerrs as the first Chair. He was very supportive, and the relationship with the parents went well initially. To me, while I had much sympathy with the concept it was simply another meeting to attend which could turn into a "greetin" meeting. It also placed me in great difficulties at times, in that the Board was the ultimate place in which decisions had to be taken, and I often found myself the pig in the middle. Like all such groups, one danger is that it can be taken over by ambitious people with an agenda of their own. The other danger is that a parent is only interested in the current situation affecting their own child, and takes no account of the needs either of the other four hundred youngsters or the long term future of the school. I could never get Al to understand this.

8. The Board

As already stated this met every month and the finance and education sub-committees in between. At first the meetings were essential but, in retrospect I realise they began to move from the wider strategic roles of a Board to getting over involved in detail. Historically the Governors had played a crucial role, but latterly were often unable to draw back and let the management team get on with it. If I have a regret, it is that I was unable to make this change and persuade them to take a step backwards. It is easy in retrospect, to see this but it must not be forgotten just how involved and committed that first Board had been in the whole setting up process. They had had to lay down a strong financial base; arrange for long term financial assurances from the bank; review the situation of St. Brides s as a grant –aided school, which had to come to an end.; to replace the existing legal situation of the two schools; discuss with the Scottish Education Department over the formal recognition of the new school. The latter did not happen for two years because of a blockage over fire regulations and required a special visit to St. Andrew House by Rab, Duncan and myself. There was continuous consultation with HMI over curriculum, staffing etc. Consideration of Health & Safety and fire regulations was required. The latter were the most difficult of all and that with the Fire Board the most obstinate to change. The fact that all these were handled by the Governors took an immense weight from my shoulders. Thankfully, I was to be involved only on the periphery. I do not think that if I had had to be part of all these matters that we could have achieved the amalgamation so smoothly. As it was twenty four hours was not long enough just for my own responsibilities.

9. Management

I had worked with an internal governing group at Greenfaulds with no regrets or major problems. This allowed healthy discussion of all areas and gave the opportunity for communication and some delegation of decision making. With so many different areas of the school at the combination – four teaching areas, if you include the nursery, and five boarding houses, this was all the more necessary. We met on a Monday at 4.15 and the Management Committee consisted of myself, Chris Higgs, Michael Howard, Elisabeth Leitch, and Roger Ball. I think that the Board regarded it as a bit of a joke at first, but later came to accept it as an important part of the governance of the school.

Lomond, today, is going strong, numbers are steady, considerable building has taken place. This has taken place in an appropriate fashion with good design features. Much of this was due to a catastrophic fire which heavily damaged the main school building. A process of reducing the number of buildings has seen considerable savings, as well as easing the whole management process. To those of us who were involved in its amalgamation and development, its present situation can only be a matter of great satisfaction.

LIFE AFTER A HEADSHIP

I expect that all those who were pupils at the various schools wondered what kind of life the head would lead when he or she left. In any kind of job there is a feeling of wondering what life would be like on retirement. I remember Rachel Drever-Smith, one of that formidable vintage of lady Heads, receiving *a* telegram from her predecessor on her retirement. It simply said that she wished her a happy time, but suggested that it was time to do something useful.

The same comment was made by Donald Fortune, an old school friend, who wrote to me and suggested that I should join the Council of the Cystic Fibrosis Trust in Scotland. Donald and Petrina had had two children who were diagnosed in the early days as having CF. In point of fact, as we have learnt, it must be a different branch of CF, but still caused major problems. Their early growing up was a nightmare, both for the children and their parents. Donald had been very involved in the early days of the Trust. He felt that my experience in the Samaritans and with children would bring a new view of the work to be done. The big question at the time was whether to go for a lay chairman or to appoint a professional Director. After a bit of questioning, I recommended that a Director could be the answer. It did not cross my mind that that the job would appeal to me, as at the time, I was fully employed with a YTS project in Dumbarton.

A Rotary friend, Charlie McCrea, had an electrical business in Dumbarton and, being a bit of an entrepreneur, he had decided to set up a youth employment scheme using government money. His director had walked out and he asked me to take over. I did that for about fifteen months. It was a good scheme that offered for young men a kind of apprenticeship with firms. The firm was paid a sum of money, the young person was paid by us, and it was conditional that they went to college for one day a week. On the girls' side, they were to be care assistants in care homes while on the boys' side, there was a big variety of opportunities.

My job was to keep in touch, to find new businesses and to keep an eye on the colleges. It was interesting and it brought in the money. The early years were worthwhile, the later ones, after Charlie's death, were not, and I had decided to get out, so the possibility of CF was very attractive. I had also become involved with Scottish Enterprise in running a scheme for young adults, with no jobs but interesting ideas. That was great fun, and the young ones had a wonderful sense of humour. In fact, Ralph Risk invited me to take on a job with them.

Sandy Raeburn, a geneticist in Edinburgh, was the driving force in setting up a Scottish Director for CF. The idea was to have an oversight of the work of the Trust with a Scottish Council of interested people and a full time Scottish Director, while the main centre would be in Bromley in Kent with a Chief Executive there. It was very medically orientated, but the purpose was to have regional Directors in Scotland, Ireland, the North, London and the South. We were there to raise money, to raise the profile of the condition, and to provide support to parents and the youngsters with CF, and to offer various services. No small job. I found it fascinating and very challenging, trying to do everything on my own, organising the various local bodies, keeping in touch with the medics and raising the money.

I was lucky that CF had become a central part of the genetic side of medicine at the time. Being related to only the single gene, it seemed to offer the best chance of a cure. The condition was blessed with wonderful medical support, literally from the cradle to the grave. Because at that time few with CF survived beyond their teens, big efforts were being made to extend life and look for new ways of helping – diet, exercises, tough drugs. Most of the clinics at the time were paediatric – this meant with small tables, chairs and beds – difficult when you are feeling awful and aged in the teenage years. So my main effort at first was to upgrade these. With the help of the civil service and the clinicians I was able to approach the Scottish Office and we had very friendly meetings, first at the lower levels, and finally with Michael Forsyth, the Secretary of State, who was most helpful. He even offered me secretarial help, as well as £1,600,000 over three years to set up adult clinics in Edinburgh and Glasgow. For everyone it was a huge step forward, and made my day. If I did nothing else that made it all worthwhile.

Cystic fibrosis is an inherited disorder, both parents having the faulty gene. Children with the disorder have a malfunction in the lungs and the digestion, which causes a thick sticky mucus that is hard to shift. It is a terminal condition that can lead to an early death. Astonishingly, 1 in 25 of us carry the faulty gene, but it is only when we join up with a partner in the same situation that there is a 1 in 4 risk. There are 6,000 sufferers in the UK. It was only diagnosed fifty years ago but it is believed to go back into the dark ages, with Caucasians and Celts worst affected.

For me, though with medical connections but no scientific education I found myself in a new world of heterozygotes, stem cells, screening, meconium ileus and the world of transplants. For parents and sufferers, treatment is tough with the emphasis on exercise, on harsh treatment of the chest and lungs, careful diet, regular drug taking and periods of hospital stays.

The first months were hectic as I had to make contact with all the small branches – Edinburgh, Fife, Dundee, Borders, Dumfries, Inverness, even Campbelltown and the Hebrides – all with enthusiastic volunteers, and to prove so supportive of me. It meant great travel – about 18, 000 miles a year, journeys to Bromley every three months, and to medical conferences in Manchester and Leeds. Each branch had an annual meeting with a medical expert as speaker. He or she I had to meet and escort round the country, and the meetings were often in the evening, so this meant much late night driving. There was also the Scottish Council in Edinburgh to be attended.

To add to the pressure, the Trust was celebrating its 50th anniversary, so that meant a trip to Westminster Abbey and then to arrange a similar service in St Giles for Scotland. I upset the minister, Rev Guillesbeg Macmillan, because I had very clear ideas of what I wanted. I turned out well with a heart-stopping moment as we came out into the sun to be met by the pipes and drums of Scottish Power. So lucky a man I was to have Duncan Maclaren, the Chief Executive of Scottish Power as an ex-parent.

CF had a patron in Princess Alexandra, who was very much into the rights of royalty. She let us down badly with a failure to go to a special concert in Inverness for CF because she could not get a royal flight. It was my first journey up there to apologise. We did manage a big evening in Stirling Castle for her in Scotland and that was a success, though it brought out all my republican instincts, with concerns over the piper, the use of a school choir, etc. However, it seemed to please a lot of people.

I found working for CF a very humbling experience, to see the care that the NHS gave, and the lengths to which people would go to support us. We ran raft races on the Tay, adventure competitions, and weekend climbs up Mount Ben Macdhui. I think that we were the first to do that sort of sponsored expedition, and it paid well. I had two trips with them, the first ending with heavy snow and a stop because of the danger. The second meant an early 3am start to meet up with an outdoor BBC programme on the summit. That was fun, with regular checks on the way up. Then there was the Teddy Bears' Picnic in Perth and an adventure camp at Ardeonaig for the kids with CF. That was a huge success but had to end in the future as the problem of infections proved a major difficulty. We were able to share with other bodies like the Seventy Wild Miles – a cycle ride from Kingshouse, a canoe up Loch Etive and a run back to Glencoe – all lifting our public image. I was lucky also to have the support of the media, with interviews on BBC and ITV all increasing our opportunities to raise money. I got to know my Scotland – Stranraer, Dumfries, Fife Ness, John O Groats, Butt of Lewis – and Ireland to see what they were doing.

There were difficulties with HQ with the arrival of an accountant as Chief Executive, and the appointment of a difficult lady as the Chief Fundraiser, but overall it was the lovely people that I met that made it all worthwhile. Sadly, the cost of medical research and treatment began to make life difficult, and simple money raising efforts like tea parties or street collections began to raise inadequate funds. This meant that money had to be raised with bigger events often requiring greater effort and organisation – big dinners, use of celebrities, etc. So much was lost in this way for the little people.

I count myself as being so lucky to have had the opportunity to play a part in such a worthwhile organisation. As in all my jobs, the support of Mary in very practical ways, and often coming with me, made all the difference.

It was also so encouraging to work with so many selfless people who had to face a day long diet of exercise, diets, drugs, injections from 6 in the morning until 11 at night for their CF children, and still stay positive and feel able to contribute to the work of the Trust.

Certainly, the time after my Headship was not uninteresting or uneventful, and it was undoubtedly useful, and always rewarding.

A Magical Brilliant Event

17/18/19 February 1998

<u>17th February</u>

In all our lives there are days – weddings, anniversaries, events – which remain in the memory as being of special brightness, washed in a warm glow all their own. They are particular, vivid and memorable. Such was the occasion of that Investiture at the Palace on the18th of February.

I felt it was important to put this on record, not just for myself and my self-esteem, or even to warm the memory in the future, though these are important, but it is a provide an outline of what happened. This was, also for Gillian, who could not be with us, in her case she had her own memorable event later that week, with the birth of Deborah.

Helensburgh was "drookit" for the ten days before the great journey South, and in contrast to the rain in the North the weather in London contributed in no small way to bathing the whole affair in a spectacular fashion – sunshine, blue skies, and a temperature that allowed us to do without coats and umbrellas. It was, of course, a truly royal occasion.

Sandy sweetly agreed to lend us the use of his stretch limo for the journey to Glasgow, perhaps he intended for us to fly away to Florida. Anyway we agreed that it was sufficient just to the Central Station in Glasgow. We much appreciated the gesture as, for some, there was a certain amount of luggage – hat boxes, long dresses etc. Now there was, also, a massive lunch box, courtesy of Seonaid.

So to the 10.00 GNER train and sank into our first Class seats – would we have travelled in any other way? Father had really pushed the boat out. Actually it only cost an extra £10 a seat for the change, but it did look good. Plus we did get endless cups of coffee and a free Torygraph. Wow!

The train was empty until we reached Edinburgh, and we had a delightful lady from Prestwick sitting nearby, on her way to visit her son, who was the Dean of Salisbury Cathedral. After she had had her lunch she leant over to me and remarked in a very conspiratorial fashion that she did enjoy the occasional cigarette. "When you are on your own it is very nice to have a cigarette after lunch and again at night- and anyway it saves the prospect of five years in a care home." A classic for the family souvenirs.

The journey was easy, but like all long journeys quite tiring. Perhaps we were all suffering in nervous anticipation. Seonaid had prepared a superb packed lunch, and swiftly curbed any comments that MBE's do not eat packed lunches. As a matter of record, Seonaid had her hands full curbing a certain effervescence in her father throughout the trip. We arrived dead on time at 15.38, a taxi to the Cavendish and a pleasant warm welcome, something that was true of our whole stay, and which made it all so memorable. It was almost as though everyone was determined to make it an event.

As mother already had a hat from Colin Moynihan's wedding, all seemed well, except that there was no hat pin! So what do you do on a rare visit to the capital, but go looking for a hat pin? Burlington Arcade was very helpful except that the hat shop there had closed..... So a little walk, and we walked, and we walked, until we found the Antiques Market in the churchyard of St James's Piccadilly, where there was wondrous array of hat -pins at £4 upwards. What a pity that in the end she did not need it. Still, a hat pin is a hat pin. When we got back to the Cavendish we did a room exchange, Seonaid had a lovely big room with two beds and we had a small room with a double bed. A swap seemed sensible.

We agreed that it was late and that a return to the hotel was sensible and a meal in their restaurant was the easiest. What a meal! There we were in our best evening wear and a sparkling wine – pink but sparkling, and cheap. The lamb and the salmon could not have been bettered.

We got a taxi and off to see, not the Wizard but "Miss Saigon". Our seats were up front but a bit on the side and we were lucky, that, with a bit of a shuffle, we made a change to some vacant seats. The first act was interesting, a bit naughty and very noisy – that was fine for Seonaid. But we all commented on its melodic charm and agreed that it had been fine and we had enjoyed it. At the price of the tickets, could we have said anything else?

The second act was much better, genuinely moving with tragedy striking Miss Saigon. I am glad that we went but I think we would give it a miss, in the future. So we slipped out into the night – warm and no coats – to seek a coffee. Mother wickedly suggested, in a moment of financial madness, that we recreate our youth and go to the Savoy. Three coffees later, and short of £ 12 for an expensive nightcap and we caught a No. 9 bus back to the Cavendish.

Wednesday 18th February

The day actually dawned bright and clear, and the view from our window over the West End was gorgeous. A cup of tea for us and a shower for Her Majesty (me not her) and a superb breakfast, with all of over-eating on the grounds that there might be no cucumber sandwiches, or the others might have eaten them. Strange that, at another table, was Bill Inglis, the MD of Strathford and lately Rotary. It was nice to meet a kent face. We got a nice smile.

By 9.15 we were all ready for the other member of the family – straight back from South Africa. Catriona arrived back with the car, after all how else would we get there – by Taxi? They, the gorgeous threesome, all looked stunning. Catriona in a stunning blue dress and a brimmed hat to match. My ladies each looked better than a thousand dollars. They did a quick check on the central character – tie straight, hair brushed, teeth gleaming, kilt straight, sporran central and the sgian dhu in stocking-to protect Her Majesty. On second thoughts it might be best to leave that at home – a bit aggressive. Off we went on the familiar route, Marlborough Street, the Mall and in through the front gate of Buckingham

Palace. Well, there was a queue of cars, so Catriona and I stayed in the car, so that I could practice my regal wave to the crowds. Mary and Seonaid jumped out to join the queue of "thousands". I am not quite sure why. Catriona just loved driving imperiously into the grounds and into the Inner Quadrangle. She did wonder about the anti-theft lock....

Into the Palace itself, with large, clear notices to all the recipients and guests, up endless marble stairs lined with Life Guards. They all stood at attention as I expected, but to Seonaid there was a doubt over whether they were really alive. A quick wink from one, brought a strangled jump. They, the honoured guests, were ushered into the Ballroom while I went on to the Picture Gallery. All a saving, of course, on any future need to see the royal gallery. My name was checked off and I was ushered onto a huge carpet with all the other waiting persons. The spread was everything – old, young, military, civilian, men, women, uniformed, plain.

About 10.30, Colonel Mather, the chief Aide, arrived to welcome and to instruct us on what was going to happen. Most important, he said, "You are here to enjoy yourselves. If there are problems, they are ours not yours. You must not worry. It will all go smoothly – have no fears". The fact that most of us were now a both moist and fearful was unimportant and irrelevant. He went carefully through the whole rigmarole, not once but twice, and very carefully warned us of all the possible slips on floors and steps. I think, by this time, that we were all so uptight that we were like kids at a prize-giving. Each of us had been given a little catch to put on the lapel to hold the decoration. Colonel Mather was dead right, my hands were ringing wet. Poor Queen, how did she keep her hands dry? We were moved in small groups slowly forward, our names once again checked, up to the door of the Ballroom. As "the one before" moved forward, we were ushered onto the carpet and the Equerry. "Don't worry, you will not slip." As our last name was read out, we were to move forward and stand in front of the Queen. "Don't go too far forward to the dais, or too far back – you would not want her to fall off as she reached to pin the medal!" She will have a brief chat with you, she will shake your hand to show that that was that, and you move off with a small bow." Oh and "don't call her 'Your Majesty', or 'your Royal Highness'." Your tongue will go into twist, and anyway, she does not like those terms." It's Ma'am as in jam not Ma'am as in marmalade!

I had time to chat to some of the others, and it also relieved the tension a bit. There was a half Colonel in Signals who had just come back from Sierra Leone, and some soldiers just back from Northern Ireland. One of those waiting lost a button – no need to worry for there was a lady with a needle and thread to help, and there were lots of safety pins! Among others there was a biologist from Cambridge, and a little lady who worked in Downing Street. Here there was a remarkable cross section of the people, and all delightful and charming, with one exception – a pushy little man who announced that he had got his for his work with the radio in Southampton Hospital. Yuck! Another Scot and I chatted about devolution and agreed that the Scots really did not need it. After all as I said, the three great Offices of state.......Chancellor, Foreign Office and Defence were all Scots anyway, and even the Prime Minister had been educated in Scotland – that is if you could call Fettes an education. "Here hold on a bit, I work in Downing Street said the little lady!"

By 11.30, my feet were killing me, so how was the Queen managing? But we were for the Off, past the incredible pictures in the Galleries – the Royal Family at the Windsors, Queen Victoria, all those painted by Winterhalter. It was emphasised that all this saved us £8! Then across the back of the Ballroom and what a relief to see that wonderful family, even managing to smile at me. I don't think I had the energy to smile back. It all went just as they had said it would – "How long have you been in the Samaritans " – "Just on forty years, ma'am." And that had been rehearsed for an hour. Shake hands, wee bow, bend and back off. Except I thought that I had gone the wrong way and had I actually bowed. I have no idea – just relief. Then off down that red carpet and "Well done, Congratulations," from everyone that I passed, and "here's a wee boxie for that medal", and a seat in front of all those elegant ladies. By 12.10, it was all over and the Queen had gone with a smile. How did she have any left? Perhaps a wee gin and tonic!

Looking back on it, I can only feel a real sense of gratitude for the recognition. This may not be true of those who get an endless array of awards, many meaningless, but for people like me it was a magical occasion. It was intimate and it was immensely dignified. The whole focus was to make it an individual event for each of us, and to surround it with dignity. That Ballroom scene had a fantastic sense, the Queen in front of the throne, flanked by the Beefeaters and the Ghurkhas. (The latter a tradition from Queen Victoria) That ceiling, the band of the Life Guards – here was value. One aspect that impressed me was that she spent no more time with the tops than with the bottoms.

Then off to the Quadrangle and relief – and how. Photos-photos, photos – and all this before the day of the digital. We escaped the professionals quickly, but we did get two prints within two days of great quality. Then the girls discovered Mrs Elizabeth Beresford, or Mrs Womble, and her clearly her autograph was desperately needed. Now who was Mrs B.? She did look like a womble, I said to Mary and the man next to me laughed – "Everyone says that, and she's my mother." Then the slow drive out through those Gates with a little wave to the massed cameras.

So where to eat, because even the honoured need to eat? Fortnum & Mason seemed to be reasonably high class – where else? I had Welsh rarebit, Mary an omelette, and Seonaid a toasted sandwich, while the growing girl asked for a roast chicken, even with a warning of twenty minutes. Where does she put that food? It was twenty minutes and the rarebit and the omelette were not that hot, but who cared. But when I collected the bill, I did quietly mention that the quality was not quite up to expectations. Unwisely the waitress argued, not sensible with four strong ladies present, and some heat rose. However the charming floor manager arrived immediately, with apologies and an offer of sweets and coffee. Graciously accepted, together with a box of chocolates. Now that's the way to smooth furrowed brows.

On our return to the Cavendish, the delightful concierge – an Irishman – wanted to see my medal, which, of course, he admired and handed me back the box, with a giggle – without the medal. From that moment we were pals, with much humour about concierges and Irishmen. The girls, of course, went off to Harrods and Mum and I went to the Overseas Club in St. James's for a seat and a quiet cup of tea. Exhaustion set in!

John and Catriona arrived at about 6 o'clock, complete with a bottle of champagne. Wow! What a start! Then off to The Waldorf Hotel, and the bright lights. The dining room looked beautiful with an array of small bright lights on the surrounds. The dinner was superb, with much laughter and joy – and no little alcohol. It was not busy and we got top treatment, with Rashid, the funny waiter who dazzled the girls, and they dazzled him with the promise of bread rolls and doggy bags. Here was charm extraordinaire. Sadly, and this is a record of truth, les girls let us down. Mary and Catriona decided on an ice-cream confection, with Chinese gooseberries on top. Catriona was knowledgeable and realised what they were, but Mum had no spectacles on and was witnessed chewing happily away at the berry. Talk of collapse of stout parties, there was laughter and more laughter, the tears flowed, but what a night. A No 9 bus and back to the hotel and bed – nae nightcaps.

19th February

A relatively quiet day with a short coffee and chat with Don Fraser Jones from CF. Mum and I went to Fortnum & Masons and a coffee. There we were warmly welcomed by the Chief with the words –"please look after my friends." He remembered my kilt from the day before, so we talked about that. Then a quick return to the Cavendish, and the bill settled, a taxi to Kings Cross and the 1500 Pullman and those endless cups of coffee – well for Seonaid anyway. All went well apart from a delay outside Central, then a taxi to Queen Street, and the train to Helensburgh and collection by Ian.

What an experience. Three days of pride, pride for me, but pride for my family, because without them I could not have done what I did. We were all sharing in an experience. Could one ask for more?

On Flanders Fields – A Journey on November 11th 1998 at Ypres

In Flanders Fields – NOVEMBER 11TH 1998

This was not about me or my doings or our journeying, but about other people which just did not take our breath away, but gave us such a sense of privilege to have been there.

I write not about French food or wine or even about their hotels – escargots, croissants or Flandres veal. It began as a strange tale of getting ourselves lost in almost every town or village that we entered, and all to find our way to the famous town of Ypres. Our sense of direction was completely out of sync – we can find our way to Valetta road, just off the M40, but can we now arrive at – Chateau Cocove, that is off the French A26, then Mount Cassell by the correct route, and even, finally, Poperinghe. And, thankfully on our way home, back in the UK we must leave Preston and get to Clitheroe – though mind the road from Blackburn is interesting. Today's generation need have no such fears in their travels – just turn on the internet, switch on the GPS!

This is a story of forty eight to seventy two hours, from Tuesday the 10th November to Thursday the 12th of November in the year of our Lord 1998. It was the tale of joining up with other Old Lorettonians, their wives and their families, on what we all saw as a pilgrimage to honour just over a hundred of those OLs who had died in that terrible war of 1914-18. Many of them had died on this same grim Western Front.

Loretto was, and still is, a small school of less than two hundred, but usually of just over a hundred and fifty boys. The thought of losing a whole generation in the space of four years is a thought to weigh heavily. No one quibbles now that war can be senseless, the problem is that they all made sense at the time. To-day is to find ourselves caught up in the religious and ethnic hatred of the Middle East, whereas in 1914 it was the senseless ambitions of the great powers of Europe, intoxicated by the long term Balkan mishmash.

The whole tragedy was caught in the stupidly incredible timetable of railway times – the Schlieffen Plan, and the German need to be the great dominant, military centre of Europe. This was a war where you can see statues and memorials raised to commemorate the deaths of hundreds of thousands of men. It was a war, when the loss of 60, 000 in a day from terrifying military stupidity, and then to be buried in those immaculate graves, But not – Haig, Foch, or Hindenburg. One small point of pride was to recognise the staunch discipline of that small British Army, while both Germany and France had been devastated.

This was not the war of poetry or the gentle reminiscence of Rupert Brook –

"If I should die, think only this of me
That there is some corner of a foreign field,
That is forever England. And in that rich soil,
A richer dust concealed...."

They are memorable and moving words, but they are from another time, another world, far from the mud, the blue clay, the gas. The year of 1998 is about the "pity of war, and the pity that war distilled." It's strange how, in a relatively short time, the whole appearance of war and approach to war has changed.

From Germany came a very immediate sense of the horror as seen by Alfred Liechtenstein in "Prayer before Battle"

"God protect me from misfortune,
Father, Son and Holy Ghost
May no high explosives hit me,
May our enemies, the bastards,
Never take, never shoot me,
May I never die in squalor,

For our well loved Fattherland.
Look I'd like to live much longer,
Milk the cows and stuff my girl friends,
And beat up that lousy Joseph,
Get drunk on lots more occasions,
Till blissful death o'ertakes me.

Look I'll off up heartfelt prayers,
Say my beads seven times daily,
If God of your gracious bounty
Choose to kill my mate, say Huber,
Or else Meir, and let me off.

But suppose I have to take it,
Don't let me get badly wounded,
Send me just a little leg wound,
Or a slight gash on the forearm,
So I can go home a hero
Who has got a tale to tell."

Liechtenstein died in September 1914, even before the leaves of autumn had fallen.

The British Army fought on a relatively narrow front, from the Channel south, so the great battles were fought around Arras and Mons, Vimy, the Somme, and, of course, Ypres. The latter town being the only part of Belgium which the Germans never captured. That Ypres Salient ran for no more than ten miles by six. In our home town terms, the equivalent of Helensburgh, bound by the Clyde to the South and Loch Lomond to the North and Garelochhead.

Within that small area of land both sides lost over a million dead, captured and wounded, of that about 400, 000 died. The famous Menin Gate records 54, 000 names, men "Known only to God" and who have no grave. It would be fair to say that the German equivalence would be over 50, 000. Every year, an average of twenty two bodies are dug up in the fields of Flanders.

So we, Mary and I, set off with different mindsets, one being the excitement of the professional historian, particularly with an interest in World War One, and the other the burden of emotions related to her own family involvement in that war. The numbers involved, the relative closeness all combined to create an unusual sense of awareness. I had two uncles who had fought in the war, and one who died afterwards of his wounds. Dad had raised 1600 men for a Carrier Corps in South-East Africa to carry supplies to the front. Mary's Dad had joined up at seventeen, became a driver of trucks in Palestine, and had, also been torpedoed off Sicily. Uncle Jack had been in the Army and Uncle Jimmy served on the Western Front. Anne's father had done the same. Another odd connection was the reaction of those around us, the mere mention of Ypres was to tell us of relatives and families who had served in that war. That war of 1914-18 has left an emotional impact that the war of 1939-45 has not. Perhaps it was the sheer hell of it, the unbelievable mud, the carnage, which has left an image of an unacceptable war.

So we drove down to London, and stayed with Catriona and John, and then on Monday the 9th of November down to the Channel Tunnel for the first time. Even though we had a reasonable knowledge of that part of France we took our time in exploring our routes. We had fixed on staying at our beloved Bollezelle, which was only twenty miles from Ypres. We were to make that journey six times over the next few days, and even then made mistakes – it all looks different at night. But we never got badly lost and indeed had a lot of fun. A time of forty minutes was not bad going. Part of our route was up a hill to Mont Cassel, this being the only hill overlooking the very flat plain of northern France. The plain stretches from the Atlantic across the Netherlands, the German plain, Poland and into Russia – the great cockpit of Europe. You can trace the footsteps of all the great European armies – French, German, Russian and even Swedish, all with battles – Agincourt, Crecy, Ramillies, Waterloo, and then all these of the last two wars. No wonder for Europe the peace of the EU is so attractive. This gentle meadow like land which can become so bleak and stricken with war.

We stopped for coffee in Cassel and learnt that this had been the HQ for the generals in the First War because of the view that it commanded over the Front. Here, General Joffre brought his chef to ensure his continuing health, and here also a rally driver to control his car and take him over the whole area, while enabling him to sleep in comfort. This reassuring position gave the saying by his reassured men – "Ah! Papa Joffre, il dort, tout va bien." "Daddy Joffre is asleep, so all must be well." For him the dreams went well, but for the poilus the nightmare remained. In our day it was all so quiet and peaceful.

From there it was down along the poplar- lined roads to Ypres. This was the town wrecked during that war, and only apportion of the Cloth Tower survived until 1918. But today the Great Square looked as it must have done over five centuries ago. We parked behind the Great Hall and found a loo – so important! The Hall housed the Flanders Field Museum. We found later that Craig, another OL that we met, had had a father who fought in the war, and had lost his best friend at Passchendaele and had buried him there. Like so many of that generation he rarely spoke of the war or the events of the time. Lynn Macdonald, a famous historian of the War, had interviewed him about Passchendaele and recorded some of those memories. Craig described how he had gone into the Hall to be met, as an introduction, by his father's voice!

The Museum was evocative, much of it in twilight, but covered so much of the war and its feelings, the sounds, for the whizz bang shot off, and the sense of danger was real. For us one bang was bad, but a week...?

About noon we drove up to the great slope of Passchendaele, so reminiscent of the great charge in 1917 and turned off into Tyne Cot Cemetery, one of those huge memorable areas

"In Flanders Fields, the poppies grow,

Between the crosses row on row"

It is surrounded by a high wall but is beautifully laid out, with grass, shrubs and flowers, but all dominated by the carefully laid out rows of crosses. Very military, very orderly. The memorials record every race who fought on the allied side – some sixty nations. Here were British, Canadian, Anzac,

South African and Indian. Perhaps the most touching are those with just the words –"Known only to God".

We could only stand in awe, yet beauty, respect, sorrow were there – and silence. We could only think that here was a memorial to man's stupidity, to his arrogance and yet to his bravery, his courage and his self-sacrifice. As we stood a youngish, stout man approached us, and in a soft Scots voice asked if we were Scots. Kenneth Macdonald from the BBC asked, rather tentatively, if he could interview us for Radio Scotland. Fame at last, but so difficult to draw back from those overwhelming emotions of the setting, and to put into words something of our reactions. Perhaps in a way we were "gutted", yet anxious to convey the depth of our reactions.

We walked respectfully round the cemetery and then drove a few hundred yards to Wetfields Farm so that we could trace the route of the Canadians who had fought, with such losses, up the slope – about a quarter of a mile, so short yet so far, to Crest Cott. In the gentle autumn light it was hard to imagine the scene of the appalling mud and rain of that day. That was the scene in 3rd battle of Ypres in November 1917. The monument to their courage lies against a cottage with a Canadian flag and a surround of wreaths, so different to the scars of craters, of mud and of bodies.

We only know that war lasts, rain soaks, and the clouds sag stormy -

"Dawn massing in the East her melancholy army,
Attacks once more in ranks on shivering ranks of gray."

It was with relief that we turned our faces to the east to join the real world of cheerful boys and girls and the welcome of friends in the Loretto group who had met up in Poperinghe Square. But even here we could not escape tragedy in that sunlit square. In the British Army there had been 2, 000 sentences of death – 327 were actually shot between 1915 and 1919. While about twenty of these were for rape, or burglary, looting or even murder, the great majority were for desertion, sleeping while on duty, or cowardice. In those white-washed cells, just off the square, twenty men would wait in "Pops" to be taken out at dawn, tied to the execution post in the yard outside, and shot by one of their own squad "pour encourager les autres." Of those who were shot two were only seventeen and one sixteen! All below the age of call-up.

It was to enter the world of sanity to cross that square and walk down the street to Toc H, that house founded by Tubby Clayton, to offer an oasis for troubled men. It was not a museum we were informed. It was "a house for the living, and you can stay here, though you will have to cook your own meals." Truly a refuge, an island of sanity, and eccentricity. "Abandon rank all ye who enter here." "If you spit at home, you may spit here!"

These signs were on the pavement outside. Here was a wonderful garden of peace at the rear, upstairs three floors of home, and a chapel on the fourth. Nearer to God? The altar was just a joiner's bench – Jesus, after all, was a carpenter. And in the corner was an old harmonium, known as the harmonium with the wonky knees, because Tubby had it carried round the trenches to play at his services. We were blessed that one of the boys tentatively offered to play it for us. The sun shone, and, for a moment, peace surrounded us. This it is not a museum, it is a place of peace. Even to-day, or perhaps more so to-day, Toc H is a haven, a place of simplicity in a world of horror, and yet it is not a land of horror, for there are people like Tubby who offer hope and sanity.

We rushed back to Bollezeele to sit and rest for an hour, and then back to Poperinghe for the band to play the Retreat at the war memorial. Here was joy and pleasure, with the pipes and drums of Loretto and those of the Belgian H Familie school. It was right, it was powerful, it was intensely moving. Dinner that night was much appreciated.

Wednesday 11th November 1998

Up bright and early to be at Vlamertinge, a small village a few miles outside Ypres. It had been agreed that midday at Ypres would be so busy that our input would be lost and that the journey to Vlamertinge would be right. In that quiet little place no pipes had sounded for eighty years, no band, no stamp of feet. As the Mayor explained, "we are but a small village of 3, 500 souls, but we have 7,000 of your dead buried here." The band was drawn up in the square, and we all lined up behind it – the pipes and drums, the banners of all the local organisations (about forty) – all the children from the schools, many of the inhabitants, and us, the friends and family. In bright, clear sunshine we marched to the church, chatting laughing, a cheerful friendly group of one mind. At the church the banners in all their glory lined the lined the way, our seats were on the right hand side. The service was entirely in Flemish, but spectacular for after each item there was music, mostly gentle pop, linked to the amazing banner co-ordinated waving by a group of twelve young people from nearby Courtrai. The Mayor read a moving account, with us having a copy in English, of the collapse nearby of a sap, or tunnel, being built under the German lines. One young man kept his head did not panic, lived for six days until rescue reached him. The other eleven were buried in the cemetery.

From the service – the Band, the pipes and a local Brass one, with all the local dignitaries – marched to play at the Veterans Home, then round the village to the beautiful small cemetery. Here we stood while the wreaths were laid and we sang the national anthem. For a moment of quiet and then the notes of Highland Cathedral were played – that haunting air, first just one lone piper, then two, then by four, and lastly by the whole band. That with the Flowers of the Forest following as a lament of the tragedy of Flodden there were few dry eyes. In an odd way to me was the sight of the graves, nearby of three German graves with their crosses. Finally, the children who had joined us, carrying a small ivy cross with instructions to lay it on a grave and to note the name on that cross. These were powerful moments.

As we had waited for the procession to start outside the church, Mary was approached by an attractive lady who explained that her son was the pipe major and asked Mary what was her connection. After a moment it came out that she was Caroline, who had been Caroline Fraser in Aberdeen. So after a number of years, we there met up with the young girl who had taken over Gillian and Seonaid to lead them to school at St Margaret's.

And so back to reality and a glass welcome glass of Flemish ale in the Commune. That is the whole parade and supporters and with a happy gesture we were invited to join them all at the local cafe for lunch at the Mayor's expense.

At this point there was a little panic over timing as were due in Ypres for two o'clock. The bus shot off with us in hot pursuit – the wrong way – East when it should have been West. Had the driver had too many glasses or was he going AWOL? A sudden screech of brakes, and an unscheduled stop by the monument to one Captain Noel Chavasse VC (twice). He was a Ramc Doctor who had earned them both for crawling out into Noman's Land to bring in the wounded. His father was the Bishop of Liverpool – did he listen to Granny Smith sing her solos?

We reached Ypres and parked near to the H Familie School. The bands met up again and began the warm up while we recovered. They were ready for the big event – the march through Ypres. At 2.30 we left for the Menin Gate, about a mile and a half down the road and then across to the Great Square. We had a few doubts as to whether we would be able to march on the Square, but to blazes, here we go! It was a long time since I had marched behind a band, and this was one I will never forget. The boys played magnificently, we followed the three OLs, Jim Hume carrying the wreath, three staff and Mary and Caroline.

The Square was packed but the roadway opened as if by magic and the crowds parted to stand and welcome us as we passed, cameras everywhere, clapping and smiles. They were powerful moments, there was pride, there was a sense that this had happened before. It was almost right to the sound of boots, of young men in khaki, with their puttees and their rifles. We were part of history, of a time past. There was sadness, there was pain, but there was also a joy that they had not been forgotten, proud that we had come all this way to remember eighty years of history. They were images, they were phantoms, but they were not forgotten.

Jim and the boys laid their wreaths and read out the names of more than one hundred of our OLs who had died, some of whose names were on the memorial. It was a dramatic scene to remember men of another generation, of another world, and for them to be remembered in turn by the young of the modern world.

For another twenty minutes the two bands played on the Square. It gave huge pleasure to all those around. Back in our own world we went for a cup of tea at the nearest cafe, and to fill the time until evensong in St George's Chapel.

This was fixed for 6.30, but, on advice, fortunately we arrived early. It was packed by the time of the start, with all of us and the Welsh Male Voice Choir. Even the walls were packed with the standing room only. Poor Rector, he had to start with a fire warning! But what a service – Highland Cathedral and the Flowers again, the voices of the Welsh Choir, a lone bugler for the Last Post. The Bishop was very good – he had five minutes and overstepped it only four, but the sermon, the sense of dedication, of memory, of being part of a huge involvement. I have never heard the singing of the 23rd Psalm to Crimond, the Nunc Dimittis and the Magnificat. These were moments to remember for all time. The sights, the sounds, the people, the warmth, the sense of pride and of hope – this was what humanity was all about. We were so privileged to be a small part. In that city, on that date the lesson was there – we are men and women, we have memories, we have sadness, we have tragedy but we also have hope we can look up to the great virtues of humanity.

On the 11th November 1998. Now lettest thou thy servants depart in peace...

"Move him into the sun-

Gently its touch woke him once,
Think how it wakens the seeds,
Woke once the clays of a cold star,
Are limbs, so dear achieved, are sides
Full-served, still warm, too hard to stir?"

THE JOURNEY OF A LIFE

1958 – 1976

"Keep me from the fatal habit of thinking I must say something on every subject.
Release me from craving to straighten out everybody's affairs.
Keep my mind from the recital of endless detail, give me wings to get to the point.
Teach me the glorious lesson that I may occasionally be mistaken."

Nuns' Prayer

There are many reasons for wanting to recall a major part of one's life – in my case the Samaritans – part pride, part satisfaction at having contributed something of value, and gratitude that I was fortunate enough to play a considerable part in the founding and development of an important social enterprise that has had a big impact not just in Britain but across the world. I suppose, too, that as time goes by the details of that story may become less sharp, as will the recalling of the names of those important others who did so much to make it what it is to-day. It is good to remember achieving something worthwhile in one's life. To-day there are an endless number of organisations which offer support and help for those facing all kinds of difficulties in their lives. In the 1950' and 60's the Samaritans were the first to offer this opportunity and in a way that was different. It was an organisation that grew in almost incredible fashion in every town. It offered the simple support of friendship and concern for every day and every hour of the day. Because a branch cannot exist without at least 60 members, it is likely that Samaritans are the biggest voluntary organisation in the world. For me, I had the good fortune to play a part in it and it became so very central to our own lives. As my parents found their purpose in religion, I found my purpose in seeing my life as being of service to others.

So where do I begin. With my church background through my father and with his emphasis on practical commitment, I suppose it would be inevitable that I became involved in life. I admit I do enjoy being part of being activite. Oddly enough Loretto was also a place which expected its boys to be involved and to play a real part in life.

I will do my best not to recall every detail or look into every reason for taking me into this organisation. Sufficient to say that my parents were very old fashioned in the belief that you should be committed to supporting and helping others, and with the Frost family, which later became so much a part of me, I had to believe the same. I am sure that Dad would have liked me to be involved in the church, and I did play a big part in a youth fellowship in Greenbank church, but my interest in my student days was with a boys club, Fet-Lor in Pilton, on the north side of Edinburgh. When I became a teacher I wanted to do more than just to be a date machine. At Melville I began a mountaineering club and the Duke of Edinburgh group. For me history is about life and the people who make it. I became involved in setting up a number of end of year schemes at both Melville College and Robert Gordons in Aberdeen. The first one was a once a year series of lectures on life – politics, religion, work, etc and these were for Sixth Year for an hour last thing on a Friday – a time notoriously difficult after exams -using outside speakers. I did the same at Robert Gordons in Aberdeen with the addition of a two day War Game and that lasted for my last 3 years at the school. That fascinating scheme arose from a famous situation during the Cuban 1963 crisis when I had a small group of 6th formers and we suddenly found ourselves discussing why we should be doing history at all when our world was about to be blown apart. For the Game I used a famous film called the War Game which revealed the full effects of a nuclear explosion on London. In all my teaching life I never intended just to be a teacher of the Past.

Among my memories, as well as the demanding round of visits, were the trips abroad. To Geneva once again, and here I found myself being organised by Elizabeth Salisbury, who was the editor of the Samaritans magazine, with all my movements being carefully managed and mapped out by her. It was lovely!

Then it was agreed that a small group of the Samaritans should attend the big conference of the IASP, the International Association of Suicide Prevention to be held in Jerusalem. That was fascinating, for it would be in the new October Break and Mary would come with me. I did get a small injection of cash but we paid for the rest. It was fantastic to see the Holy Land, Tel Aviv, the Sea of Galilee, Bethlehem and finally Jerusalem. Wow! Mary and I walked up the Mount of Olives and came down to the Garden of Gethsemane, passing a little monastery as dawn broke, and to see a solitary monk praying over that City for which Jesus had wept. It was incredibly moving and memorable, except to youngest daughter, Catriona, whose birthday was due and so she was "dumped" to a friend.

I also learnt that for many of those who attended these conferences, that they gave their address, so justifying their expenses and then went off on the tourist trail. We, in contrast, attended most of the talks. Mike gave his usual party, despite much banging on the room wall and then we all paid a ceremonial visit to the Inn on the road to Jericho. That was after a dip in the Dead Sea. All in all it was an incredible and wonderful trip. We had a memorable dinner for 22 which produced one enormous fish on a huge dish surrounded with vegetables and sauces.

My other expedition was a little different. For some reason the very professional American suicide organisations were highly suspicious of the Samaritans, and it was not helped that they viewed Chad with personal suspicion. At regular intervals he would launch one of his onslaughts on volunteers to get more involved with sex and the sexual problems of the callers. Unfortunately, Chad himself loved being surrounded by beautiful ladies. As a celebrity he had little difficulty in achieving some success in that area. Chad did have the habit of always assuming that sex was a dirty word. At one of our conferences in Scotland he had made an incredibly inspiring talk under the heading of Bisons, while the next talk in Dundee was entirely devoted to sex. The Executive spent some time discussing this problem and Richard Fox, the psychiatrist, suggested that, as he was to be in the US for their big conference, it would be useful for me to go with him and so represent the usual normal approach of a volunteer to life and the other... Wow! The Executive agreed, simply explaining that my attendance would be perfectly normal, and agreed to pay some of my expenses. I suggested that I would combine my visit with a call on an old friend in Wisconsin who had worked with me placing American teachers in Scottish schools and so give a talk on Scottish schools – that went down well with the Education Committee. It was suggested to me that an approach to the Churchill Foundation in New York might bring in some money and, thank goodness it did. The journey over two weeks took in Boston with their new Samaritan branch and a stay on Cape Cod with the delightful Monica Dickens, and to spend time in San Francisco looking at their work on suicide which was an eye-opener. I would add that the excellent lecture that I had prepared on Scottish education was brutally dumped and I was asked everywhere to talk about suicide prevention!

It was an incredible journey, starting in Boston with Monica and finishing in San Francisco with Charlotte Ross, a formidable but friendly Director of San Mateo, with in between, New York, Washington, Saint Louis Missouri and Wisconsin. The conference was held in the enormous Stouffer Towers, that cost me 2$ just to get to my room for my infra-red suntan. It was all very interesting, with some great presentations and some awful ones, and I made some good friends. One soon learnt that US friends are instant, warm and positive but last only for the time that you are with them. I made a naughty note – “Americans are neurotic and self-analytical, they will dig up everything including themselves to see what’s going on, and if it’s wrong getting rid of it. They love jargon – schizoid, paranoid, psychotic. Their language can be foul – arse, crap, Jesus Christ....But they can be lovely. I covered 12, 000 miles, nine states, three/four/five cities, slept in four hotels, used seven airlines, ate in nineteen restaurants. Only in the US can you order a delectable sweet and 20 spoons. Great!!

So four years as Chair of the national organisation and 41 years in the Samaritans proved to be a major part of my life. Later when I stopped being Chair I found myself being responsible for setting up a letter writing branch in Scotland, it was to be the precursor for the present internet service. I also did two examinations on behalf of the Executive, one into the problems facing big branches. That was fascinating and took me to Liverpool, Dublin where I was greeted with as much enthusiasm as if I had been the Pope, to London, which by this time had moved to Soho and where I got a great welcome, and, as a balance to Glasgow who would not even let me into the office! The other study was into the means of communication, always a very difficult one, but one which the national body was very concerned about.

Those 41 years were incredible ones, with Samaritans becoming a national institution and offering a real and effective answer to the tragic problem of suicide. Its success must lie with Chad. It was his energy, his dedication, his hard work, and his vision that captured that moment in the tide of human affairs that would lead to the contribution of ordinary men and women to such an effort achieving so much. He was an incredible, impossible, great man. At a big church meeting on the day of the 9/11 atrocity the news of what had happened came through to total stunned silence and horror. Chad, aged 80 + rose and started with the words – "Lighten our darkness, Oh, Lord, defend us from the perils of this night.....in the name of Jesus Christ, our Lord…" They all joined in the words.

Yes, looking back I was blessed to have shared with a remarkable man and so many good and humble people the journey of a lifetime.

For me, my contribution to some lightening of that darkness was only made possible by that total support which

Mary gave to me. She later became a Samaritan herself, but it was her love and the time that she devoted to the family and to always being there for the craziest exercises into which that husband entered. Only that made it all possible.

CREDO

No child of my era could not but be affected by living and growing up in a manse. We had short prayers for the whole family, and any visitors, every morning of life. There was church every Sunday, regular discussions with Dad about religious matters. He and my Mum had very simple straightforward beliefs which had no doubts, they were very very biblical and, I suppose fundamental. Both Dad and my granddad, who I never knew, had had Damascus Road conversions, and I got the impression that they thought that this would happen to me. Then, I went on to school at Loretto and there was chapel twice on Sunday and another service midweek. It was not possible to grow up in a manse and not to become immersed in religion, and following on to that, it was at University where I joined Greenbank Church, because I liked the minister David Reid, an ex- POW who went on to the States and was replaced by a charismatic minister whose name I cannot remember, but I think was Rev. Montgomery. There was a very good youth group – Quest, in which I became very involved. As I grew older and Mary became important to me, so I spent a lot of time with Mary's family at St John's Episcopal. Again both Frosts held very straight beliefs, as did Mary though she was also very practical.

When we went to Aberdeen I became very involved with Rev. Bill Cattanach at Beechgrove Church and took part in a BBC TV programme "Word for Living". This was a programme which lasted for about two months and as a result of which I was ordained an elder. It was an interesting programme, which gave us each a verse over the week to study and left us to think about it, and we then returned to discuss it in detail. I think looking back I realise that much of my thinking has been affected by the person presenting it. Bill Cattanach and David Reid are examples of why I was moved to see Christianity as one that I could accept. I suppose my commitment to shape my belief was the need to see in Christianity the message of love which, of course, took me into the Samaritans. Forty-one years of very challenging work there sharpened and focussed those views.

The next important step was when I became a Headmaster and I then had to face up to the way in which I would work my morning assemblies. It would have been very easy simply to read a bit and mumble a prayer, but it was one occasion on which I spent a lot of time in trying to make these moments relevant. They must have a been a reasonable success as Jim Malcolm told me that he had tried to do the same when he went on to be a Head. Particularly for the seniors I tried to do a five to ten minute "homily" – that is the Anglican way of presenting an argument in short fashion and which had to be a very carefully thought presentation. This was always combined with an appropriate prayer – not always one from the Book.

So was it over immersion in religion that turned me to query much in religion? I don't think so. It was a result of an increasingly changing view of the world as a result of all my experience. I am not against Christianity. I just cannot accept much of the shallow matter of the basic beliefs and practices which surround it. I find many of the hymns are over simple, and that much of the thinking and preaching is just not borne out or even related to the reality of life. Much of it does not face up to the major questions of life – the whole concept of the Beginning, then there is war, pain, tragedy, bereavement, and evil with all its consequences.

As one example, I took strong exception in May in a service in Sweden, to the young man who preached on Abraham taking his son up the mountain to sacrifice Isaac. Could anyone ever imagine taking one of your children anywhere to cut their throats to satisfy God?

Now though I do not go regularly to church I read widely on philosophical matters. I listen to "Thought for the Day" on the BBC, and the hour long programme, every Sunday morning. I do go to the West Kirk on the first Sunday in the month because it is thought provoking and is quiet – it is a time for reflection.

What I am really saying is that I have thought and thought and continue to think very deeply on matters religious and attempt to work my life and to mould my thinking on the results. I think that the most important part of creating a better world is in the practical use of love and its honest expression of concern for others. I suppose that I am a Justified by Works man rather that by Faith. I sometimes think that Faith as presented in so many sects can become nothing but an excuse for condemning the way of life of others and not thinking carefully enough of the true meaning of life. My concern in all religions is the concept of Absolutes. Life is too complicated for too much dependence on Absolutes' While we must have standards, we also need to see them with love, for none of the problems that we face are easy – to name but a few difficult issues – abortion, the end of life.......

I think that I have moved away fundamentally from traditional Christianity because the concept of an all powerful and supernatural God is to me just not acceptable. The cruelty, the devastation, the hatred which is evident everywhere in so much of life cannot come from a Loving God. In practical terms I just cannot accept the lack of real evidence of so much. My training as a historian is that you must look at the facts and at the evidence. I remember someone saying to Deborah, my grand-daughter – "thank you God for a lovely day." On that very day one million people were losing their homes in Mexico with floods. If God can make a lovely day for one, how can He cause such chaos and pain for others? You cannot blame the floods on Man's sinfulness, not all the dead or losers were sinful.

The evidence for the evolution of the world is overwhelming, whether scientific or philosophical, or archaeological. We can see evolution in the way that bacteria is changed by other bacteria, so to me the evolution of two cells in a muddy pool into man is not so impossible. You can see tremendous evolution in the development of medicine –

from Dad's cutting open tendons and stretching them to Gillian's extraordinary long distance surgery.

First, I find it very difficult to believe in the all- powerful, loving God that Paul describes. There is no one or nothing that I believe could provide the ability to control everything to the extraordinary extent which would be required to control the whole world. I know that it is a matter of faith to describe it as beyond human understanding, and that we should not apply our limited understanding to something that is beyond understanding on our terms. I feel that that it is too easy an escape from the question. How could any being have an overview or control of the vast areas of the physical dimension – the rivers, the tides, the winds the storms? How could any being record and monitor all the activities of the billions of us individuals? How could any being or force exert the powers that would be required to do all this. I know that this freedom is explained by free will, but why would an all powerful God ever have given up such a vital power that could negate everything for which He had worked?

Because I cannot believe in such a God and I do not therefore blame him for the death of Mary and Catriona or for the loss of Lomond. That would be too cruel to consider that anyone could do such a thing. It links in with what I wrote earlier of the enormous impossibility of such a task of oversight and all the contradictions that are a part of life.

That does not mean that I do not accept that there is a power or a force which impacts on human life. I see it as a power that is within us to move forward and for good. I cannot, however, accept that evil is the result of some sort of Fall. That was a handy myth for simple people to explain away man's weakness. This power is an evolving one which builds on what has gone before. It is all part of the whole evolutionary process that has moved man from the beliefs in many gods to the concept that there is one, and now to a much less complicated view that that there may be no overall power. We have moved from mythology to religion and now to philosophy. That does not mean that we ignore the build-up over the centuries of thoughtful people trying to seek the truth and to live by it.

Did I write it was all less complicated?

This leads one to take the view that for me there may not be another dimension to life in the sense of an afterlife. If there is where is it? What happens to the earthly body in heaven, and how do we relate to those who have gone before. I love my children, as did my parents, as did their parents and so on. How would we disentangle all those complicated relationships at the meeting at the End? What is eternity like? Near to Hell if it is unfulfilled. I would think. I always remember Dad describing Hell as being a trout stream without fishing rods or a golf course without golf balls. I know that it is silly to think of a spot-lit place with angels and light all around, but what exactly is Heaven? It is not simple. I still find myself wishing for a miracle. I speak to Mary, I tell her that I love her. Is there a spiritual dimension? I do accept that. I certainly feel that we are not just matter, that there is much more to us all. I don't discount prayer, I am sure that the mass concerto of thinking has an effect.

So what of that extraordinary man – Jesus Christ. Divine or just a very remarkable man? So were Mahomet and Buddha? Summed up in one word, that magical converter – Love.

These all raise lots of questions and I know that I do not pretend to have all the answers. Probably I never will, but is not that what the search for meaning is all about? If belief is about Faith, Hope and Love then I entirely accept Hope and Love. Hope has been at the heart of my life or I would never have started Samaritans, or two schools, and Love is central to my life and my living of it, then perhaps Faith is the acceptance of those two concepts as being central to all else?

Journey Through The Valley

Dante's *Inferno* was a desolate picture of fire, hate and vicious small figures. The Valley of Death is not very different, it is desolate, it is cold, it is lonely, a vale filled with tears and sorrow. It seems at times that there is no future, nothing to which you can look forward. I know that this is a road that many have travelled, and that much of the journey is common to us all, yet for each of us it is a journey that is filled in different ways and differing difficulties that must reflect the relationship that we shared with the one who has died. It is a journey which is unique to our own character and background. I wonder if filled is therefore the right word, perhaps emptied would be better? It is much easier to look at the grim side and to forget the wonderful love and support that I have received. As Laurie Campbell said, that to him Love is the Love of God and I accept his point. There cannot be many ex "Heidies" who have had so many hugs in the streets. To go to Gartocharn coffee hall, and be met by the tall, stringy lady who runs the coffee area with a kiss and a cuddle when she heard about Mary, and then the jewellery one who said that she did not always connect with people, but for us……! The Valley does have its green shoots.

Over my life, I have suffered five harsh blows. Four of them relate to the death of a near one, and one to the end of my time at Lomond. The latter was, of course, quite different and while it was a terrible blow, it was and is not part of a grieving process, it has been something to be conquered, which it has. My father died aged seventy-one, and I was twenty-two, and serving as a Signalman at Catterick doing my National Service. I was still in initial training at 3 TR, with a very good and supportive group of young men, and on being notified that my father was dying the Army was exceptionally helpful. They not only gave me immediate compassionate leave with a warrant for travel to Edinburgh but extended my leave to cover the interment and still retained me in the same squad when I returned. That was important for the support and companionship of that particular group – the alternative of being held back would have involved new faces and new situations. Dad had angina and had not been well latterly, he also felt that he had had a good "three score years and ten" and was then ready to die. Nowadays a simple heart operation would have saved him. I was with him just before he died and I never forgot the change from a vital powerful man to a nothing. I decided then that I did not want to see a dead body again. I know that I wept and often, and was very sad and that Mary, as ever, comforted and loved me. She was already my tower of strength. Dad was so important to me, even though he was a bit aloof and formidable, but he had a giggle and he laughed and we talked. He and Mum handed on to me the need to get involved with people, partly why I went into teaching, but also as a student into working with the Fet-Lor Boys Club in the High Street and then later into forty-one years with the Samaritans. It is the practical involvement that attracts me. I am also a deeply spiritual person who is still searching for the truth – whatever that may be. I have dozens of books on looking for whatever is out there. I listen to talks and search into the other possible worlds. Mary was far too practical, if it's there, it's there. Why get all het up!

Mum died in 1973 when I was forty-three and Rector of Greenfaulds, with a wife and three children. I had never had a warm relationship with Mum, she was not a very warm person and very independent. She had many wonderful qualities – loyalty and total commitment to the work of a minister's wife. She was very time-conscious, and nothing must come in the way of that. The kids remember most her determination to leave the cinema before the Anthem, even if Mary Poppins was still going! Her passing was difficult as being long drawn out because the doctors thought that they could save her, despite the fact that she had made it abundantly clear that she did not want to live. Indeed Jo and I had agreed at one point that we would refuse entry to that particular doctor if he showed that he had not listened to what both we and she had said. That was not a pleasant experience. I know that I was sad, and that I did miss her but I do not recall being overwhelmed with grief in the same way that Dad had affected me. I suppose in some similar way the deaths of Father Frost and Grannie Frost did not affect me so much emotionally, and Mary was her stolid self-contained self though I know that she felt deeply both deaths. It was not in her nature to weep, it was something that she locked up in herself. Such things were to be borne and to be faced and overcome.

As to Catriona's death. I think that we both knew, as we waved her goodbye after that pain-filled Christmas holiday, that the end was near. But what a blow – we loved her so. Her warmth, her vitality, her love. It wasn't that she was particularly special – we loved the other two equally – it was just that she was our third and we probably knew her better as she had spent so much time with us on her own. We both wept and wept and comforted each other – I suppose that that was the first painful step on my road to hell. I still open the front door at night, look to the stars and talk to her up there. And me an unbeliever in that other world!

My upbringing was tough. My parents were Victorian and did not believe in cosseting or physically cuddling. My first experience of any warmth and of a cuddle was with the Frosts and with Mary's warm love. For me boarding school – one a very tough one, a lonely youth, and the Army taught me that I had to be self sufficient and independent. I had to be tough, to stand on my own two feet, life was to be faced and overcome. I should not rely on anyone else. My relationship with Mary was my first experience of a deep and physical and emotional loving, of a total dependence on another, of being part of a family. Grannie Frost, before the change was such a warm, happy, cheerful lady, and so wise. I have this picture of her sitting in the armchair at Braid Road, close to the fire to keep warm with a cigarette in her mouth, chatting and laughing. I cannot remember what it was about but she once took me aside and very sweetly suggested that I think about some line of action. She was not being critical or annoyed simply so wise.

Her daughter inherited that gift. Perhaps my first upbringing has been a poor preparation for the Valley? Someone wrote of the "unmapped self". We know so little of what we are really made – our genetic makeup, what we have learned, of the disciplines through which we have passed, and the various experiences through which we have lived. All these have made us what we are and left their mark. We are not just flesh and blood, but of something more. Perhaps all the barriers that we develop and use as shields to help and to protect ourselves bring their own problems.

I think that my friendship with Mary was the right one for me from the off. I am very aware that I am, and always have been, a one woman man. It was not love at that stage it was just fun and warmth. She was so mature, so sensible. I cannot remember whether the next step was that she asked me out or I asked her again but from that moment we both knew it was right and we never deviated. It was hops, it was the Union, it was local dance halls the New Cavendish and the Cosmo at Morningside, it was formal university dances, it was meals with her parents at the Caledonian, the Aperitif, the Café Royal. They were so good to me, I had never before met anyone with a wallet packed as Father Frost had with cash!

We got quietly engaged in September 1951, somewhere out towards Carlops on a hillside if I recall, but kept very private – to be honoured for 55 years. It became public in June 1952. Mum and Dad gave me the money for the ring.

So what was she like that girl? She was always my model, so wise, so honest, so physical, so funny, so capable at everything that she did – mother, cook, seamstress, tennis player, companion. She was much more sociable than me, much more clear in her views on everything and always prepared to argue her case. That was a point very much obvious to others – poor Chris on his first encounter thought that we were on the edge of divorce! But our arguments, our discussions were never heated or angry simply rather complicated interactions. She was more religious than me, not more spiritual. Just very practical, if there is a heaven – fine. If there isn't, then equally fine. If something was not right she said it. We were so good for each other, we shared so many tastes, we liked each other's company. We wanted to be together. I remember so vividly when I knew that it was love. It was walking up from Woodburn Terrace to Braid Road and passing a garden with lilac and the scent was over-powering. Simple yet haunting.

She was very sharp –"born in the knife box, you'll cut yourself one day" was her father's remark. I recall doing an intelligence test at Moray House in 1957 and boasting that I was a genius with a score of 140. Promptly she demanded that she sit the same test – bother, 141. And she never forgot to rub it in. Figures she loved and the bank and computers were right up her street. She let me run the budget – once! Disaster and she took it over. Home Banking was just what the doctor ordered.

She suffered badly in health. First acne, then painful periods. Those will be cured when you have a family, said Dr Morton, and he was right but it did not make life easy for once a month with violent headaches and weariness. Then the stones – two in her lifetime, painful backs. She never complained – you just have to get on with it, she said. The births were extremely painful but she never once discussed it, all due to a misshape in the birth canal.

She was so good with children. With Seonaid's dyslexia she got into children with area of special needs. Even at the end, small children became a focus for her attention in cafes, and in the street. She loved them. She was so warm. She loved a cuddle. That was the first law of our marriage – a cuddle last thing at night and first in the morning. She was a very physical lady, she loved to love and to be loved, even up to ten days of her death. She adored all her grand-children, they were something special, and to be prized. She constantly talked of them to her friends.

I don't suppose that she was perfect, but she was for me and my life was for ever there for her – that was the purpose of all that I did – the house, the garden, the holidays, the trips. They were for her and only for me in so far as she was with me. She made the decisions about purchases- she had very clear ideas about what she wanted and what was right – and the cost!

She loved driving. She was nicknamed Demon Hill by Colin. She loved fast cars and driving fast. The two Renault 11's were her dream of perfection. She reached 120 on the M4 after a late ferry just to be in time for lunch with Laurie and Sheena at Bath. That was the day that Michael Heseltine was fined for doing the same. She did have the knack of getting scratches on the new cars as Catriona remarked at our Golden, but she was never dangerous and two of her daughters are like her. I have an abiding memory of that last holiday in France. Yes, I was wicked and did the illegal, but sorry I cannot feel any regret. She drove only on the autoroutes. I had made a mistake, and had not taken over as we got to the terrifying roads round Lyons. She never turned a hair, drove at a steady 70 in the middle lane, while the inner lane was filled choc-a-block with huge trailers and giant camions, and the outer lane was equally full of shining Mercedes and BMW's hammering along at 100mph. Technically she was superb, her reactions were as in the old days – very sharp. I know it was naughty, but what a memory?

What else – the beautiful girl who got off the plane in Dusseldorf in 1954 to start her holiday in an army camp and take over the Adjudant's quarters and be an army wife, though she had never had any such experience, and she was to the manner born, an instant success with the Colonel and the rest of the officers and their wives. The glow on her whole face after the births of the daughters. She did want a boy, not for her but for me. I could not have cared less, each daughter was a miracle. Her cheeky interventions at the net in tennis. She prided herself on a mighty leap and putting the ball away, followed by a hop skip and a little jump and that grin – Pity, you cannot do the same she would remark! She loved working for Black Horse, and I can see the same characteristics appearing in Seonaid. She was so good with people, she was always welcomed with a smile and a joke. Never at a loss and so efficient.

People have asked me whether her being in care made it easier for me in the grieving process. It has in a way been worse as I have grieved for longer and there seemed to be no end. I often wept after leaving her in Argyle Lodge and was driving home. I hated leaving her in the home. It was just awful, it was like dropping me being dropped off as a child at boarding school with all of that pain – a dereliction of my duty. Unfair – of course but we cannot control how we feel, rationality does not come into it.

I read that people feel that death is like a dream or a nightmare from which they feel they will wake. It is so true. I feel that my existence now is dreamlike and that Mary will walk through the door with that smile. I wait for her in the pool and to come up the stairs for her coffee, "peching" away from the climb. I see her organise the kitchen and get cross because I have got it wrong. Well not cross, just disapproving. And then there was always that smile, the laugh, the joke. It is being alone for the first time in my life, I have no one in the house to share – the TV, the beauty of the garden, the magnolia, the daffodils, the cherry trees, just the beauty of the world.

She was a perfectionist unlike her husband, she liked things to be right and was happy to work at it until it was right – she would unpick knitting or tapestry if it was wrong. Her eldest daughter, Gillian, with her seeking for perfection and her nimble fingers has inherited that gift. She loved colour, but not too violent like her husband's ties. It had to be tasteful. Flowers were her life and the arrangement of the unexpected mass of shrubbery and colour was always right. Now I find that I must have flowers in the house – that is all that is left of her.

She was known as a sharp dresser, though her everyday trousers and shirt were not that wonderful, but going out. Wow! The colours were right, the clothes matched, she was a beauty. A look at her wardrobe is enough evidence of that. She loved music, concerts, opera, choir and playing the piano. She was very shy of playing in front of others, I could never understand why. She loved singing with Roger Clegg in his small group.

She was always willing to get involved in working to help – Samaritans, Macmillan Nurses, Inner Wheel, Beacon Old Girls, LADFAS. She was a good committee woman but hated public speaking.

I cannot think of any more loyal wife than Mary. She was happy to talk through our numerous moves, she knew what kind of house we needed, she was clear. Once we had made the decision she stood by it unflinchingly. She was my woman and she backed me one hundred per cent. She sat at in at so many of my talks, conferences, speeches, she never complained and she always came up afterwards and clasped my hand. If it had really been a good one, she glowed and her eyes lit up. Conferences at Swanick, Hull, York, Lancaster, Loughborough she was always there, my girl, my life-line. Could any man not feel god-like?

Will it help to put it all on paper? Will it be a catharsis? I don't know. My problem is that I am not convinced of an afterlife, so I fear that I will never see that lovely girl again. We were so truly one. I weep. I am so lucky – I have had fifty five years of the most wonderful woman, I have memories of so much. But they are each memories that bring with them pain, at what cannot be again. At times she is a shadow, a representation from a photograph. Never is an awfully long time.

When I think of all that I put her through in terms of moving I do a little shudder, but it never fazed her. She thought about it and agreed – Fairmilehead was a joy but to move to Aberdeen, never seen the house or the work done, two weeks after a baby, and then the joy of a move to Bridge of Allan. Though in her case she felt a real sense of loss of the many lovely friends; and then finally to Helensburgh, after a distinctly wet viewing of St. Bride's. I think that she had the greatest compliment paid to her at the interviews – wives as well. There were six of us hopefuls, with partners, lunch at the Royal Northern with all the Governors et al. present. She was never obviously powerful, she was just quietly that.

I think so much was brought home to me at a recent funeral of a friend, who died of motor neurone disease. I could only sit at the funeral and marvel at how Mary's was a celebration of a wonderful life, the sun shone, the crematorium was filled with flowers, the place was packed to overflowing, the hymns were right, the words spoken were magical and so heart-felt, the music that filled the church. There was beauty, there was mystery, there was dignity, there was love. The tributes from Seonaid, the reading by Gillian, the rose from Ruth, and, of course Laurie. Truly, for an unbeliever like me we were surrounded and uplifted by the love of God. As Keith said afterwards that, as the curtains closed on her to the haunting "Ave Maria" we all crossed the bridge with her. That tribute to a truly lovely lady was so right – "Fur Elise" and that gentle smile as she took her place in the Eightsome.

They say that grief is the price that you pay for love. My God, it is some price.

For all that she did and all that she meant – "Ave Maria".